M000045047

# THE CHINESE OXYMORON

VERONICA S. PIERCE



A BROWN BAG MYSTERY
FROM COUNCIL OAK BOOKS

TULSA

Council Oak Books
Tulsa, Oklahoma 74120

 Published 1990
Printed in the United States of America
97 96 95 94 93 92 91 90 5 4 3 2 1

Library of Congress Catalog Card Number 90-81818
ISBN 0-933031-29-7

Designed by Carol Haralson

To my husband, Ron,
whose love and encouragement
made all the difference.

ox-y-mó-ron:
n. Gr. a smart saying which at first view appears foolish, (from oxys, sharp and moros, dull or foolish) a figure of speech in which opposite or contradictory ideas or terms are combined (eg., thunderous silence, sweet sorrow).

*Websters New 20th Century Dictionary*
Unabridged 2nd Edition

*Things are best perceived by contrast.*

# Author's Note:

The Cremonese violin maker, Giuseppe Guarneri, (better known as 'del Gesù') a contemporary of Antonio Stradivari, is accurately portrayed in this book. His violins are acknowledged by experts to equal or excel the famed Stradivarius. However, the particular violin attributed to him in these pages, and its history, are fictional.

# 1

# THE TALL MISS SMALL

THE LOW-SLUNG CAR DOWN-SHIFTED neatly around a hairpin turn, then roared up the steep incline, the dizzying alpine scenery falling rapidly below. Expanses of snow-peaked Alps and sun-lit valleys stretched in all directions. The brightly colored little car gathered speed and shifted smoothly into high gear, cresting the mountaintop, its momentum lifting all four wheels from the road. The precarious mountain track leveled briefly, and the small car gained traction and hurtled forward, then — driver and car operating as one — down-shifted expertly into the next quick turn.

A loud crack rang out, like the report of a rifle, and the driver used the curve of the road to cut the wheel sharply and apply the brake, sending the car into a controlled brodie. The spin caused the engine to stall.

The driver restarted the car, bumped to the shoulder of the road, and shut off the ignition. Dust still swirling around her, Minikin Small got out, slammed the door and walked slowly around the car. The right rear tire was flat. *Damn* it, she thought angrily. Well, at least the view here was worth stopping for.

She set the emergency brake, donned gloves and removed the spare tire from the trunk, leaning it against the rear bumper. She looked around, spotted the missing hubcap beneath a bush and carried it back to the car. Using the lugwrench, she loosened the lug nuts and fitted the jack to the frame of the underbody. She cranked quickly, lifting the car, removed the five lugnuts and dropped them into the upturned hubcap. She took a deep breath, lifted the wheel from its axle, taking care not to brush it against her clothes, and leaned it against the side of the car. She noticed that the blowout had torn a foot long gash in the tire, perhaps caused in part by the skid. She rolled the spare to the rear fender and lifted it carefully into place. Long capable fingers spun the lugnuts home. She tightened the lugnuts, dropped the car to the ground and meticulously stored the jack, wrench and flat tire in the trunk. Then, gently, she tapped the hubcap back into place.

Minikin Small stood up and walked to the edge of the precipice, her long wheat-colored hair whipping wildly around her face. She breathed deeply and peeled off the soiled gloves.

Pigskin leather is biodegradable, she thought, dropping them one by one into the valley far below. They were supple and functional for a time, then conveniently disposed of, and forever afterward forgotten. Dark green eyes watched as the wind caught the gloves and carried them toward the valley floor. She realized if it had been impossible to control that blowout, she would have gone hurtling over the edge of the precipice, down to that valley far below. She might have experienced a long moment of surprise, but no great loss, for she felt a lot in common with those ephemeral gloves. The tall Miss Small folded her long legs into the tiny car, shifted into gear and pulled away. She decided to take it a little slower. To her, life was only enjoying the trip, but now she had no spare.

About dusk Minikin Small turned into the snow-encrusted driveway of a large chalet in Gstaad, parked and got out of the car. The frosty air was rich with the heavy tang of pine. Bellmen ran to help her unfasten her skis from the roof of the car, and carried her bags into the hotel.

The concierge, a tweedy little man with a handlebar mustache, smiled and rubbed his hands together vigorously. "Fraulein Small, what a pleasure to see you again. A telegram has arrived for you this afternoon. Here it is. Your reservation is quite in order, of course. We have been looking forward to your visit."

Minikin nodded to him, tore open the envelope and scanned the two lines. Then read the wire again more slowly. And read it once more. She steadied herself against the counter while she thought a moment, and then she chose her words with care, "Wait, Herr Sauer. Wait. I have to make a flight reservation, right away. And then I must send a wire. Please put everything back in the car — I'm afraid I won't be staying."

The experienced Herr Sauer gave her a penetrating look, then quickly covered his surprise. "Of course, Fraulein. Right this way to the phone. You have had some bad news, I perceive."

Everett Orson Stallworthy raised his bulk from the rear seat of his limousine, with the help of the chauffeur's strong arm, and stepped heavily onto the pavement in front of Kennedy's Swiss Air terminal.

"Please wait here, Omar. She should be coming through customs, now. We won't be long."

Omar touched his cap, and Everett Orson plodded slowly through the doors into the terminal, heading for the customs' gate.

Mr. Stallworthy would be forty-five on his next birthday, but looked considerably older owing to his colossal girth. He would have been a handsome man for he was tall, with tight auburn curls and classical features, but alas, life was an irresistible cornucopia of gourmet delights to him, and he intended to savor them all to the fullest. When his bathroom scale indicated he had passed three hundred pounds and was still climbing, he had merely sighed and ceased to weigh himself.

He paused at a gift counter and purchased a couple of large Cadbury chocolate bars. As an afterthought, he also picked out a gift assortment of bon-bons for Minikin.

He continued on his way, chewing as contentedly as Ferdinand among the flowers. Then he saw her coming toward him, her head above the crowd, that wonderful mane of hair.

"Minikin! Minikin, over here," he called.

She was beside him in a moment, they paused awkwardly, then he hugged her to him.

"Hi, Rhett," she said.

"Minikin." He blushed with pleasure at the old nickname. "Omar is waiting outside with the car. You remember Omar." He exuded the rich aroma of warm chocolate. "How was the flight?"

The fatigue of an all-night drive through bad weather to the Geneva airport was evident in her face.

"Fine," she shrugged. "Seven hours in the air, but only two hours on the clock."

He took one of her bags. "Come, we'll talk in the car. Oh, yes, here's a little something for you. Sweets for the sweet."

Outside, New York City was enjoying an exceptional day. It was late April, a spring shower had cleansed the air and a mild breeze blew. Passing over the bridge into Manhattan, they saw the East River sparkle in the sunlight. A strange day for a funeral.

Everett Orson continued speaking in his mellifluous tones, "It was completely unexpected. No indication, at all, that anything was wrong. Your father had dinner as usual with Miss L' Amoureaux, then went home and to bed. And went like *that,*" he snapped gracefully tapering fingers, smartly. "I beg your pardon," he added hastily. "Heart, the doctor said. Dear me, your poor father."

Minikin patted his hand, absently. "Where is Miss L'Amoureaux now?"

"She's been very upset, as you can imagine. I mean, ahem, he literally died in her arms." He averted his eyes, delicately. "She's been under sedation, but told me she would see us at the funeral. All the arrangements have been made. Wherever possible I deferred to her judgment. She has such wonderful taste, and she cared for Max so."

"Thank you, Everett, I know it was difficult for you." She gazed unseeing at the approaching skyline. "I'm very grateful your wire reached me in time."

"You've been away too long, Minikin," he said sadly. "This is a most unhappy way for you to return. Dear me." He took her hand, and the remainder of the ride into the city was spent in silence, each with his own thoughts.

At last, the gleaming limousine slid smoothly in to the curb. Omar carried Minikin's bags into the house on East 64th Street while Everett Orson gave her directions to the church where the ceremony was to be held. Minikin stepped onto the sidewalk, and with no more ado the car pulled away.

Inside the empty house, the rooms were dusty and the curtains drawn. There was just time before the funeral for Minikin to take a bath and change her clothes. Suddenly she realized that somewhere along the way she had forgotten her skis.

Later that afternoon, at a sunny vine-covered chapel on Park Avenue, a small group of acquaintances gathered with Minikin to pay their last respects to Max Small. No other family members attended — there were none.

From her seat in the front pew, Minikin glanced around the small, modern chapel. The day was incongruously bright and cheerful, and had it not been for the traffic outside, she was sure she could hear birds happily chittering away. She supposed birds still happily chittered in New York City.

She had been to the casket and had peered down upon her tall, silver-haired father. She felt uncomfortably detached, as though she were gazing at a stranger. He was as remote to her in death as he had been in life — his lack of feeling a source of pain to both of them. The peaceful face looked unexpectedly smug. What a macho way to go, she thought, and so unlike him. She knew it probably would have amused him if he had known beforehand the manner of his demise, and she felt oddly comforted.

As she returned to her pew, Minikin saw Lacy L'Amoureaux enter and be seated. Lacy was a slender, lovely vision in gray silk; her ash-blonde hair gathered in curls atop her head, with wispy tendrils escaping around her face. Her eyes were covered by dainty, gray designer sunglasses but Minikin could see, beneath the light makeup, the unnatural pallor of her skin and the trembling lips. She had been much closer to Max than Minikin ever was. She would undoubtedly miss him terribly. Poor Lacy.

They had met at an auction several years before, Minikin reflected, the widower Max Small and Ms. Lacy L'Amoureaux. Lacy had been a famous model, and was sole owner of the L'Amoureaux Model Agency; a remarkable lady whose beauty was unexpectedly coupled with a shrewd business head. She had set her stylish chapeau for the shy, retiring Max, and pursued him with all the zeal and imagination of a liberated woman. Max had been genuinely alarmed by her attentions at first, but gradually had warmed to her, until in recent years they had become loving best friends. To Lacy, Max had meant respite from the daily frenzy of a busy career, someone who wanted nothing from her but to spend time in her adorable presence. And also, perhaps, he represented that most elegant of lady's accessories: a handsome, attentive man at her side. To Max, Lacy meant reentry into the world of fascinating people, amusing diversion, and companionship — a walk in the sunshine. It was clear to Minikin that Max had had the best of the exchange.

Minikin knew that Lacy had refused to marry Max because she had already been divorced several times. But Max, being old-fashioned, had still proposed to her at irregular intervals.

The minister entered and spoke knowingly, in beautifully modulated tones, about a perfect stranger known to him only as Maximilian Small. Minikin slid down the length of the pew and took Lacy's hand in her own, while tears escaped from beneath gray sunglasses and flowed unchecked down Lacy's cheeks.

Funerals are for the living, Minikin thought. They help us realize that our loved ones have gone, and give us an opportunity to weep for them. Sometimes, it seems, they intentionally provoke the cathartic emotions. Perhaps it does some good. Perhaps.

One day when science has cured all disease, she mused, and people only *occasionally* die by some accident from which there is no recovery, one day they will look back across time and think what a brave and courageous race of people we were, to live our brief lives in the shadow of imminent death, having to watch those we love dying around us. She felt better, feeling a member of a brave and courageous race of people, and tried to follow the minister's words.

The life and essence of Max Small varied greatly from the words spoken there. He had been the only child of an eminently successful criminal lawyer. As a boy Max had been immoderately tall and painfully thin; a shy introvert, alternately tyrannized over and ignored by his domineering father. With an intense appreciation for the beautiful things in life, Max had withdrawn into the world of art and books, and eventually he became one of those people who seem to relate better to things than to other people. He attended Princeton University and, much to his father's disgust, majored in Art.

When his father died, Max sold their summer estate in Newport to help finance an insurance business. Being unable himself to create the rare and wonderful things he so admired, Max decided to have a hand in protecting them. The Small Agency insured *objets d'art* while on loan to exhibits, or en route to be sold at auctions, or in other unusual circumstances. In that branch of insurance known as the Excess Liability Market — covering the loss of or damage to property with a very high value — the name of Small soon became quite large. In fact, The Small Agency became to the world of valuable antiques and works of art what Lloyds of London was to shipping.

For a time life was kind to Max. His business prospered, his spindly frame filled out, and his hair became touched with premature silver at the temples. In fact, he grew quite handsome.

When he married he brought his lovely and accomplished wife, Ariana, home to live with his mother — a potentially explosive situation that was defused when Ariana immediately became pregnant. Unhappily, the doctors were concerned to discover an unsuspected heart condition, and the fragile Ariana was bedridden throughout her term. In spite of every precaution she suffered her first stroke in the delivery room and a massive one three days later that killed her and nearly destroyed Max as well.

The day before she died she held her baby in her arms, whispering softly, "My little one. My sweetest one. My minikin." She raised beautiful eyes to her husband, "Oh, Max, let's name her Minikin." A caprice of fate that probably would have been rectified had she lived.

Not long afterward Max's mother also died, and the baby was cared for by a long succession of nannies. When she was old enough, Max sent her to the best and most prestigious boarding schools and then to the most renowned universities on both continents. Max spared himself no expense, his daughter had the best education money could buy.

When it came to their private lives, however, Max retreated into his shell. He had armed his daughter as best he could against the pitfalls of life — there was nothing she was not at least competent in — but of himself he gave nothing. He simply had nothing left to give the daughter that had cost him his wife.

Minikin was a friendly, outgoing child, and probably would not have been the loner she became had she not attained her full height, five foot ten inches, by her fourteenth birthday.

Outside on the sidewalk, the late afternoon sun had softened in intensity. The muscles in Minikin's face felt unreliable as she thanked the last mourner for attending and listened at length while the miserable man tried to express his undying friendship for her father. When at last he turned away and descended the steps of the chapel, she stood uncertainly for a moment, then moved slowly to the limousine parked at the curb.

In the rear seat Everett Orson held an urn of ashes uncomfortably on his lap, and Lacy L'Amoureaux lay back against the cushions, her eyes closed.

Indicating the urn, Everett Orson said with uncharacteristic discomfort, "They gave me this, inside. Do you want to take it now, or shall I leave it at the office for you with the rest of your father's things?"

"At the office, please, Rhett. I feel like taking a walk, just now."

Without moving or opening her eyes, Lacy said, "Minikin, let's have lunch tomorrow."

"All right."

"Meet me at my office around one, dear. All right?"

"Okay." Minikin reached through the window and squeezed Everett Orson's hand. "Thank you, my good friend," she said. Then she was gone.

# 2

# FORCEFUL DISARMAMENT

THE PRESIDENT OF THE UNITED STATES ducked under the still-revolving blades of the helicopter and strode purposefully across the tarmac to the waiting cars. He was effectively shielded by a wall of living human flesh as four bodyguards walked closely in front, back, and on both sides of him to the open door of his limousine.

His aides were waiting inside, and as the door slammed behind him, the caravan of cars moved immediately onto the road in prearranged formation.

He secretly revelled in the attention and the attendant feeling of power that always accompanied such a demonstration of importance. He leaned back in the corner and crossed his legs watching the New Jersey countryside sliding past the bullet-proof windows of the stretch limousine. Then he sighed contentedly, "Well, it looks like spring is finally here."

There was a gratifying murmur of agreement to this banality throughout the car, and he turned with a satisfied smile to the aide on his left.

"They tell me you're a pretty smart fella. I suppose you had better brief me on what we're going to see today."

"Yes sir, Mr. President." The nervous young man appeared to sit at attention. "Naturally there isn't time to explain everything technically, but in layman's terms it isn't very complicated. I'll try to be brief. The ray you are about to see demonstrated is an X-ray laser. As you probably know, the name 'laser' is derived from the first initials of the words *Light Amplification by Stimulated Emission of Radiation.*" The President smiled wisely, "Yes, of course."

The young aide tried to keep a pedantic tone from his voice as he continued. "A regular laser is a device — about the size of a flashlight or smaller — that can produce an incredibly intense, pencil-sized, sharply focused beam of light over extremely long distances. It is a coherent light source in which atoms are pumped simultaneously into excited states by an incoherent light flash. They return to their ground state with the emission of a light pulse for which the energy flux may last about 10 nanosecs. The first continuously operating laser was the gas laser produced by Bell Telephone Laboratory in 1960, and it utilized a low-energy discharge in a mixture of neon and helium gases to produce a sharply defined and intense beam of radiation."

The President nodded slowly, and the young man wondered fleetingly how it was possible that *he* was explaining anything to the President of the United States. And also how much the other man actually understood.

He went on, "To give you some idea of the immense speed at which laser rays travel, American scientists shined the beam at the moon and timed how long it took for its reflection to make it back to Earth — two and a half seconds, round trip. Of course, a beam of regular light would never make it to the moon and back."

The President shook his head gravely.

Nervously, the young aide saw the approaching building in the distance and hurried to finish his talk. "The newly developed X-ray laser takes the power of a small nuclear explosion and channels it into laser rods that will emit lethal bursts of coherent radiation. Regular laser beams can bore through metal and bounce off the moon, and now X-ray lasers can efficiently tap the enormous power of a nuclear bomb. When nuclear fire strikes the laser rods, the rods are filled with energy and their electrons become so excited that they spin about the nuclei of the atoms in expanded orbits, then return to their normal orbits with cascades of greatly increased energy — which creates a beam of radiation equal to a focused nuclear blast. And that is what you are going to see demonstrated this morning." He had finished the briefing with little time to spare.

The President was gracious; he blinked rapidly and refocused his eyes. "Fascinating," he said. "Thank you for a most enlightening talk."

The Presidential aide collapsed back against the seat. He felt wet under the arms and hoped they would allow him to ride back in one of the other cars.

They turned into the long driveway and approached a Cyclone fence topped with barbed wire. An armed guard opened the electrically controlled gates to let the caravan pass inside, then immediately reclosed them.

Up close, the massive building resembled a fortress with ominous stone towers and battlements. From a private estate it had been transformed into a corporate headquarters for a time, but had recently been reconverted into a vast laboratory used exclusively for research.

The Secret Service had sent men ahead to check the laboratory and grounds, and they were waiting at their various posts, conferring into hand-held radios, as the President entered the gray stone building with the customary flurry. In the vaulted entrance hall he was joined by two important-looking men who had arrived at the same time in separate cars.

Another distinguished man, with theatrical silver streaks in his hair and the professional bearing of a diplomat, hurried forward to greet them.

"Mr. President, gentlemen, welcome. I am Baker Forbes, head of research and patents for the Labs." He indicated a shorter, younger man with the features and coloring of a fox, "And this is our director of research, Dr. Ridley Rhyne."

In turn the President of the United States, with the understatement of great power, politely introduced his Secretary of Defense, Walter K. Dunkle, a mild-featured man wearing tortoise-shell glasses. And his National Security Advisor Sanford Baddash, an arresting presence with a black widow's peak and pointed eyebrows.

No one shook hands.

Baker Forbes said, "If you will just follow me we'll go straight to the demonstration room."

They set off down the hall at a brisk pace.

Dr. Forbes said, "I believe this is your first visit to our center. We are very proud of our facilities here. Last year we spent nearly two billion dollars on research. We don't have departments in the ordinary sense, we have laboratories — over one hundred of them. And our researchers have complete access to each other in whatever project they are working on. We find it sparks creativity."

They entered an elevator and descended to the lowest level as Dr. Forbes continued urbanely, "You might also be interested to know that we have over three thousand Ph.D.'s and close to six thousand Masters working for us here, and a large back-up staff devoted to relieving our creative people from administrative chores. Of course, for security reasons, we are nearly alone here today."

The elevator opened with a bored sigh, and Dr. Forbes indicated a door on their left. "Ah, here we are."

There were two Secret Service men standing in front of the door, and they parted to let them enter.

The small room was part of an underground test site far below the building. The dull black walls appeared to be reinforced, and several brightly-colored chairs had been gathered at one end.

With a flourish, Baker Forbes indicated the young man standing beside a strange-looking device. "Mr. President, allow me to introduce one of our researchers, and the man most responsible for what you are about to see, Dr. William Telford Grow." He twinkled at him, "Will, I'm sure you recognize these gentlemen."

Will Grow nodded to them, boyishly. He was a slightly built man with sandy hair and a closely trimmed beard. There was a bright, bird-like quality about his eyes and an intensity of manner that was betrayed in painfully bitten fingernails. An intuitive observer would guess the reason for the tightly wrapped Band-Aid around each thumbnail.

"Gentlemen, please be seated." Dr. Forbes ushered them into chairs. "Ridley, I'm leaving this demonstration to you and Will," he said, as he took his seat with the others.

Ridley Rhyne joined Will Grow in the center of the room. He brushed back his red mustache and cleared his throat, but before he could speak the President chuckled and held up his hand.

"Dr. Rhyne, my head is still spinning from my briefing. Please don't make your explanations too complicated. We don't need to know *how* it works, only what it will do."

Ridley Rhyne smiled and relaxed somewhat. "Well, that makes my job a lot simpler. In a nutshell, we have been able to develop a ray that could stop the entire force of strategic enemy missiles in the world today." He paused for dramatic effect. "The X-ray laser is fueled by nothing less than the energy of a nuclear blast. We don't yet know the limits of the ray's power, but it is very, very powerful. The new beam is made up of coherent waves of light so firmly parallel that it can travel through untold distances in space without lessening in intensity. The narrowness of the beam means that a great deal of energy can be focused into an extremely small area, and in that area the temperature will reach extraordinarily high levels. And it is smaller, cheaper and more powerful than any comparable device conceived of to date." He paused to let his words sink in.

"The X-ray laser moves toward its target at the speed of light — 186,281 miles per *second* —

nothing in the universe travels any faster. In that split second between enemy launch and our laser impact the enemy missile could travel, at most, only a few *yards*. The burst of invisible light would explosively evaporate the enemy booster's skin and effectively vaporize the electronic controls, rocket fuel and engine parts. And there would be no radioactive after-effect — it could be used any place, any time."

There was complete silence in the room.

Before it became uncomfortable, Baker Forbes broke in conversationally, "Not long ago Will Grow went to Dr. Rhyne and said he had an idea how this could be done, so we gave him the go-ahead. Frankly, I expected the trial and error process to take some length of time. However Will, here, seemed to know from the outset how it would work. His logic was flawless. He actually skipped a couple of steps in construction and refined the device into the compact model you see before you."

All eyes were drawn to the device on the table. Will Grow reached out shyly and gave it a possessive pat.

It was about the size and shape of the ship's wheel on an ocean-going liner, but without the handgrips. Nearly four feet in diameter, it was erect, circular and open in the center, with three crossing spokes dividing the space into six pie-shaped pieces. The somewhat broader horizontal spoke had a silvered coil wound symmetrically around it. The rest of the device was painted dull black. Close scrutiny revealed a small opening, about the size of a quarter, at one end of the horizontal bar. The device was mounted on what appeared to be a computer console.

Will Grow moved to a control panel at one end of the console while Ridley Rhyne pressed a button that opened sliding doors along one side of the room. The open doors revealed a wide, brightly-lit tunnel, perhaps half a mile long and fifty feet high. It was empty except for several large, widely-spaced pieces of equipment at the far end.

Ridley Rhyne said pleasantly, "Let me draw your attention to the four objects at the extreme end. You may wish to refer to the large video screen on the right of the door for a closer view. On the far left you will recognize our standard ionospheric weather satellite — compliments of NASA — used by both super powers to keep an eye on their neighbors. Will, if you please." Will Grow was adjusting dials on the panel in front of him. The wheel-shaped device pivoted in place on the table, then revolved slightly, like a ferris wheel making one stop, until the small opening was pointing directly at the satellite.

Will said in a soft voice "We have already figured the trajectory angles by computer, and the blast will be timed in milliseconds in proportion to the density and distance of the target in order not to damage the wall behind it. We insulated the wall, anyway, just in case."

To the President it seemed anticlimactic. He saw the red button depressed, had a momentary impression of sizzling grease and saw the object disappear completely, without light, without noise.

"My word," breathed the Secretary of Defense, quietly.

Ridley Rhyne said, "Next, you see a mock-up of the latest American ballistic missile, the Midgetman. So new that it is still not yet in production. It is forty feet tall, about seventy inches in diameter, weighs about 22,000 pounds, has a range of 8,000 miles, and is intended to carry one warhead of undetermined kilotons. It is unarmed, of course. Will?"

This time the President watched the missile. Again, there was no flash, no thunder — it simply disappeared with a quiet thump. After a moment the President thought he could detect the acrid odor of burnt metal. He looked uneasily at the boyish figure standing at the control panel: Will was smiling.

"Next," Ridley Rhyne continued, "we must demonstrate an unforeseen hitch. It was originally intended that the beam would bounce off mirrors on satellites in space to destroy incoming missiles, but see what happens, instead. Will . . ."

All eyes focused on the large reflector disk in the distance as Will Grow adjusted the controls.

"Zap," he said, and the disk vanished without a trace.

"Good God," exclaimed Sanford Baddash, in spite of himself.

Like the good showman he was, Dr. Rhyne had saved the best for last. All eyes turned to the silver rocket standing alone at the far end of the tunnel.

"That, I'm sure you know, is an atomic missile from our nuclear submarine base in Groton, Connecticut. We needed your authorization to obtain it because we wanted to end this demonstration with a bang." He grinned a fox-like grin, and stroked his red mustache. "I hope you won't be alarmed when I tell you that its atomic warhead is fully operational."

The President exchanged a nervous look with Walter Dunkle.

"And now, Mr. President, if you will just step to the control panel, we have everything ready for you. This one is all yours."

The President smiled good-naturedly, "Oh, fine. If anything goes wrong, I'll get all the blame." Everyone laughed, quietly. If anything went wrong, no one would ever know anything about it — a large portion of New Jersey would simply disappear beneath a radioactive mushroom-shaped cloud.

Dr. Rhyne said, "All calculations have been checked and rechecked. I assure you there is no possibility of error."

The rest of the party clustered around them. Will smiled encouragingly at the President and indicated the red button. The President tried to control the slight tremble of his hand as he reached out and pressed the button. He felt a barely perceptible thump, and when he looked up the rocket was gone.

"I've just cost the taxpayers a fortune," he observed dryly. "Are you sure this isn't done with mirrors?"

Everyone laughed loudly with relief.

Baker Forbes said, "Now, I thought we'd check the target area with Geiger counters for any traces of radiation, and then we have arranged a luncheon for you in the executive dining room where we will have a question and answer period. If everyone will please follow me. . . ."

The executive dining room resembled the banquet hall of a medieval castle; it was long, with ornate fireplaces set at each end and a row of Gothic windows along the length of one side. The room was paneled in dark wood and filled with circular tables and high-backed chairs. There was a fresh scent of spring flowers from the arrangement on each table, and the view from the windows commanded an expanse of lawns and rolling, tree-covered hills as far as the eye could see.

The six men were gathered around a table by the center window, and the food had grown cold on the plates in front of them.

"What I want to know is why I didn't see any light. I expected a bright, thin ray, or at least a flash when the beam made contact with the target."

Baker Forbes answered, "You didn't see anything for two reasons, Mr. President. First, X-rays are invisible to the naked eye, and second, the impact simply happens too fast. A millisecond is one thousandth of a second, and nothing you saw vaporized took long enough to actually see."

Will Grow said, "We had to be excruciatingly careful all during testing. The only accident we had was when we tried to bounce the ray off a reflector. We were expecting to receive the ray in a different place, instead it vaporized the disk, ate through steel reinforced concrete, about sixty feet of earth, and set fire to some trees outside."

Baker Forbes frowned at him slightly, then turned with a smile to the President. "Of course we use the computer, now, to gauge exactly how much energy it takes to vaporize any known volume."

Secretary of Defense Dunkle asked, "How will we lick the problem of, er, non-reflectibility?"

Dr. Rhyne answered, "When we perfect ground controls, I see no reason why we couldn't launch the device itself into space — let it fire directly at its targets. Until that time, the ray could be deployed on land and at sea pretty much as you see it."

"Have you tested it over any distance?" asked the National Security Advisor.

Will Grow answered, "No, but there should be no problem. You see, the Earth's atmosphere actually *filters* the intensity of the ray, while space of course is a vacuum and offers no resistance. Most of our efforts have been to contain it. Frankly, I'd be afraid to see what it was really capable of."

"How much will it cost?" the President wanted to know.

Baker Forbes replied easily, "About two million apiece; half for the bomb and the rest for the hardware. Moreover, one X-ray laser would be able to knock out about a thousand *billion* dollars worth of enemy ICBMs."

"Did you say they cost two *million,* not *billion?*" the President asked.

"That's correct," Baker Forbes assured him. "They are quite energy-efficient, you see."

The men smiled at one another around the table.

Sanford Baddash said, "Do you realize, if we can use this ray as an effective defense against nuclear attack, it spells the end of the arms race and the threat of nuclear war? Perhaps the end of war of *any* kind. It means that we no longer have to worry about the extinction of our species and our planet."

"We must be years ahead of the Russians in the development of this type of beam," said Walter Dunkle. "We could clear the earth and skies of all major weapons and prevent anyone from building more. We could eliminate the means of making war."

The President mused, "Forceful disarmament — I like it! It could be the beginning of a new era for mankind. However, it must be tested further."

Ridley Rhyne interrupted, "I'd like to make a suggestion if I may. The remains of a rocket launched about five years ago will be making its reentry into the Earth's atmosphere in the next few days. In the normal course of events it would simply burn up in its fall to earth. I would like to suggest we have a ready-made test object there. What do you say, Will?"

Will Grow gaped. "We'd need to be sure we had a clear shot at it; know the airlines' schedules and so on. And it would have to be over some remote area." He tried to keep the excitement out of his voice, "We could do it, all right."

Ridley Rhyne nodded, watching him, "It would go easy as a hot knife through butter." The President turned to Baker Forbes. "Do you think you are ready for a test like that?"

"If anyone knows what our ray can do, it's these two," he replied proudly. "If they say it's ready, you may be sure it is."

The President exchanged a look with his two advisors. "You'll have an answer within twenty-four hours," he said.

At the close of the meeting, the President asked Sanford Baddash to accompany him on the ride back to the airport. The glass partition between them and the security personnel ensured their not being overheard as they discussed what was probably the most sensitive military secret in the history of weaponry. "It's like the Martian ray gun in an H.G. Wells' fantasy," the President gushed. He pointed his index finger at the National Security Advisor and said playfully, "Zap!"

Sanford Baddash grinned at him. "You may be interested to know that around the Labs this new invention is named after you; they call it 'Rayburn's ray.'"

"Is that so?" the President flushed with pleasure and modestly changed the subject. "Sandy, I'd like to hear more about that fella, Will Grow."

"Yes, he's quite something, isn't he?" agreed Baddash. "I liked his sound effects, too. Zap!" he said, and chortled softly. He removed a folder from his attaché case. "Here is his dossier."

"Just give me the salient points," the President said, crossing his legs comfortably.

Baddash folded back the cover and read aloud, "William Telford Grow, born February 25, 1953, in Hartford, Connecticut. Only child of Gerald and Matilda Telford Grow. Republican. White Anglo-Saxon Protestant. Et cetera, et cetera. As might be expected, Dr. Grow is one of those egg-heads with a scary I.Q. Bachelor of Science from Brown University at nineteen — Phi Beta Kappa. Masters and Doctorate degrees from MIT by the time he was twenty-three — a double Doctorate, in fact, in mathematics and applied physics — *summa cum laude*. Wrote some papers for his thesis that attracted the attention of the scientific community and won him his job at the Research Labs. Met his wife, Gloria Greenstreet, at MIT. Born September 26, 1952, in Atlanta, Georgia. Republican. Presbyterian. She has a Masters degree in mathematics. They married June 20, 1974, and have one son, Gerald Albert, eleven — a normal kid, bright, but not brilliant — and another child expected in the fall. They are hoping for a girl." He glanced up smiling and turned the page. "There's also a lot of psychological jargon here, but it all boils down to the fact that Dr. Grow is a little high-strung owing to the rather narrow focus of his life. It seems that marriage is agreeing with him; his wife is well-adjusted and gregarious, and she is drawing him into the 'real' world in a healthy, positive way." He paused and looked up. "Want more?"

"Anything else of interest?"

"Not really. They have a mortgage on a house in New Jersey, two economy cars and some modest charge accounts. Here are copies of their IRS statements — boring stuff. No police records. Nothing unusual." He sighed and closed the folder. "Normal everyday people, who invent death rays."

"Okay, what are we doing to protect our investment?"

Sanford Baddash became deadly serious. "As of five p.m. today, Dr. Grow will be under round-the-clock surveillance. Very inconspicuous, of course. His wife has quit her teaching job to prepare for their new arrival, so it will be a simple matter to keep an eye on her and their house at the same time. Both his office and home phones will be tapped, naturally. Also the phones of several of the key personnel at the Labs. Security at the Labs will also be tightened. For the time being, regarding the ray, no more of this 'complete access among the researchers' insanity. After we see how the ray tests out we can make further decisions. I'm putting one of our best men in charge: Homer Rohm. He'll report directly to me."

"Ah yes, I've met him. Capable fella."

The National Security Advisor's eyes narrowed, "Of course you realize, there is no way we can keep this weapon secret from the Russians indefinitely. So, if the ray checks out, I propose we start Dr. Rhyne working on a dummy set of plans — one that we can feed to a known double agent — designed to delay the Ruskies until we can finish manufacturing ours."

The President hesitated, "Interesting concept, yes. You've got my go-ahead."

# 3

# ICY FIRE

THE FOLLOWING DAY, PROMPTLY AT ONE o'clock, Minikin Small pushed through the glass doors of the L'Amoureaux Model Agency.

The broad, windowless room was decorated top-to-bottom in beige; the walls were covered in durable-looking beige suede which exactly matched the twin sofas, occasional chairs and wall-to-wall carpeting. The monotony was relieved by the many Kodacolor blowups, lining the walls, of the covergirls represented by the L'Amoureaux Model Agency.

The room was full to bursting with loudly chattering, animated females. Behind a counter of blonde wood, four booking agents answered incessantly ringing phones. Underlying all the hubbub was the sweet warm aroma of cosmetics and perfume.

Minikin moved through the jostle to the counter and waited patiently until she got the attention of a fine-featured mulatto who flashed a photogenic smile and perfect teeth.

"Hi, I'm Ricki Ann, may I help you?"

"Yes, I'm here to see Miss L'Amoureaux, she's expecting me. My name is Minikin Small."

"One moment, I'll see if she's available." Ricki Ann lifted the receiver and dialed inter-office. "There is a Miss Small here to see you." She glanced up at Minikin, nodded, and replaced the receiver gracefully. "Go right in, Miss Small, it's the first door on the left. Next, please."

Minikin went through the beige door, down a short hall and took the first left. It was like climbing above rumbling thunderclouds into a serene sky. Lacy's quiet, sunny office was pale blue with white and gold antique furniture; as exquisitely feminine and carefully chosen as Rebecca's morning room at Manderley. The daughter of Max Small could discern that the furnishings were only good copies, but she also knew that Lacy had the authentic Louis *seize* at home.

Lacy was speaking into the phone, "My dear, she's perfect for you. Just the right hint of decadence in a pouting baby face, and a neat little ass that will look sensational in your jeans." She waved Minikin into a chair.

"Of *course* she can talk; beautiful bell-like tones." She paused a moment to listen. "That's what I said, a husky chime. Oh, Gloria, have I ever steered you wrong? Just see her, trust me. Good. What time?" She made a note on a slip of paper,

"Fine, I'll send her right over. Bye, darling." She hung up, dialed again, and held up one finger to Minikin, who nodded.

"Ricki Ann? Send Chichi Castenago on that designer jeans commercial, right away. Tell her there's dialogue, and if they sign her she'll get national exposure. This could be her first big one. Thanks, and hold my calls, dear, I'm going to lunch." She hung up and turned to Minikin, "It's a madhouse this week. The people at Vogue Patterns are doing their new catalog. We've called out *all* the reserves."

She rose from her chair, walked around and sat on the edge of her desk. Lacy was beautifully dressed in a lilac suit with matching shoes and a white silk blouse that tied in a bow under her chin. A large amethyst set in baroque pearls was pinned to her lapel. She asked, "Where would you like to eat, Minikin? I'm taking two hours today."

Minikin watched Lacy's quick assessment of the dove gray cashmere sweater and slacks she wore with a silver fox vest. She replied, "You're probably a better judge of New York restaurants than I am, Lacy. You choose."

"Good, then we're going to Lutece. I've already made the reservation."

In spite of the bustling lunch hour business, Lacy L'Amoureaux and Minikin Small were seated with dispatch at a table near the rear of the restaurant overlooking a brick patio. Outside the windows, yellow daffodils were already in bloom, and purple tulips promised an early appearance.

Lacy ordered a Southern Comfort Manhattan and Minikin, a glass of white wine.

Minikin felt vaguely apprehensive; although she was fond of Lacy, she was half expecting her to turn the conversation to reminiscences of Max. Minikin wasn't sure she could bear hearing Lacy extol her father's virtues today, and she knew she would not be able to share her feelings with Lacy.

Lacy put down the menu and sipped her Manhattan. There were lavender shadows around her eyes, and she looked as if she had slept badly. She set down her glass and raised candid gray eyes to Minikin.

"The relationship between you and your father was already established when I met Max," she began, crisply. "Personally, I have always felt the surest way to turn a man off is to try to tell him how to raise the children of a previous marriage." Unexpectedly, she smiled, "However, you and I always seemed to get along, Minikin — that is, you didn't get on *my* nerves — and well, I thought there might be something I could do now to help you find yourself, so to speak."

Minikin tasted her wine. "You make me sound like a lost lamb, Lacy. I'll be able to get along."

Lacy waved away a hovering waiter and continued, more gently, "You may not be a lost lamb, as you put it, Minikin, but you *are* alone now and without a direction. In my opinion, life is too short not to know where you are going every minute. And, if you'll forgive my saying so, dear, you are running around in circles. Dangerous, inflammable circles."

So it was going to be a lecture from an affectionate aunt, Minikin thought, and leaned back in her chair. "I suppose you mean the racing."

"Precisely. Statistics show . . ."

"I've given up competition driving," she said simply. "I proved to myself I could do it."

"Really? That's wonderful." Her relief was genuine, but then she frowned. "However, one shouldn't always be dropping out, either, you know." She aligned the forks neatly beside her plate. "I remember thinking, a few years back, that you were really going to amount to something as a skier. I even read about you in the papers, once or twice. What actually happened? Didn't you nearly qualify for the Olympics or something?"

With an effort Minikin remembered that Lacy was only trying to be helpful. She replied, slowly, "My trainer said I have weak ankles. We tried everything to strengthen them, exercises and so on, but at top speed they just wouldn't support me."

Lacy looked contrite. "I *am* sorry. How disappointing." She paused. "But then, it's really more important for a woman to have nice *looking* ankles, isn't it?" She used the stemmed cherry to stir her Manhattan. "I mean, who wants muscular ankles anyway?"

Minikin felt moved to make some response. "I actually enjoy skiing more now that I don't have to take it so seriously."

"Now there's your mistake, darling. One should always take oneself seriously."

Minikin laughed, "Give me a break, Lacy. I know this is leading up to something, come to the point."

"Precisely what I intend to do," she said, smiling brightly. "What do you think about a career in modeling?"

"*Trompe l'oeil,*" Minikin answered good-naturedly, before she could stop the words.

Lacy stiffened, "Well, that's honest."

Her smile vanished, "Sorry, Lacy, it's just not for me."

"Before you reject it so quickly, think a moment. You'd be perfect, your height would serve you very well there."

Minikin winced inwardly. She caught the implication that her height didn't serve her well in much else. In fact, it had always made her seem awkward and ugly to herself, her discomfort enhanced by the foolish travesty of her name.

Lacy went on enthusiastically, "Your face is good, you probably inherited your mother's cheekbones. You'd have to do something about your hair — have it styled or layered — you look like a mustang. Otherwise . . ."

"No, Lacy, it's no good. Whenever I take too much notice of the way I look I just make myself unhappy. I need something else, something apart from myself." Something that would challenge her *intrinsic* worth, Minikin thought. However, she kept that to herself; she wasn't sure Lacy would understand.

Lacy sighed, "Minikin, I could give you a career that would make you rich and famous. Do you know how many girls would give their firstborn for an opportunity like this?"

"I couldn't handle fame, Lacy," she answered quietly. "I'm still shaky with anonymity."

Lacy hesitated, then went on carefully, "In the past, it has seemed to me I sensed a sadness in you. I believe if you had work you enjoyed doing, you would get a lot more satisfaction out of living."

Minikin was silent for a moment. Finally she said, "I realize that you are completely right. I'm drifting —I need to find something productive to do, make a commitment somewhere. But this is wrong for me."

Lacy was at a loss for words; she hadn't expected Minikin to turn her down. After all, it was her business to understand young girls, and she thought a touch of narcissism would be good for Minikin. Lacy felt she owed it to Max to try to help the girl; now she had run out of ideas and sat frowning into her cocktail. Finally she said, "Oh hell, let's order lunch." Then she smiled up at

Minikin. "I don't want you to think my offer was *all* unselfishly motivated — I could probably make a pile of money on your commissions. If you change your mind before you get wrinkles, let me know."

Minikin thanked her, promised she would let her know if she changed her mind, and ordered sole Florentine from the menu. Lacy chose quiche Lorraine with a green salad. To bolster their spirits they decided they would indulge themselves with a well-iced bottle of vintage champagne.

As they ate, Lacy said, "I suppose you are going to let Everett Orson continue as general manager of The Small Agency?"

"I naturally assumed he'd want to. He's been with Max for years."

"If he stays it might be a good idea to give him a percentage of the business, whether or not you plan to involve yourself with running it."

"You're probably right, I know very little about it. How much do you think he should have?"

"I think twenty-five percent would be generous. You might request a token payment. People always have a higher regard for things that cost them something."

"All right, if you think so," Minikin agreed. She cast an appraising glance at Lacy; her past, like her age, was a mystery. She seemed to have materialized full-grown onto the covers of high fashion magazines and never alluded to her early family or origins. Minikin wondered what early conditioning had formed her. She couldn't resist asking, "Where did you learn to be so practical, Lacy?"

Ms. L'Amoureaux gracefully daubed the corner of her mouth with her napkin, "I never discuss my past, dear. *Toooo* depressing. More champagne?" Minikin nodded, and Lacy summoned the waiter to pour.

"What will you do with the townhouse, Minikin?"

"I hadn't thought about it. I don't suppose you would be interested in buying it?" Minikin asked, half in jest. "I'd give you a good price."

"What? That white elephant?" Lacy grimaced. "No, thank you. I prefer my little penthouse; high and bright, with all the modern conveniences." She thought a minute. "But, if you are serious about selling it, I can get you the name of a reliable real estate agent."

Minikin suddenly had the panicky feeling that her few remaining ties to life were being neatly severed, one by one. The old house on East 64th Street had always been home, her point of reference, no matter how many schools she went to, or how far she traveled when she was away. In a moment, she thought, she would just float away from the world she knew into space, like a balloon filled with helium.

With an effort she shook off the illusion; the house was an inanimate object that would burden her with unwanted responsibility. Homemaking bored her, and housekeeping was a thing she had not disciplined herself to. The best thing was to sell it, of course. When she was ready to take care of one, she might buy an apartment in Paris, or a chalet in Switzerland. Until that time she would continue to drift, and follow her fancy.

She replied, "Yes, thanks Lacy. If it's not a lot of trouble I would like the name of a good agent."

"Not at all." Lacy again summoned the waiter. "Will you have a dessert, dear?"

Minikin surprised herself by accepting, "Yes, I think I will." She thought a moment then asked the waiter, "Do you do crêpes Suzette flambé at lunch?"

He glanced at Lacy, a regular and valued customer. "I think in this case we can manage, Mademoiselle."

Lacy laughed, "Outrageous! If I had just one taste of those I'd want more for weeks afterward every time I opened a menu. No dessert for me, Emile, just coffee."

Minikin smiled and felt a sudden wave of gratitude toward Lacy. Minikin would pursue her own destiny, but she would not forget this gentle wake, and that Lacy had been there in case she needed her. She didn't trust herself to thank her today, but she would remember that Lacy was a friend.

She held up her glass, "Let's drink a toast, Lacy. What shall we drink to?"

Lacy raised her glass from the table and lifted her chin, "How about 'absent friends.'"

Minikin's voice caught, "Absent friends." They touched glasses and drank the icy fire.

# 4

# BITTER SWEET

IT WAS A FRESH MAY AFTERNOON IN SUBurban New Jersey. The Blue Sox little league baseball team was playing last year's champions, the Cougars. Once again the Blue Sox were in second place, but if they could win this game they would take the lead, for a time at least, in the league's standings.

It had been a hard-fought game. The Cougar pitcher, a flinty-eyed little twelve year old who based his style on Luis Tiant, had shut-out the Blue Sox. But in a surprising show of control the Blue Sox pitcher had limited the Cougars to one run, an uncomfortably narrow lead. It was the bottom of the sixth, the final inning in little league ball, and the Blue Sox were at bat.

Disappointingly, the first batter struck out, and the Cougar pitcher spat contemptuously into the dirt and straightened his cap. Then Danforth "Dandy" Desmond walked slowly to the batter's box. He was the best the Blue Sox had, batting third in the line-up. Chances were good he might hit a home run and tie the game. There was complete silence in the stands as he took his batting stance. The pitcher stood frowning at him, thinking it over. Here was a good strong hitter looking for a high fast ball, but ready to swing at anything. He gave him one low and outside, and sure enough he went for it. Strike one.

The pitcher's second ball nearly got away from him, and for a moment he thought Dandy might hit it, but he only got a piece of it. It popped up in foul territory, bounced to the ground, and the catcher fell on it. Strike two. Now only one more strike and the game was as good as in the bag. He took his time adjusting his cap. He wished he could spit again, but his mouth was dry. He wound up slowly, glancing skyward like the good Luis Tiant, and let it fly. Craack! A long line drive straight up the middle, deftly fielded, and Dandy was safe on first base.

The pitcher's eyes immediately went to the runty little red-headed kid who walked briskly from the on-deck circle and took his position on the left-handed side of the plate. A new kid this season, could be tricky if he was any good; but from the look of him, no sweat.

The first two pitches were balls, low and outside, and the little runt watched them go by without turning a hair. The pitcher removed his cap, wiped his face with his forearm, and resettled it again on his head. Dandy's hit had unnerved him somewhat, and now the winning run was at the plate. At moments like these he sometimes wondered what in *hell* he was doing there. He steadied himself, a cocky nod from his catcher encouraged him, and he blazed one at the little runt that should have bowled him over. Instead, with a fourth of July pop, it vaulted skyward beyond the third baseman, directly toward the left fielder. The little outfielder danced with glee, it would be an easy catch, and to him would go all the glory for winning the game. He stood confidently beneath the ball, head back, arms extended, and then he lost it in the sun. It dropped beside him on the grass. Rats. He scooped it up, and in his haste he bobbled it. Oh no. One run scored! The crowd screamed, his father was watching; he would throw directly home. With a mighty effort he threw straight as a laser beam to the dependable Cougar catcher — who lost the ball in the headlong slide of the little red-headed kid.

It was all over but the shouting, and there was plenty of that. The underdog Blue Sox had bested the champion Cougars, 2 to 1! When the dust settled everyone behaved like the good sport each was learning to be, and the Cougar pitcher made a mental note in future to watch that miserable X-rated little runt, Gerald Grow.

It was a twenty minute walk from the baseball field to Gerald Grow's house, but on this day his feet had wings. He fairly flew up the tree-lined street, his mitt cradled under one arm like a football. He was a natural athlete, he thought proudly. Anyway, that's what his dad always said. And his dad would be back from his trip today — was probably home already — and he couldn't wait to tell him about the game. Hooray! He gave a happy leap in the air.

"Gerald! Gerald Grow, wait up."

Gerald threw a glance over one shoulder, stopped in his tracks, and turned around. A youthful man with chestnut curls and a bushy mustache was hurrying to catch up with him. He wore a red and white Hawaiian shirt, blue jeans and sneakers, and carried a sack full of groceries.

As he came nearer, Gerald cocked his small red head to one side and asked, "Do I know you?"

The man's blue eyes twinkled, and he smiled with handsome white teeth. "Sure, I'm a friend of your dad's. Harry. Harry Balding, don't you remember me? I live over thataway," he said, and waved vaguely in a direction up the street.

"Uh, not really. *Harry Balding?* That's a funny name. I'm afraid I don't remem —"

"Oh, that's okay, Gerald, you were a lot younger the last time we met. My wife and I came to your house for dinner. Boy, Gloria sure knows how to cook. I'm surprised ol' Will doesn't get fat." He grinned down at the boy.

The man had the names right, and Gerald relaxed and smiled back at him.

He continued, "I just wanted to tell you, I stopped to watch the game on my way home from the supermarket, and I saw the final inning. That was a great hit you made, kid, put 'er there."

Gerald laughed and slapped the man's extended palm, and then they laughed together.

"Come on, I'll walk along with you," the man said. They turned and started up the quiet, residential street.

"Yessir, that was one fine hit. You're a natural, Gerald my boy, a real natural."

"Thanks, Mr. Balding," replied Gerald, privately agreeing with him and basking in his admiration. "It's my first year of little league ball, you know."

"Is that right?" the man asked, surprised. "Well, you certainly show a lot of talent. It's probably because you're left-handed. There are lots of famous left-handed athletes, you know," he said, glancing down at the boy. "Who's your favorite player?"

"I like Wade," Gerald answered, immediately.

"Who?"

"Wade Boggs. He's got red hair. And he's left-handed."

"Oh, yes. Good choice. Plays for the Red Sox, doesn't he?"

"That's right. My dad knows everything about baseball, and he says Wade is one of the all-time greats. Last year Wade had the highest batting average in the major leagues."

"And I bet you know what it was."

"It was .368!"

"Young man, you certainly know your stuff," Harry Balding said, and waggled his bushy eyebrows at the boy in a comical fashion.

Gerald laughed, delightedly. "You know," he said, "you look a lot like Magnum on TV."

"Do I? Well thanks, Gerald," the man replied, and looked pleased. "As a matter of fact, people have told me that before."

"I'm not surprised," Gerald said, smiling. He liked Mr. Balding; he was nice.

Suddenly Mr. Balding exclaimed, "Say, I'd like to do something special for the winner of that great ballgame." He stopped, set down the sack of groceries, and fished out a little bag of candy. He opened the bag, shook out a piece of candy wrapped in shiny red foil, and held it out to Gerald.

"Oh, my mom doesn't like me to have candy, Mr. Balding. We're health-food nuts, you know."

"Yes, I remember," the man answered quickly. "But this is a special occasion. It's your award for being 'Most Valuable Player.'" He stood smiling down at the boy, the candy extended to him.

Gerald really had no desire for candy; it wasn't something he was accustomed to. He took it reluctantly.

"Well, thank you," he said. He started to put it in his pocket, but the man removed a second piece from the bag and began to peel off the green foil.

"Come on, MVP," he smiled. "You earned it." And he popped the whole piece into his mouth and chewed with relish. "Um, chocolate covered cherry!"

Gerald shrugged, inwardly. He sensed he was being manipulated, but he didn't want to hurt the man's feelings, and what was the harm of one piece? He clasped the mitt between his knees, peeled off the foil and, emulating the other, popped it whole into his mouth. Wow. Good. Very sweet, and a little bitter.

"Um," Gerald said, chewing.

Mr. Balding said, "Give me the foil, old son. Can't be litter bugs." And he took the red foil from Gerald and dropped the colored bits of paper into his bag of groceries. Then he gathered up the sack, and they continued on.

"I haven't seen Will lately. How's your father doing these days?" he asked.

"He's fine," Gerald answered, sucking the bittersweet taste from his teeth. "He had to go to Montana for three days, but he should be back today."

"Good. Give him my best, will you? Tell him I'll be in touch."

"Sure will. Well, this is where I turn," the boy said as they neared the corner. "It was nice seeing you again." He smiled, "And thanks for the Most Valuable Player award."

The eyes that studied Gerald were very serious now. "Take care, boy. You keep hitting 'em."

"Yes sir! 'Bye." Gerald turned and walked away. When he glanced back half a block later he saw Mr. Balding was still watching him, and he turned and broke into a run.

Will Grow pulled up a stool to the kitchen counter and climbed aboard as his wife began to prepare dinner.

"I wish you could have been there, Glo," his tone was boyishly excited. "We were on top of a Montana mountain with pine trees all around; it smelled great. Off in the distance, where it was still light, you could see Canada. It began to snow. It was just beautiful! Ridley and I were shouting orders left and right. The NASA personnel were falling all over themselves making the final adjustments to their equipment, and then we were ready. After a time, I could see it through their telescope. The satellite had reentered the atmosphere and was beginning to incinerate, trailing a long rooster tail of red and gold flames. We waited till it entered the mesosphere — about fifty miles up and about three hundred miles distant — it was falling to earth at twenty-six miles per second. NASA's tracking equipment gave us the coordinates and, ZAP!, I let it have it. I guess I gave it a microsecond less than was necessary, and it exploded like an incandescent fireball. Showers of fiery bits all over the sky!"

Glo smiled at her husband, put her arm around his waist and gave him a squeeze. Her short copper hair curled under in a smooth pageboy; her sleeveless, yellow sundress barely revealed the budding figure beneath it.

"Golly. I wish I could have seen it, Will."

"Oh, it was beautiful! You *will* see it — we got it all on film. And look, this morning before we left, in the newspaper." He removed a clipping from his wallet and read the title aloud, "'Meteor Showers Over Montana.' How about *that!*"

They laughed and hugged each other, and she took the newspaper clipping from him and began to read it.

The rear screen door slammed shut.

"Mom, is Dad home yet? Dad!" Gerald Grow hurled himself across the kitchen into his dad's outstretched arms. "Dad, guess what? I hit a home run in the bottom of the sixth inning and won the game for the Blue Sox!"

"You did!"

"Yep. The coach even said it was a good hit. Dandy was on first, and . . ."

Glo Grow put down the clipping and watched her menfolk with a contented eye. Today, all the Grows were hitting home runs.

The following morning, Will Grow left for work later than usual. Gerald had unexpectedly regurgitated his breakfast, and Glo had decided to keep him home from school. Probably all the excitement of yesterday, Will thought, as he started the car and backed carefully into the street. He wondered again about the mysterious Mr. Balding and decided Gerald must have gotten the name wrong. Then, he noticed a new cassette in the car radio and pushed it in to engage it. He was quite startled when a pleasant voice began to speak.

"Good morning, Will, Harry Balding speaking. Gerald may have mentioned running into me yesterday, but in case he did not I must inform you that yesterday afternoon, after the ballgame, I administered a complex and quite lethal poison to him in the form of a small piece of candy. This poison, if untreated, will surely kill him, but not until he suffers convulsions violent enough to cause brain damage."

Will's car jerked to a halt in the middle of the quiet, tree-lined street. He stared at the small plastic cassette with eyes that seemed unable to focus. The voice continued pleasantly: "However, you have it in your power to save him, Will, for you see, I have the antidote. And I will give it to you, but I want something in return. I want the plans, Will, your plans for the ray. I will give you the antidote in exchange for 'Rayburn's ray.' "

Will felt he was suffocating and opened his mouth wide and struggled for breath.

"I will phone you at nine-thirty this morning at the lab. Please be available to take my call. I will ask to borrow your picnic hamper this afternoon after work, and you will agree. You will put the plans inside, and I will come and collect them."

Will's thoughts raced; it couldn't be a joke — no one would be that cruel.

"I advise you to watch what you say from now on, Will, because your office and home are bugged, and if you are careless they will try to stop you.

"If you follow my instructions exactly, by eight o'clock tonight your son will be out of danger. By midnight it will be too late to save him, though he will take another agonizing day to die. I assure you the poison in his bloodstream is too complex to have analyzed in time to help him, and — if you try — you will only draw attention to yourself, and they will prevent my coming to you. Remember, I'll call you just once, at nine-thirty this morning at the lab."

The voice hesitated, then added an ironic afterthought: "This tape will *not* self-destruct in case you want to play it again, Will."

## 5

# SELLER IN THE ATTIC

MINIKIN OPENED THE FRONT DOOR AND watched the eyes of the little man opposite her crawl from her midriff, up, up to her face. His head was tilted far back, a note of incredulity in his voice, as he asked, "Miss. . . *Small?*"

Minikin fought down the familiar feeling of discomfort and answered quietly, "Yes?"

He allowed the laughter to show in his eyes, "I am Ralph T. Smerkers of Sills and Dore's Realtors. My card."

She took the white rectangle. "Yes, Mr. Smerkers, please come in."

Ralph Smerkers was about forty years old, short, with capped teeth and a curly black toupee. He had the even all over tan that comes with the regular use of sunlamps. Minikin decided that he probably jogged with sheep-like regularity and wore ascots to singles bars. She closed the door behind him.

"I don't need to tell you what a wonderful location this is, Miss Small. Right off Fifth Avenue in the mid-sixties," he said, as if she were unaware of the location. "You could hardly do better."

"You think the house will sell quickly, then?"

"Oh, there may be some minor haggling over price, but we could sell anything at this prime *situs,*" he assured her.

"I suppose you want to see all the rooms?"

"Yes, indeed. These old houses are invariably well-crafted with materials and workmanship you don't often see these days. Helps them to sell, you know." He smiled up at her. "We'll need to write a glowing description for the catalog. For example," he indicated the floor, "black and white marble in the entrance foyer. Good, very good." He whipped out a small notebook and made a note. "Small, winding stair-case," he wrote furiously.

Minikin said, "I understand there is a new central heating system, and the plumbing is in good repair."

"Excellent." His ball-point flew across the page.

She opened double doors on the left. "This is the living room."

She sensed his disappointment at once. The room was gloomy and airless and crowded with faded Victorian furniture. There was a humpback divan capped with lace doilies, heavy carved tables with clawed feet, maroon lamp shades with dusty fringes and red flocked wallpaper above mahogany wainscoting. Mr. Smerkers drew a deep breath.

Minikin said, "The black and white tiles continue under the rug."

"Yeess," he said slowly, "and the fireplace is nice; white marble, handsome detail. Wainscoting, mahogany." He wrote it down.

Minikin wound her way through the dusty, cluttered furniture and opened sliding doors into the dining room. It was also dark — the tall, broad window heavily draped with faded green velvet — and crowded with massive furniture. The room was dominated by a huge Dutch marquetry display cabinet crammed with dusty ornaments, and an old Victorian sideboard. Against a third wall stood a large black lacquer *chinoiserie* armoire full of dishes.

"Here, I'll turn on the lights," she said helpfully.

The old chandelier sprang to life, throwing harsh shadows into the corners and highlighting the dusty neglect. The lace tablecloth was yellow with age, and a spider had built a home in one of the table candelabra.

Minikin said, "My father lived alone here. His regular housekeeper retired last year, and I'm afraid there hasn't been a permanent replacement."

"Oh, well, it's a big job to keep up a house like this." He lifted a corner of the threadbare rug. "Parquet floors. Need refinishing."

Minikin said, "Though there are several fireplaces in the house, I have always thought this was the prettiest. It's pink Carrara marble."

"Ah yes, lovely." He made a note, then moved to the window. He pulled aside the heavy drape and looked through the dirty glass at the long narrow back yard. The grass was patchy and brown, and the stepping stones to the tiny greenhouse at the far end were broken or missing altogether. A multitude of boxes stacked untidily along the wooden stockade fence on both sides of the yard.

"Nice leaded-glass window, don't you think?" Minikin asked.

"Oh, yes. Very pretty." He dropped the curtain and turned away. "Is that a dumbwaiter in that wall? Well, I'll be. I haven't seen one like that in years. Looks like it works, too. Handy thing in its day; brought the food right up from the kitchen."

"Yes, indeed. Although the catch is broken now, and the door doesn't stay shut. When it's closed, the paneling fits so well you'd never know it was there."

A side door led them back into the hall.

Minikin said, "There is a small elevator here where the servants' stair used to be."

"Yes, yes. Charming. Look at that lattice work. A real antique." He laughed, "If you don't mind, though, I think I'd prefer to use the staircase in the front."

"I assure you it's quite safe."

"I'll take your word for it."

They ascended to the second floor by the front stair. "This floor was used more, as you can see. The room in front has always been the family room; my father called it the 'withdrawing room.' It overlooks the street. I guess I should mention that all the ceilings on the first three floors are twelve feet high. Those windows are eight feet tall, and framed in antique *verde* marble which matches the fireplace, as you can see."

Mr. Smerkers scribbled in his notebook while Minikin gazed at the shabby, overcrowded furniture and the hideous wallpaper glaring from beneath ponderous, unrelated wall-hangings.

They reentered the hall, and Minikin opened the door to a small, windowless room containing a horsehair sofa and her father's eighteenth-century mahogany cylinder desk. Rolltop, she had always called it, to tease him.

"This was my father's study. Here's a bathroom. And at the rear of the house, the library."

"Ohhh," gasped Mr. Smerkers, stepping down into the sunken room. "Look at that. Floor to ceiling books. Leather bound volumes. Marvelous redwood paneling. Wonderful snob appeal, you know. Of course no one really uses libraries like this anymore. But *so* delightful to show. Look at the little balcony that runs all around three sides. Gives access to the books higher up. Just too gorgeous. And I love the tall windows. My, my." He walked closer. "Pity about the view of the back yard, though." He made copious notes.

Minikin walked with him to the third floor.

"This floor was done over some time ago into two master bedrooms sharing a central double bath with dressing rooms. The room facing the street was my grandmother's room for a while; now it's kind of a guest room," she said, her eyes on the scattered disarray of her open suitcases. "There is a wall of closets behind the fruit wood paneling and twin French windows with Juliet balconies. Uh, the fireplace is alabaster."

Minikin waited while he wrote it all down, and then they moved on.

"Here's the master bath."

"This is more up to date, I see."

"And this was my father's room." The scent of Max's aftershave cologne swept over her as she opened the door. She walked to the windows and opened the curtains. Though it was decidedly a masculine room, Lacy's hand was apparent in the subtle harmony of the blue draperies and bedspread with the blue slate fireplace. The Chippendale furniture and Aubusson carpet was all Max, however.

"Now *this* is more like it. A beautiful room. I'll bet you got this bedroom suite from Bloomingdale's. I can always tell. Either there or W & J Sloane's. Am I right?"

"I'm afraid I don't know; we've had it a long time."

"Are there any more floors?" he asked, mopping his forehead carefully not to disturb his toupee.

"Just one. It was my old nursery and playroom. There's also a bath and another bedroom up there that we use for storage now. No more fireplaces."

"Okay, let's take a look." He followed her out.

Minikin had to marvel at the man's patience, and the lack of any personal curiosity on his part. She couldn't help but wonder at the number of homes he must have combed through to be able to exhibit such indifference to the private lives laid bare to his casual scrutiny.

The fourth floor was worse than Minikin remembered. Long unused, it was a regular haunted attic, with dusty toys and cobwebs in the dormer windows. Her former nannies' rooms were airless and filled with old furniture and steamer trunks. The seller in the attic gave a quick look around, and they returned to the stairs.

"The roof didn't show any signs of leaking, I'm happy to say." He glanced through his notes. "I think we've about covered everything — no, we seem to have missed the kitchen."

"Oh, yes. It's in the semi-basement, I guess you would call it."

"Down five flights?"

"Correct."

The door to the kitchen opened with an Inner Sanctum creak, and a dim light dangled from a cord in the center of the large room. Minikin noticed the old chipped porcelain sink was filled with dirty dishes, and a peculiar odor emanated from somewhere beneath it. It suddenly occurred to her that food was also rotting in the old refrigerator. Her eyes fell on a few blackened pans on top of the stove; she had been taking all her meals out. Oh lord, she thought, I should have looked in here before. A tiny window above the sink was on a level with the yard in back, the filthy glass choked with weeds, the whole prospect starkly depressing.

Mr. Smerkers kept a carefully straight face. "Is there any more?"

"Well, yes. That's the door to the garage, just up these steps. Oh, the light's burned out. And the housekeeper's room is in the front with a small adjoining bathroom."

In the housekeeper's room, the barred window looked out upon the street at knee level. The sparse furniture was bare, the single bed pushed back against the wall and the mattress rolled up.

They returned in silence to the foyer.

Mr. Smerkers put away his notebook. "As I mentioned earlier, Miss Small, you may have to wait a bit to get the proper price, but we'll sell it for you, never fear. If I may be frank, in its present trashed-out, ahem, I mean, neglected condition, the customer that buys it will probably expect to break it up into apartments or co-ops. They would be very much in demand because of the location."

"Yes, I see."

He fumbled in his breast pocket and brought out a sheaf of papers. "Here is the standard contract allowing us to show it with the standard six percent commission for selling it. If you will just sign where I've *X*ed the line, we're in business." He offered his pen.

Minikin frowned at the pen and drew a shaky breath, "Could I call you in a few days, Mr. Smerkers? I'd like a little more time to think it over."

"May I give you a bit of advice, Miss Small?" His eyes were not unfriendly.

"Yes, of course."

"If you decide you do want to sell it, it's a good idea to fix it up a bit. Open all the curtains, turn on all the lights, and get rid of some of the furniture. Try to make everything seem as bright and spacious as possible. You'll get a good return for your efforts."

"Thank you, Mr. Smerkers. I'll bear that in mind."

As soon as the door closed behind him, Minikin turned on her heel and descended the stair to the kitchen. This poor old house certainly hadn't shown to its best advantage today, she thought. It hadn't been a real home in years, of course, but it didn't deserve to be destroyed — the paneling ripped out, the library gutted, and the fireplaces sold piecemeal — to be rebuilt into box-like models of sterile efficiency. A little care and polish might restore it to its former beauty and give it a chance to become a gracious home again. She realized she had always loved this old house. Tomorrow she would hire a young and strong live-in domestic to help her, but today she would clean up some of this mess, starting with the kitchen.

# 6

# WILL WON'T

WILL GROW SAT AT HIS DESK AND watched the perpetual flashing of his digital desk clock. It said 9:28 a.m. FRIDAY, and he realized suddenly that he had been sitting there for some time with no clear memory of the drive to work, only the words of the tape replaying over and over. Even now he clutched the cassette tightly in his jacket pocket. His chest felt constricted and he was unable to breathe freely. Tremors played across his spine, and his thoughts circled like a kite in a high wind. It was 9:31 a.m. FRIDAY.

The phone rang, sending an internal shock through him so violent that for a moment he sat frozen in his chair. It was like being doused with cold water, but suddenly his mind began to function again.

"Hello. Hello, this is Dr. Grow."

"Hi, Will, this is Harry Balding. How've you been, ol' buddy? Long time no see." It was the now familiar voice of the recording.

"Oh, hi Harry. Okay, I've been okay. And yourself?" In spite of himself, Will's voice trembled.

"I can't complain, Will. Listen, can you do me a favor?"

"Sure, Harry. Anything."

"I'd like to borrow your picnic hamper. I've got in-laws coming for the weekend, and it will be an excuse to get them out of the house. Give us something to do."

"Sure, Harry. Of course."

"Great, Will. I'll stop by your house after work today and pick it up. Is that okay with you?"

"Uh, you can stop by earlier if you like," Will said in a strangled voice. "I just got back from a business trip yesterday, and I'm taking the afternoon off. Jet lag."

"Sorry. No can do, ol' buddy. I won't be able to get away till later. But I'll definitely see you about five-thirty, quarter to six. Is that all right?"

Reluctantly, Will said, "Yes, fine. I'll see you then."

"Give my best to Glo."

"Right. Right, Harry," Will waited, unwilling to break the connection. There was a click and then the dial tone. He hesitated, and as he was about to hang up he heard another click. Almost absentmindedly, he unscrewed the mouthpiece of his phone and sat staring at the bugging device. A remote corner of his mind nagged at him: it was true, his phone *was* tapped.

Though it was strictly against all regulations to take classified paperwork home from the Labs, Will had been indulging in this practice for as long as he had worked there. It was impossible *not* to take work home when it occupied most of your thoughts, waking and sleeping. Some of his best ideas came to him while he was doing some mundane chore around the house or just before he fell asleep. Reference notes were essential to him at those times. Weighed against the positive aspects, he felt his deception to be no more serious than a childish prank.

To avoid being caught by the occasional spot-check at the gate, he had devised a space beneath the glove compartment in his car large enough to hold the thickest notebook. More than large enough for the specifications of Rayburn's ray.

At noon, briefcase in hand, Will left the Labs pleading fatigue and drove home. The search of his car at the gate had been cursory.

He pulled into the driveway of his house, went inside and up to Gerald's room. Their son was dozing fitfully. Glo was standing at the foot of his bed, a worried expression on her face. She glanced up quickly, took Will's hand and led him out of the bedroom, closing the door softly.

"Oh, Will, I'm glad you're home. Gerald's beginning to worry me; he's running a high fever, and I think he's really sick."

Will took her arm and put his finger to his lips. They descended the stairs as he said, "Glo, there's something I want to show you. Something in the car." He led her protesting out of the house.

Once in the car, he said, "I've tried to think of the best way to tell you, and I can't think of a better way than to simply let you hear it for yourself." He removed the cassette from his pocket and played it for her.

There were no tears, no hysteria. After the first few moments Gloria Grow put her hand in Will's and sat listening, motionlessly. When it was over she remained staring into space.

Will said, "I took the call at work. He's coming here at five-thirty. I have the specs for the ray in the car."

She put her hand to her throat and whispered, "I understand."

He took her hands in his, and they sat together in silence.

Finally, she said flatly, "We have to face the fact that, even when we give him the plans, he may not give us the antidote. It will increase the risk to himself."

"It's all we can do."

"I know."

After another long pause, he cautioned her, "We mustn't forget, he warned us that the house is bugged, and in fact I found a bug in my office phone. The house may even be under surveillance."

"I'll be careful. Will, who's watching us? And why?"

"The Labs, I guess, or maybe the government. It's probably something to do with security because of the ray. Are you all right?"

"I think you may have to help me back in the house."

It was an interminable afternoon for Will Grow. His wife had gone upstairs and put her arms around their son. Gerald's sleeping face looked flushed, and his skin was hot to the touch. After a time, Glo had fallen asleep on the bed beside him — a healthy animal dealing with an insoluble problem. Will marvelled at her strength.

The words, *he may not give us the antidote,* ran through his head. There, she had said the unthinkable. It was the first time he had admitted that possibility to himself.

He retrieved the specs from their hiding place in the car and, putting them into a briefcase, carried them inside the house. In the kitchen he transferred them to the picnic hamper, all the while wondering at how much Harry Balding knew about them: he knew Will liked to play musical cassettes in the car; he knew about the new picnic hamper from Hammacher Schlimmer; he knew about the secret plans; he even knew their nickname — Rayburn's ray; he knew Will's phone was tapped; and he knew where his son played.

Like most Americans, Will realized, he was apolitical and had always taken his good life and citizenship for granted. As a scientist, he felt himself to be a member in good standing of the human race, and it had long been his dream to make a lasting contribution to the world through his scientific endeavors. To him, the X-ray laser was an idealistic answer to nuclear war; one that would benefit *all* mankind. But now it began to dawn on him that, in an opposing hand, its potential for destruction was as great as for preservation. It was an unsettling thought. Added to which, Will was accustomed to thinking of himself as an honorable man — and he really couldn't face the implications of what he was about to do, now, to try to save his son.

He felt he had to expend some energy or go crazy. He changed into dungarees and a sweater and went to his workbench in the garage. With an effort he forced himself to stop chewing his nails and began to tinker with his gadgets. "Gadgets" was a humble term for the toys in his repertoire, he thought to himself; not for nothing was he the creator of Rayburn's ray.

Suddenly the germ of an idea began to form in the back of his mind. Where was that device he and Gerald played James Bond with? His hands trembled with apprehension. A few modifications would be all it required. Perhaps he should discuss it first with Glo? No, there wasn't time, and she would only advise against it. He checked his watch to be sure he could be ready.

Shortly after five o'clock Glo came out of the house and watched as Will threw a tarp over his motor scooter. Her face was puffy with sleep, and her sundress was wrinkled.

She said, "I saw the picnic hamper on the kitchen table." Will held a finger to his lips to remind her to watch what she said. "Yes," he replied, "Harry Balding asked if he could borrow it. He should be here, soon. Let's take a stroll around the yard."

Together, they inspected the shrubbery away from the house.

"How is Gerald?" he asked.

"He seems nearly delirious. I have ice packs on his head, and I bathed him in alcohol to help reduce the fever."

"It's going to be all right, Glo. I've got an idea how we can have our cake and eat it too."

"Oh, Will," she pleaded, frightened, "don't let's take any chances."

He smiled reassuringly at her, "Now just a minute, who's the genius around here, anyway?"

Promptly at five-thirty Harry Balding strolled into the backyard, seeming to appear from nowhere. He was wearing the same red and white Hawaiian shirt, blue jeans and sneakers that he had worn the previous day, and his resemblance to Tom Selleck was striking.

"Hi, guys!" he said brightly, like an actor entering on cue. "Say, I really appreciate you folks lending me your hamper. It's a real chore entertaining my in-laws, and I promise to find something *extra special* to do for you in return." He stood smiling down at them, stroking his chestnut moustache, and seemed to enjoy his playacting.

As the impact of his words hit her, Glo recoiled as if in pain, but then replied sharply, "We're glad to lend it to you, Harry, just as long as you keep that promise. The hamper is on the table in the kitchen, I'll get it for you." She spun on her heel and walked stiffly into the house.

Harry Balding's eyes followed her with an admiring look. "Spunky little thing, isn't she?"

Will was suddenly overcome with rage and loathing. His face turned a deep red, and he clenched his fists.

The tall stranger gazed at him with mild concern, "Steady, ol' man. Steady. If you keep your end of the bargain, I will keep mine."

"I've only your word for that," Will said between clenched teeth.

Glo returned carrying the hamper. Wordlessly, she thrust the wicker box into the stranger's arms.

Deliberately he unfastened it, glanced inside, and then reclosed it. His blue eyes twinkled at her. "Thanks, Glo. A messenger will call on you this evening with a little expression of my gratitude for what you've done." He sauntered across the yard, waved, then turned and disappeared through a neighboring hedge.

For a moment they stared after him, then Will turned slowly and took his wife by the shoulders.

"Listen, Glo, I've left something for you on the dining room table. I'd like you to go inside, now, and read it."

Gloria looked at him uncomprehendingly, "I don't understand. You want me to go inside and read something *now?*"

"That's right."

"What have you done, Will?"

"Don't worry, it's going to be all right. Go on, now."

She turned and stumbled toward the house, tears beginning to blur her eyes. Inside, she opened the letter and read, in her husband's tiny, cramped handwriting:

> Glo —
>
> I couldn't let them get away with this. I glued a homing beacon to one of the illustrations in the specs — it looked like it belonged there. I will use my laser homing toy to follow it — at a safe distance — to wherever it goes. I will wait until eight o'clock to be sure you have time to receive the antidote, and then I will call you and tell you where we are. Call Ridley Rhyne at the Labs. Tell him what's happened and to alert the police to

be ready to close in when I call. I love you.
Don't worry, I'll handle this.

Will.

She raced to the front door and flung it open in time to see Will, in brightly-colored helmet and goggles, roar off up the street on his red Yamaha.

Down the street an exterminator truck started its engine, made a U-turn, and went after him.

Glo sat down quietly on the front steps and began to cry.

# 7

# MERCILESSLY CHARITABLE

MINIKIN TACKLED THE RESTORATION OF the old townhouse with a vengeance. She had spent a week just labeling furniture and sorting and boxing dusty ornaments and bric-a-brac; the quality items had already gone to Christie's for auction. Some of the pieces, like the old Dutch marquetry cabinet, were extremely valuable. She would use the money they brought to help pay for the improvements to the house. It needed no major alterations, she decided, just an embellished facade, some landscaping, and a new kitchen. The finances would be tight, but by doing much of the work herself she felt she could swing it. She had kept a few furnishings that would show the house to best advantage; all the rest of the accumulated clutter had been picked up by the Salvation Army and Goodwill. She had been mercilessly charitable.

She noticed the house was beginning to echo. It was a thunderous silence. Good, she thought grimly, the ghosts were at peace.

The second week had been the hardest — sorting through all the closets and drawers — deciding what to keep or sell and what to throw away. The nursery and attic had been especially difficult. So much useless stuff, she thought, but it had to be gotten through if she was to be free of it — whether of the house or of the memories it held wasn't clear to her.

Her father's room she had left undisturbed. She would deal with it later and, she hoped, at leisure.

It had not been as easy as she had anticipated to hire a new housekeeper. One after the other had presented themselves from the agency — neatly dressed, with glowing references — to view her Herculean task with horror. Each time, Minikin's offer of employment was refused even before she could explain that the position was only temporary until the house could be restored and sold.

Minikin felt she needed the moral support of someone working alongside her to be able to finish what she had set out to do. Before continuing the interviews, to give the applicants a little more encouragement, she had decided to redecorate the living room. Now she surveyed the room with pride. The threadbare rugs were gone, and the black and white marble floor shone with polish. She had removed the flocked wallpaper and spent most of the previous evening painting the walls off-white, taking care not to spot the shuttered mahogany windows and wainscoting. She found her first experience at house painting quite restful, even therapeutic. The room was still redolent with the smell, in spite of the open windows.

She had decided to use the black and white color scheme dictated by the marble floor, and the empty black lacquer armoire stood next to the sliding doors that led into the dining room. Its *chinoiserie* trim — inlaid mother-of-pearl, silver and copper — evoked tranquil scenes of oriental gardens. She thought it would make a handsome bar. A matching three-leaf Chinese screen undulated in the opposite corner, sporting *chinoiserie* pictures of a tiger hunt mounted from elephant back.

She had ordered two white modular sofas to be delivered today. They would face each other across the carved ebony coffee table she had just manhandled down the stairs. It was a little eclectic, but *House Beautiful* would love it.

From the attic, Minikin had salvaged three portraits in oil of her Puritan ancestors. Stern-faced, homely, and dressed all in black, they gazed unseeing from ornate gold frames. They would fill the blank spaces on the walls.

The *pièce de résistance* she placed on the mantle of the white marble fireplace: a Louis XV bronze mantle clock depicting the kidnapping of Europa by Zeus disguised as a bull. The clock itself rested upon the back of a majestic bull cast in dark bronze, while graceful Europa, in brilliant gilded bronze, sat atop the clock streaming garlands of flowers down the sides of the clock over the back of the bull to the gilded base. It was signed by Saint-Germain.

As she stepped back to admire it, the doorbell rang. "You Miss Small?" the very hirsute man on the doorstep wanted to know.

"Yes?"

"I got two sofas for ya in the truck." He jerked a beefy thumb toward the van parked at the curb.

"Yes, I was expecting you. Please bring them right in."

He turned and yelled over his massive shoulder, "Okay, Fu, this is the place. Bring 'em on in."

Minikin watched in amazement as a tiny, fine-boned Chinese man, wearing dirty white overalls, hefted a modular unit onto his back and, placing his small feet carefully, strode ponderously toward the door.

The hairy man made an important business of holding the front door for him, and the smaller one followed Minikin into the living room where together they lowered the unit carefully to the floor. Then he returned to the truck for another load. On the third trip Minikin noticed that the large hairy man had wedged a wooden block under the front door, to hold it open, and disappeared. Curious, she walked outside and found him sitting in the truck, consulting a clip board.

She asked casually, "Don't you think you ought to give the other fellow a hand?"

"Nah, lady, he don't mind the work. He's a lot stronger than he looks." He glanced at her quickly. "Anyways, I hurt my back last week and I'm givin' it a rest." His earnest little eyes pleaded for sympathy.

"I see," she replied impassively, and turned and walked away. It was none of her business, but the injustice of the thing rankled a little.

Minikin returned to work in the living room deep in thought. As she helped guide the final section of sofa gently to the floor and watched the young Oriental fastidiously align it with the others, she made up her mind. Here was one hard worker, worthy of his pay, and just what she was looking for. Could she hire him? She decided to give it a try.

"Er, would you care to have a seat, for a moment?"

"Excuse please?"

"Uh, my name is Minikin Small," she began, "and I'm looking for a domestic worker."

"My name is Li C. Fu, how do you do?" They shook hands solemnly, but remained standing.

"Would you like something cold to drink?"

"No thank you." His voice was a musical sing-song.

"Er, have you been in this country long?"

"I am almost here three years."

"Oh. You speak English very well," she lied.

"Thank you," he responded with dignity.

"How long have you been moving furniture?"

He hesitated, "I have been moving furniture five months."

Amazing stamina, she thought distractedly. "Do you. . . I don't suppose you have any references?"

He looked blank and asked, politely, "What references?"

"Oh, never mind, it's not important." Minikin could see the growing confusion in his face. "Could you just tell me what other jobs you have had?"

"Excuse please," he inquired, "is this friendly conversation?"

Minikin tried to smile reassuringly, and spoke slowly so that he would understand. "Listen, I have seen that you are a good worker, and I am looking for someone to work for me. To live here and help me take care of this house. Temporarily. I think you might prefer to do this instead of moving furniture because I will pay you whatever salary you are making now, and in addition you will have your own room here, and meals. And when you leave I will give you very good references." She took a deep breath. "If you are interested in this, please tell me what other work experience you have had."

Minikin knew she was taking a chance, but she liked him. He appeared to be in his early twenties, about five foot four or five, with delicate, fine-boned features. His skin was smooth and beardless, and at close hand his eyes were quite remarkable; wing-like brows tilting above thickly fringed cat's eyes. There was something almost effeminate in the length of his eyelashes, and she wondered briefly if he was gay.

While she studied him he blinked rapidly. At last he answered, "Have worked two years in Chinatown as busboy and waiter while learning to speak in English. Last summer was assistant gardener on Long Island, until people sold house. Plan to save enough money to learn computers. What work you want done here?"

It was Minikin's turn to blink rapidly. "Well, there would be some cleaning and painting. You see, I plan to do a lot of redecorating. Also, there would be some gardening and maybe a little cooking."

"Could see room that would be mine, please?"

"Yes, of course."

Minikin led the way down the stairs. The large, gloomy kitchen was a tired clean, but the housekeeper's bedroom and bath had been scrubbed and aired, the bed crisply made. Minikin snapped on the light and stepped back to let him enter. She watched his face carefully, but his expression told her nothing. She held her breath, until finally there was a nod of approval. Hot dog!

He said, "Must finish work today, but could start here tomorrow morning."

With great restraint she replied, "That would be most satisfactory."

# 8

# GOT LOST

SEVEN O'CLOCK, FRIDAY EVENING, HOMER Rohm entered his office in New York City, set down his attaché case and moved to the window. Lost in thought, he stood looking down on the tiny people far below. His closely cropped hair was pale gold, almost white. His eyes were somewhere between light brown and gray. In fact, everything about him seemed indeterminate — he appeared to be in his middle thirties, but could have been younger or older. His build was slender, but he moved athletically and when he straightened up he seemed rather tall. He was everything a good spy should be: well-trained, capable, and instantly forgettable.

When the phone rang he answered it without looking.

"Homer Rohm."

"Mr. Rohm, this is George Zengo. I've been trying to reach you for nearly an hour."

"Sorry, George. I was attending a seminar on supporting the agent in the field," he said.

The person on the other end of the line took a deep breath. "Well, that's pretty funny, because there's been a snafu in the field regarding our scientist."

Rohm sat down at his desk, turned on a tape recorder, and grabbed a pencil. "Okay, tell me what happened."

"Well, the party under surveillance went home at noon and did not return to work. He spent what appeared to be a normal afternoon in his garage, tinkering with some sophisticated-looking electrical equipment. We watched him with binoculars. No phone calls. At five-thirty p.m., a neighbor named Harry Balding came over to borrow a picnic basket and left. Then the party in question decided to take a ride on his motor scooter, license number PGW 760. Gonzales and I followed him in the truck.

"It's hard to explain what happened then, Mr. Rohm," he continued, the words coming more slowly. "At first, it seemed like he was just learning to ride that darn scooter, because he kept doubling back, and going around in circles. Then Gonzales says, maybe he's taking evasive action — he might be trying to spot us! So we redoubled our efforts to look inconspicuous; darting our old truck up driveways, bouncing across lawns, and sneaking around hedges." He cleared his throat, nervously.

"The only result was, he nearly ran us down without even noticing us. It's really hilarious, now I think about it; we were following him, and we couldn't get out of his way."

There was an awkward silence. Homer Rohm said, "I'm *not* laughing."

"No, sir. Well, then we realized what we should have seen all along: *he* was following something. We noticed he had this queer-looking gismo on the front of his bike, about the size of a large portable radio. It was a sensing device of some kind; looked homemade, and whenever he came close enough we could even *hear* it. It was humming, no, beeping."

"I see."

"Well, it was easier going after we got on the turnpike. We went over the George Washington Bridge, into Manhattan and down the Westside Highway. Then, somewhere along in there, he must have made us."

"Oh, no," Rohm groaned.

"Well, you said not to let him out of our sight. Top priority. And he must have seen us when he was acting so screwy. I guess it finally penetrated."

Rohm sighed, "Right. Go on."

"He made a detour through the Times Square area for the express purpose of losing us. The crafty little guy threw off his helmet, and I think he reversed his jacket. Anyway, we passed him going the opposite way on 42nd Street and there wasn't a thing we could do about it. He got lost in the traffic. We looked for him, but he simply vanished."

"I see. What about his wife, where is she?"

"Still at home. Apparently the kid is sick, because he stayed home from school today, and at 6:03 p.m. she tried to reach his doctor by phone. Left an urgent message about high fever. Also, she's been trying to reach Dr. Rhyne at the laboratory, but he hasn't been available."

"Okay. Where are you now?"

"We've rejoined the team at the subject's house."

"Fine, I'll be with you as soon as possible."

With trembling hands Gloria Grow lifted the receiver and began, again, to dial Ridley Ryhne. She hadn't been able to get through to him at the Labs, but knew he usually got home from work about seven and hoped she would be able to reach him there. She kept her desperation rigidly in check, letting the phone ring for several minutes. Finally she replaced the instrument in its cradle and sat staring into space.

She must not panic, she told herself firmly. There were always alternatives; if she couldn't reach Ridley before eight o'clock, then she would call the police and explain it all to them.

Oh no, she reconsidered quickly; she could already see their polite smiles and the disbelief in their eyes. By the time she had made them understand, it would be too late to help Will. Oh, Will, what a mess!

Ridley would know who to contact. He had the power of the Labs behind him. She'd just have to wait until she could reach him. She would have to wait.

She considered calling Gerald's doctor again, but the patient voice of his answering service ran through her mind, "I'm sorry, Mrs. Grow, you know the doctor always leaves early on Friday. I promise to give him all your messages just as soon as he calls in."

I've already made a nuisance of myself, Glo thought. She rose and went quietly into Gerald's bedroom. The pale blue shade of his bedside lamp cast an eerie glow over him. He seemed so still, now, and he lay so heavily in the bed. She realized she was afraid to take his temperature again; it would surely register above the 105' mark it had shown last time. With dread, she wondered how high fever could go without causing brain damage. Soon he would go into convulsions, and . . . She moved the ice packs closer around him and walked out of the room.

She could call a paramedic team, but over her frantic protests they would whisk Gerald off to a hospital somewhere, out of reach of the antidote. She would never be able to make them see that his best chance was to wait here in case it came.

What time was it? She glanced at her watch: nearly seven-thirty. Time to try Ridley again. Oh, Will, where are you?

The doorbell chimed. Will! She raced down the stairs and opened the front door.

A square-jawed youth in the uniform of a Federal Express messenger stood blinking at her in the porch light.

"Are you Mrs. Grow?"

She couldn't answer, all she could do was stare. He had a package for her. He actually had a . . .

"Are you Mrs. Grow?" he repeated.

"Yes. Yes, I am."

"Got a delivery for you, please sign here."

She signed quickly and closed the front door. Brown wrapping paper covered a rectangular shape about the size of a shoebox. She placed it on the dining room table and unwrapped it carefully. It was too big, she kept thinking. It wasn't what she had expected. Shouldn't it be smaller? What if someone had actually sent her a gift? "Oh God," she groaned aloud. The brown paper came away. She lifted the lid from a white cardboard box, pulled back the tissue paper and saw an exquisitely carved wooden casket. The top was inlaid with large pieces of lilac jade carved into clusters of grapes and connected with coiling silver vines and leaves. She lifted it out. This can't be it, she thought in despair. She placed the casket carefully on the table and opened it slowly. There, nestled on the purple silk lining, wrapped in cotton and sealed in cellophane, was a hypodermic syringe. The vial was full.

Glo put both hands over her mouth to stifle the sobs. Then she grabbed the box and stormed up the stairs and into Gerald's room. She removed the syringe from the casket. Someone had written on the cellophane in marker ink, "inject intravenously." She wiped the tears from her eyes and collected herself. She needed alcohol and a cotton swab. She ran to the bathroom and returned, stopping to remove Gerald's red elastic suspenders from his bureau drawer, and carried all to his bedside table. Something was buzzing in the back of her mind as she bound his arm with the suspenders and swabbed alcohol into the hollow of his elbow. As she removed the cellophane wrapping she realized what was bothering her: What was she doing? She could be injecting *anything* into her son's arm! What if they had found out that Will followed them, and . . . No, she was wasting time — they had *already* poisoned him.

The vein stood erect in the small arm. She pushed the hair back from her forehead and quickly wiped her streaming eyes. Then she lifted the syringe, sprayed a few drops of serum into the air, and carefully inserted the needle into the vein. She depressed the plunger until the vial was empty, gently removed the needle and placed it on the bedside table in the casket. Finally, she untied the suspenders.

She wiped her eyes again so she would see clearly; there seemed to be no change. She sat on the bed beside the boy and took his hand. At first, she thought she must be imagining it; but, no, his skin was becoming mottled with color — now it was blotchy and angry-looking. She drew in a ragged breath that was more of a sob. Oh, what have I done? she thought, rocking back and forth in desperation. I can't bear it, he's going to die! She leaned forward to brush the hair from his forehead, then drew back her hand and stared stonily at her fingertips — they had come away *wet.*

Now she began to see it: beads of perspiration springing up all over his face. His color was returning to normal, and he was perspiring — the fever had broken.

Will Grow shut off the motor of his scooter and quietly coasted to a stop. He lowered the volume on the homing device; he was very close to the plans now, and the humming was too loud. He parked the scooter quietly and looked around. This was a section of Manhattan that was unfamiliar to him; he was in a narrow alley somewhere in Chinatown behind a small camera store. Apparently this was as close to the homing beacon as he could come on the scooter — he would have to go the rest of the way on foot.

He took out his penknife, unscrewed the device from the handlebar of his bike, and pointed the sensor at the building. The humming was louder above street level; he would have to find a way to get inside and upstairs.

Holding the device casually under one arm, he walked around the corner of the building to the front of the camera store. At dusk, the street was deserted and the camera shop closed. The items for sale in the window looked faded and forgotten. Under a dim neon light a violet-hued cat glared back at him through the glass, its tail curling angrily back and forth. Will turned and glanced around.

The dingy little street was well off the main thoroughfare and lined with brownstone buildings. There was a Chinese laundry next to the camera shop and a small vegetable store across the street. At the far end of the block loomed a forbidding warehouse.

He returned to the rear of the building, the humming of his device clearly indicating the space above the camera store. The rear door was covered with heavy grillwork, padlocked, and obviously burglarproof, but there was a rusty fire escape clinging precariously to the building next door.

Will removed his jacket, wrapped the sensing device inside, and tied it around his neck by the sleeves. He rolled his bike beneath the ladder of the fire escape, carefully stood upright atop the seat, and caught onto the bottom rung with both hands. The weighted jacket hung like an anvil from his neck. Sweating and cursing, he swung his foot overhead, hooked his heel over the rung, and swung himself upright — the device cracking him in the teeth as he rose.

He smiled with a grim humor. Geniuses do not make mistakes, he told himself. However, the next time I try that I'll let the jacket hang down my *back.*

Quietly, he climbed the ladder to the second floor and peered warily in the window. The shade was drawn, and the room was dark; it seemed completely deserted. In the quickly fading light, Will Grow scampered up the remaining two flights of the fire escape and stepped off the ladder onto the roof. From there it was a simple matter to cross the roof and climb over a small parapet wall onto the adjoining roof of the camera store next door.

Moving carefully, trying not to make a sound, he crossed the dirty tarpaper to a skylight and looked down. The attic room beneath him appeared rarely used; it was sparsely furnished and lit by a single bulb. Through the slanted, filthy glass he could see two men below. He looked at once for Harry Balding, but with a sinking heart realized he was not there. Both of the men below him were Chinese; one much better dressed than the other in a three-piece business suit.

Suddenly Will noticed that the better-dressed man was examining the specifications for Rayburn's ray! The man removed his glasses, stood up and nodded his head enthusiastically. The other man — in a dirty white technician's smock — smiled, and then the two men shook hands, congratulating each other.

It took all of Will's self-control to restrain a war whoop of excitement. He'd done it! He had followed them back to their hideout.

As Will watched, the man in the dirty technician's smock ushered the other man from the room. The equipment had already been assembled. The technician placed the plans on the prearranged stand, turned on a floor lamp, and began to photograph them — turning the pages quickly.

Will glanced at his watch; it was time to go. He had to get to a phone at once, but it was all moving too fast. What if one of the men left with that film before help arrived? The secret of the ray would be lost; there would be no homing beacon to follow this time!

Will stared. There, beneath him, the best work of his lifetime was being stolen from him. In his mind's eye, he saw copies of that film being sold to militant countries all over the world. He knew — no one knew better — that without responsible, benevolent control of that weapon no one would be safe; at whim, entire cities of people could literally be eradicated from the planet with no loss of manpower and no radioactive ill effects to the aggressor! The original plans for the X-ray laser were safely on file at the Labs — if only Will could find a way to destroy those copies.

Glo didn't know how long she sat there gazing at her son, but suddenly she looked at the clock on the night table; it was after eight o'clock. She stirred, removing the icepacks from the bed absentmindedly. Gerald was sleeping peacefully now. He was going to be all right. But when Will called there would be no one ready to help him. *Why hadn't he called?*

Glo rose and walked restlessly into their bedroom. She told herself she must keep the line open, now, to give his call a chance to get through. She paced the floor by the telephone until she could bear it no longer. At eight-thirty she tried Ridley's home number again — no answer. She felt nauseated with worry. Why hadn't Will called? What should she do?

At nine o'clock she decided it was time to act. Our phones are tapped, she reminded herself. Whatever she did next, she had to be careful what she said. She sat down on her bed, lifted the receiver, and froze.

Who *was* tapping their phones, anyway?

Glo cleared her throat and spoke into the mouthpiece, "Is there someone on this line?" She waited, feeling foolish and hearing only the dial tone. There was no reply.

Then, in a voice suddenly shaking with emotion, she demanded, "If there *is* someone there, please answer me. I need help badly." She felt stifled, overwhelmed, and to her vague surprise she found herself tumbling off the bed onto the floor, and into unconsciousness.

As if from a great distance Glo thought she heard voices, then an Amyl Nitrate was broken and thrust beneath her nose. She coughed and struggled away from the powerful fumes, and at last her eyes opened. She was on her own bed, but the room seemed full of strangers. Wearily, she closed her eyes again; she was just too tired to deal with this now.

Again the Amyl Nitrate was placed beneath her nose, and this time she became fully conscious and pushed it away.

An Italian man, with prematurely gray hair and beautiful Medici eyes, smiled down at her. "It's all right, Mrs. Grow. You asked for help and here we are, just like the U.S. Cavalry."

He moved away and was replaced in her view by a fair-haired man with neutral features. He extended a card case holding identification to her; it said his name was Homer Rohm.

"Mrs. Grow, we represent a government agency assigned to protect your family. Evidently we haven't done a very good job. Could you please explain what has happened and where your husband has gone?" He lifted the jeweled casket containing the hypodermic needle, "And what this is?"

Gloria moaned and struggled to sit up. The man with the Medici eyes moved to her side and arranged a pillow for her. "Would you like some water, Mrs. Grow?" he asked.

She tried to focus her thoughts. "I need coffee."

"Gonzales, go make coffee," Rohm ordered.

A small Latino, with shiny black hair, glided from the room with a spectral grace.

"Please, Mrs. Grow," the fair-haired man prompted her, "try to remember. Where did your husband go?"

"I don't know," she replied truthfully. "He followed Harry Balding."

"And who is Harry Balding?"

"He. . . he's the man who poisoned our son," her voice broke, and she looked from one to the other of them in confusion. Glo knew she was stalling. Whatever she said would compromise Will — Will, who was still missing. Waves of helplessness swept over her as she realized they would have to know everything to be able to help him.

Slowly, she said, "I think the cassette is still in the car. If you listen to it, it will explain what's happened. And Will's letter is on the dining room table, under the wrapping paper."

Homer Rohm snapped his fingers, and George Zengo hurried from the room.

Gonzales reentered with a thermos of coffee. "I got this from the truck," he said softly, "it was quicker." He poured a cup of coffee and handed it to her.

Impatiently, Homer Rohm lifted the hypodermic syringe and asked for the second time, "Now, Mrs. Grow, please tell me, what is this?"

Glo Grow took a sip of the hot, sweet brew and sighed, "It's the antidote."

# 9

# DREADFULLY HAPPY

MINIKIN LAY ON HER BACK IN HER grandmother's four poster bed and stared at the ceiling. She ached with fatigue, and it was difficult getting to sleep.

After nearly a week, she decided she was more than satisfied with her new domestic worker, but admitted to herself that he was an enigma to her. He insisted upon calling her Miss Small — he pronounced it "Mees Smawr" — and in turn wanted to be called by his full name: Li C. Fu. When asked what the C. stood for, he explained patiently that it was his middle name. Period. And Minikin hadn't pressed it.

To her daily discomfort, Minikin had discovered Li C. Fu worked in complete silence. As he worked, frowning with with concentration, twin horizontal lines formed across the bridge of his nose, and all communication between them was limited to coordinating the work at hand. At first Minikin had looked for ways to ease the formality between them, but Li C. Fu had no small talk — she grinned at the pun. He smiled only rarely and never laughed — except once, she reminded herself, when he first saw the backyard. Then his quiet laughter had gone on and on, and Minikin had flushed and hurried to explain that this yard would require a *creative* gardening effort. He had wiped the tears from his eyes and told her not to worry, disappearing again behind his dignified reserve. In an effort to relieve the heavy silence between them, Minikin had gotten in the habit of playing a radio softly in the background while they worked. Although she counted her blessings for his many other attributes, she began to form the private opinion that Li C. Fu just didn't care much for women.

However no job was too menial for Li C. Fu, and he approached each one with order and precision. When it came to house painting he was an artist, and he had visited the hardware store with her and chosen his brushes with care. Under the closest scrutiny his work was perfect — even in the smallest places — and soon Minikin confined herself to working with the roller and left the fine work to him.

In less than a week they had finished work on the entrance hall and staircase of the townhouse. They had painted the walls and ceiling off-white, restored the mahogany finish to the stairs and banister, and polished the black and white marble floor to a high sheen. Then she had proudly remounted the leaded-glass lighting fixtures to the walls — aware for the first time they were signed Tiffany & Co. It had been backbreaking work, but now the entrance to her house looked gracious and inviting.

Minikin groaned aloud and threw back the covers. She rolled carefully out of bed, slid into her robe, and padded quietly downstairs and into the kitchen. She would take some aspirin for her aches and pains, she decided, and hot milk for her insomnia. She had too much to do tomorrow to lose any sleep tonight.

While the milk warmed in a pan she leaned against the kitchen counter and thumbed through the day's paper, stopping to read:

*NUCLEAR SCIENTIST STILL MISSING*

Dr. William Telford Grow, 33, still missing from his home in New Jersey after one week. He was last seen wearing a blue and white Adidas jacket, yellow sweater and blue dungarees, and riding a red Yamaha motor scooter, license number PGW 760.

The police do not suspect foul play, it was revealed today. A spokesman for the family said Dr. Grow was known to have been under considerable pressure at work where he was completing a difficult research project. This stress, combined with the fact that his wife is expecting the birth of their second child and his son just recovering

from an unspecified illness, is believed to have been the cause of his disappearance.
If you have seen this man, or have information as to his whereabouts, please notify the authorities at . . .

The milk hissed in the pan, and Minikin poured it into a mug and carried it, with the newspaper, to the table.

Her eyes returned to the photograph above the article: a youthful, bearded face with a bird-like tilt to the head. Nice eyes, she thought. Poor guy; life is all in the way you look at it.

The opposite page showed an advertisement for a furniture auction at Christie's: Estate Sales and Oriental Rugs. It reminded her that her things were due to be auctioned in a few days, and she hoped they would bring enough money to pay for the improvements necessary to attract a buyer for the house. She finished the paper and her warm milk, returned to bed, and fell into a deep sleep.

The following day was gloomy and overcast. Rain had fallen in the night, and a pewter sky sulked over its reflection in the mirrored puddles of the streets.

Minikin cooked breakfast for herself and Li C. Fu, and they spent the morning taking down and disposing of all the faded, dusty drapes in the house — the gloom outside adding a new dimension to the echoing silence within. The drapes in Max's bedroom were new, so Minikin left them as they were.

Thunder grumbled overhead and rattled the tall, naked windows as Li C. Fu made sandwiches and heated canned soup for lunch.

At one o'clock Lacy's interior decorator, Chalfonte St. Giles, presented himself on Minikin's doorstep. Minikin's eyes widened in surprise as he swept across the threshold. Lacy hadn't prepared her for the splendid presence that calmly surveyed the entrance foyer and strolled languidly into the living room, removing his hat.

"*Do* call me Chalfonte, dear Minikin. Lacy has told me *all* about you."

St. Giles was tall and elegantly slim, dressed head to foot in British tweeds — complete with cape — and carrying a slender furled umbrella. He had long sideburns, finely chiseled features, and his manner was unmistakably that of a handsome Victorian fop.

Minikin tugged at the sweater of her gray warm-up suit and quickly tucked a few stray hairs into her red bandana sweatband.

He revolved slowly, absorbing the ambience of the room before speaking. "I have great admiration for what you are attempting to do, my dear. I see you've made a valiant effort, so far. A *valiant* effort." He paused to stare at the fireplace. "*Ex*quisite mantle clock," he murmured, and continued on through the room, stopping at the entrance to the dining room.

Li C. Fu, in black T-shirt and denims, was standing barefoot on the dining table carefully removing the dusty crystals from the chandelier, one by one, and placing them in a large leather handbag hung round his neck. The Splendid One eyed the small upturned face, powerful little shoulders and tapering hips with a sensual curl at the corners of his mouth.

Minikin said, "Li C. Fu, this is the decorator who will create a new kitchen for us: Chalfonte St. Giles."

Li C. Fu gripped the handbag, put both heels together and bowed from the waist.

*"Enchantez,"* the decorator responded, one eyebrow cocked. The sexual invitation was obvious, and Minikin waited to see the response.

Very slightly, Li C. Fu turned his back and went on with his work. In spite of herself Minikin registered surprise; it wasn't what she had expected.

Chalfonte turned with a sigh of resignation to Minikin and smiled seductively, "Well, shall we go to work?"

As she led him downstairs into the lowly kitchen, an amused Minikin Small felt very much the second choice. She snapped on the kitchen light. "Well, this is it."

A business-like gleam came into St. Giles' eyes. "Ahhh, I do love a challenge." He set aside his hat and umbrella, and removed his cape with the grace of a matador.

"I know it's pretty grim, er. . . Chalfonte. Do you think you can do something with it?"

"Of course, dear Minikin, it will be *gor*geous. Naturally we'll have to enlarge that window." He was all business now. He whipped open his tape measure with the dexterity of de Sade and inquired briskly, "Do you prefer a modern look, or something more rustic?"

"Whatever," Minikin drawled, "as long as it's valiant."

In the evening it began to rain again. From the tiny balcony of her unlit bedroom, Minikin watched the raindrops tap dance across the street and quickstep into the streaming gutters.

She tried to shake a feeling of moody unrest and told herself she was content with her progress on the townhouse. The kitchen *was* going to be gorgeous. There would be golden oak cabinets and counter tops, and a huge greenhouse window that would replace the present kitchen wall and require special reinforcement. There would be a lavish assortment of built-in appliances, including a built-in desk with personal computer — Chalfonte had insisted after noticing Li C. Fu's interest. It was going to be all right, she told herself. It was only that she was finding all the changes a little unsettling.

She laughed to herself softly in the darkness — the joke was on her — she was unable to turn on the bedroom lights now, without curtains at the windows. Tomorrow she would have to speak to Chalfonte about ordering some more. Stupid not to think of that before hauling down the old ones and throwing them away, but she had lately thrown away more intimate things without giving herself time to dwell on them. She realized she was afraid to allow *too* much time to think; she seemed to be racing to finish in an effort to outdistance her feelings. After the Splendid One had left today, she and Li C. Fu had painted the entire dining room, and she was over-tired.

Minikin sensed the razor-edge of her emotions and knew this experience was affecting her on a more personal level, one that she was repressing and didn't yet understand. Crying wasn't her custom, so she laughed again in the darkness, trembling slightly with fatigue.

Suddenly, something across the street caught her eye. She seemed to have been watching the subtle movement for some time, without really being aware of it. There it was again! A fleeting figure darted out from a doorway, ran a short distance up the street and again took cover. It's just someone trying to run between the raindrops, she told herself.

A car eased slowly down the block: a laundry van, seeming to look for a house number. As it cruised by, its headlights momentarily illuminated the doorway occupied by the fugitive from the rain. That's odd, Minikin thought — the man had actually prostrated himself on the sidewalk beneath a stoop! She began to watch more closely. As the van passed, he rose stealthily and ran bent-over into the next doorway. When the van stopped at the end of the block and two men in raincoats got out, Minikin got slowly to her feet, alarm pulsing through her. She watched as the two men separated, each taking one side of the street, and began to walk back toward the one hiding.

Minikin turned and ran to the stairs — *muggers were stalking someone on her block!* She hurried in darkness down the stairs to the front door, opened it a crack and peered out just as the smaller figure crossed the street on the run, the two larger shadows following in hot pursuit.

She flicked on the porch light and flung wide the door, shouting angrily, "Hey, you two! What do you think you're doing?"

The smaller figure veered toward her, racing up the three steps of the entrance, and rushed by her into the house. For a long moment she stood facing his pursuers, surprised to see two oriental faces streaked with rain, before slamming and locking the front door.

She snapped on the foyer light and whirled to confront the youthful figure she had seen enter, but he was nowhere in sight. She walked slowly around the winding staircase, and there beneath the arch crouched a small bearded man, dripping rain, and staring up at her with insane eyes!

Minikin froze. There was no mistaking the madness in his face nor the shattered mind behind the crazed look. She drew in her breath and took a step backward, glancing toward the door. I've let an escaped lunatic into my house, she thought in panic. The men outside must have been trying to recapture him!

The bearded man seemed to read her thoughts and gave a muted cry of anguish, covering his head with his arms.

Minikin turned back to him, forcing herself to appear calm, and spoke quietly, "It's all right. You are safe here."

He peeped up at her for a moment, then to her astonishment he lowered his arms and began laughing. It was hysterical laughter, dreadfully happy, and completely out of control. Minikin felt her skin crawl.

"Stop that!" she shouted at him, frantically. Then, in a calmer tone, "Don't do that. You're all right now."

He stopped just as suddenly as he had begun and got slowly to his feet. He looked at her, a bird-like tilt to his head, and came toward her. She thought, *don't run from a wild animal — it will chase you,* and held her ground.

He faced her, frowning with concentration. Forming the words with great difficulty, he said, "It's behind the bridge in the shadow of the sun. Behind the bridge in the shadow of the sun." The words became a chant, "Behind the bridge in the shadow of the sun. Behind the bridge in the shadow of the sun." But then the words became gibberish and were choked off with insane laughter — beginning as a low cackle and rising to a frightening shriek. His face was distorted, his eyes bored into hers.

Minikin felt a scream building inside her.

With a terrific crash the front door splintered open, slamming back against the inside wall. The hulking form of an oriental man fell to the floor of the entrance foyer, revealing the second man immediately behind him, his hand poised. He gave a quick, expert flick of the wrist and Minikin heard the smaller man beside her gasp. She turned to see the hilt of the knife protruding from his chest, blood beginning to bubble around it and spreading slowly down the filthy yellow sweater he was wearing. She tore her eyes away and looked back at the door, but the two attackers had disappeared.

He swayed and she caught him as he fell, lowering him carefully to the floor. He was still breathing and, to her horror, he clung to her like a furry young primate to its mother — it was both touching and loathsome. For a long moment his glittering eyes stared at her in shock before finally fluttering closed. She felt for the pulse in his neck. It was still beating!

She knew if she removed the knife he would hemorrhage and die, and so she left him lying on his back on the-gleaming black and white tiles and ran for the kitchen phone.

She collided with Li C. Fu on the stairs. "Li C., go and close the front door.

There's an injured man up there. Don't touch him!"

A few moments later the ambulance was on the way, and she stood trembling beside Li C. Fu, staring down at the bearded young man. An elusive thought flickered into awareness: he was the missing nuclear scientist. What was his name, William Tell?

# 10

# PRETTY AWFUL

MINIKIN STEPPED FROM THE REAR OF the ambulance and watched as white-clad attendants rolled the firmly buckled stretcher through the Emergency Receiving entrance of Lenox Hill Hospital. The small bearded face was barely visible to her above the folds of the blankets.

Inside, at the admissions desk, she was asked to wait. A few minutes later, she looked on with foreboding as the bearded man was wheeled rapidly into surgery.

She pulled her damp raincoat closer about herself and took a seat on a plastic chair in the small, impersonal waiting room. It must be nearly midnight, she thought. It had been a long day and she realized she was exhausted; in fact, she couldn't remember ever having been so tired.

She watched an elderly woman with a cut over one eye being rolled past in a wheelchair. The white hair was mussed, and one leg was elevated by the support attached to the chair. She was weeping softly.

Going the other way, a Puerto Rican youth hobbled slowly by on crutches. His ankle was encased in a plaster cast; his family encouraged him.

Minikin looked at the only other person in the waiting room, a black man reading a dog-eared paperback with hands that shook. She wondered briefly what emergency had befallen the one *he* waited for. It was a grim diversion.

Suddenly, from a distance, she heard the screams of a child. She got to her feet and stood helplessly as two attendants carried by a three year old boy, screaming in pain, his small penis caught in the zipper of his brightly-colored overalls. His frantic father was trotting beside him, wringing his hands and bellowing, "Put him to sleep. Put him to sleep!"

Behind closed doors the awful screams continued. Tears sprang to her eyes, and she sat down shaking. His concern evident, the black man passed her a package of pocket Kleenex. As she reached out to take one the cries suddenly stopped, and they smiled at each other in relief.

Minikin sighed and blew her nose. What a night.

A tall, tired-looking man in a trench coat approached her.

"Excuse me, are you Miss Small?" he asked.

"Yes?"

"My name is Detective Kake, Nineteenth Precinct," he said flashing a badge. "I understand you came in with the knifing victim. I have to ask you a few questions."

Minikin had steeled herself for this ordeal. "I understand," she said. "Okay, fire away."

He seated himself next to her and took out a leather-bound notebook and a pen. In a dispassionate voice, he began: "Full name and address, please."

Minikin told him, spelling her name slowly for him.

"Did you see the mugging take place?"

"Yes."

"Would you recognize the assailants if you saw them again?"

"Probably not, I only saw them for an instant."

"How many were there?"

"Just two."

"Please try to describe them."

"They were Asian. I don't know what kind, I can't always distinguish between them. But they seemed taller than average. Tall as I am. And they wore dark-colored raincoats."

"Is that all?" he asked quietly, still writing.

"I'm afraid so."

"In your own words, describe what happened."

"Well, I first saw the muggers chasing the bearded man from a window of my house. I ran downstairs and let the man in, and then I locked the door. The muggers broke down the door, and one of them threw the knife from the doorway.

It . . . it struck the bearded man in the chest." She swallowed quickly and went on. "Then the muggers disappeared."

He wrote in silence for a while. Minikin took a few deep breaths to steady herself; dimly, she noticed the clean smell of fresh, damp air from his raincoat.

Without looking up, he continued, "You said the assailants broke down the locked door?"

"That's right," she confirmed. "One minute it was closed and locked, the next instant they broke through."

He wrote it all down, then glanced up at her, "The ambulance attendant said you knew the victim."

"Well, not exactly. I mentioned that I thought I recognized him from a picture in yesterday's newspaper. The article said he'd been missing for several days. I'm not sure about his name, but he looks like the photograph of the scientist who had the nervous breakdown and disappeared."

"Exactly when did you think you recognized him?"

"While I was waiting for the ambulance."

"Can you recall the name?" he asked and waited patiently, pen poised.

She rubbed a hand over her face and struggled to remember. "It was something like William Tell. Dr. William. . . er . . ."

"Telford Grow?" he said, surprising himself.

"That's it," she smiled. "Dr. William Telford Grow."

His eyes narrowed, and he looked her over carefully. Then he rose to his feet, "You wait here," he told her, and left.

A pretty black woman carrying a sleeping baby entered the waiting area. The black man stood up quickly and went to her. She smiled reassuringly at him and said in a soft voice, "It was nothing. It appears our daughter is just cutting her first tooth." They peered happily at the sleeping infant. As they left the man nodded politely to Minikin, and she smiled her farewell.

Detective Kake returned. The tired look was gone; he seemed more alert and more dangerous.

"Miss Small, I'm afraid I'm going to have to ask you to wait here until this man is officially identified. And then we're going to have to take a more complete statement from you at headquarters."

"Why?"

He hesitated before answering. "It appears your Dr. Grow is someone special."

For over an hour Minikin sat in the waiting room trying unsuccessfully to read one of the worn and dated magazines. Detective Kake sat nearby, his attention buried in the sport section of a newspaper. Minikin yawned, and her eyes watered with fatigue. The hospital corridors emptied of people and seemed to grow wider and longer.

Just as Minikin's eyes were closing involuntarily in sleep, a trio of people hurried by. A man with beautiful Italian eyes and a small Latino accompanied a tousled young woman with copper hair. She wore an overcoat thrown hastily over her nightgown, and her bedroom slippers were visible through transparent galoshes. Minikin could see she was four or five months pregnant. The men on either side seemed to support her as they propelled her forward; her face was frozen in shock.

Minikin no longer felt like sleeping and sat staring at the floor in front of her.

Finally, a police sergeant appeared; his name badge proclaimed him to be one Horst Mosshammer. Together with Detective Kake, he escorted Minikin through the rain to a waiting squad car. It was painted baby blue and white. Minikin found the color disturbing somehow; the pastel shade seemed to rob the law enforcement vehicle of all authority.

One of them held the rear door open for her. She got inside and found herself trapped in an upholstered cage. Heavy wire mesh separated the front seat from the rear, and there were no handles on the insides of the car doors. The back seat smelled faintly of vomit; the floor was filthy. Exasperated, Minikin thought, a fine way to treat a stand-up citizen.

At the station house she was released from the back seat and taken inside. They hurried her past the booking room filled with gaudy people and up a flight of bare wooden stairs. On the second floor she was marched into a large, dimly-lit office that faced the street and ordered to take a seat.

Sergeant Mosshammer closed the door and took his position beside it. Detective Kake introduced her perfunctorily to several other men wearing plainclothes. Nothing was explained to her. Instead, suddenly *she* was doing the explaining: what she had seen, what she had heard, what she had thought. What kind of van? How big? How far? How fast? Why did she open her front door? Describe Dr. Grow's actions. How did he look? What did he say? Why had he laughed? Why? Why? Why *did* she open that front door?

Minikin had always perceived herself to be a reasonable human being. She understood that the police required all the details of the attack for their records because the scientist was someone important, and the thing that had happened to him was pretty awful. So, in spite of nearly overwhelming fatigue, she tried to answer all their questions patiently and was as lucid as possible for as long as possible. But when the questions dragged on and on, she began to feel their curiosity had gone beyond the bounds of good judgement. Fatigue overcame her, and her patience ebbed as her temper rose. In spite of herself, her answers became more and more sarcastic.

Just as she was beginning to think the interrogation was coming to an end, there was a knock at the door. The towering Sergeant Mosshammer opened it and admitted three more men. She heard whispering; someone said, "This is Homer Rohm, CIA."

Minikin was led protesting to a smaller office down the hall, and the questions began all over again with new variations. Was she a citizen of the United States? How long had she lived at her present address? Where was she before that? Why Switzerland? Where exactly did she go to school? When did she graduate? What did she do to support herself? What did her father do? What did he die of? How long ago? Had she ever been a member of the Communist Party? What *were* her political affiliations? The bland face of Homer Rohm became hateful to her, and she was close to screaming with rage and frustration. It was daybreak before they finished with her.

Detective Kake held her raincoat for her while she put it on, and then he walked her down the stairs and out the front door. Wordlessly, he held the door of the squad car for her — the front door, this time. Minikin got stiffly inside.

As he started the car, he said, "I'm sorry about all that; they were pretty rough on you. Everyone gets excited when the CIA is involved." He pulled smoothly away from the curb into the empty morning streets.

"You are taking me home?" she asked, hoarsely.

"Of course," he answered in surprise.

"Then why don't you ask where I live?"

He glanced at her sadly, his triangular face and tired eyes reminding her of Robert Mitchum in his prime.

"Because, lady, by now I know it by heart."

Minikin was too drained to muster a sarcastic reply.

At her front door, she summoned the energy to ask, "Do you know if Dr. Grow is still alive?"

He studied her in silence before answering, "The last I heard he was still hanging on."

She nodded, let herself out of the car, went inside her house and shut the door.

There was evidence of temporary patching inside the front door. Must have been Li C. Fu, she thought gratefully.

Minikin couldn't decide whether to wait for the elevator or take the stairs, and slowly climbed the stairs while she thought it over. As she opened the door to her bedroom, the sunrise nearly blinded her. She groaned aloud as she realized there were no curtains on the windows. Not funny today, she thought.

Wearily, she turned around and went into Max's quietly beautiful bedroom. The smooth counterpane looked cool and inviting. Carefully, she removed her gray warm-up suit, folded back the covers and lowered herself wearily onto the bed.

Everything hurt. She was going to sleep for a weary week.

11

# A REAL NIGHTMARE

MINIKIN DREAMT OF JEAN-LOUIS FOR the first time since the accident; the sensual, protective curve of his arm, the smell of his skin; the thousand things between them that they shared; and her awakening sense of self-worth. She felt, too, the awareness of personal danger — her overwhelming vulnerability — but her emotional commitment to him was no more dangerous than the sport they were so light-heartedly involved in. Perhaps the very lack of a certain future of any kind was what made her commitment possible for the first time. Then, she heard again the deafening crash on the far side of the track — saw his racing car upside-down and in flames. Running, running to get to him, she became disoriented in the milling crowd and lost sight of the burning wreck. She couldn't find him, and she realized he was lost to her. She searched frantically, but all at once she couldn't recall his *face!* Then, racetrack officials were asking her questions, terrible questions about the meaning of life. Interminable questions, and she couldn't find the answers.

She woke at two p.m. that afternoon. Li C. Fu was knocking lightly at the bedroom door. She pulled the covers closer around herself and told him to come in.

He put his head timidly around the door and blinked at her. "You sick, Mees Smawr?"

She shook her head, "No, just very tired. The police questioned me until dawn, and I didn't get any sleep."

"I bring you something to eat, you wait there," he said, and closed the door softly.

Minikin got up, put on one of her father's pajama tops, and got back into bed. When Li C. Fu returned, she was sleeping again.

He came briskly into the room with the old breakfast tray and set it beside her on the bed. He had made hot cereal, toast and frozen orange juice. She was touched.

"Why, this is wonderful," she said, sitting up carefully. "Thank you, Li C. Fu."

He bowed impassively, but seemed uneasy, and stood fidgeting by the foot of the bed as she began to eat.

"Police come very early last night," he told her. "They take flashbulb pictures of broken door."

She swallowed some juice. "It's okay, Li C. They probably needed them for evidence."

"Also they yell at me for fixing it," he confessed solemnly.

"Well, forget about it, you did the right thing. We can't have our door hanging off the hinges in New York City."

He peered at her for a moment, his cinder-black hair falling in elfin points around his face. "Did man with beard die?"

"I don't think so," she told him quietly. "He was alive this morning."

He hesitated. "Police suspect us?"

"I hope not. Frankly, it never occurred to me," she replied in surprise.

He shifted from one foot to the other while Minikin thought to herself, he's working up to a difficult one this time. She bit into her toast, sipped the juice and waited.

"Mees Smawr, why you let fella in?"

She drew in a deep breath and let it out slowly. "I thought he needed help," she answered for the hundredth time.

He nodded his head in agreement. "He needed help, all right."

Li C. Fu watched her eat the rest of her breakfast in silence, his golden cat's eyes studying her. Disappointed, she thought, darn, just as he was turning into a regular chatterbox.

When she had finished eating, he took the tray and let himself out quietly. Minikin rolled over, fell into a deep and dreamless sleep, and when she woke again it was Monday morning. She felt guilty about sleeping so much. She got up quickly, showered, and dressed in faded blue jeans and a blue sweat shirt that drawled in oily black letters, "Foat Wuth Ah Luv Yew." She combed her hair into a ponytail, realizing that she felt terrible; her head ached, her hands trembled, and she was vaguely disoriented.

As she started hurriedly downstairs, the room spun and she lost her equilibrium. Minikin sat down on the steps, hung her head over and stared at the dining room furniture in the foyer. The dining room furniture in the foyer?

When things came back into focus, she rose slowly, went the rest of the way downstairs and on into the dining room. She found Li C. Fu on his hands and knees, painting the already sanded parquet floor with Polyurethane. The smell made her sick to her stomach.

He got to his feet and greeted her with a smile. A *smile,* she thought in disbelief; either he's getting lonesome, or I'm still dreaming.

"Man with machine came yesterday and sanded floor while you slept. Looks great, huh!"

She had forgotten. "Oh, yes," she answered weakly. The man had been paid double to work on Sunday. "Listen, Li C., I don't feel very well today. I must be coming down with a virus."

The smile vanished. "Oh, sorry. You go back to bed, I finish here. You want breakfast, I bring later." He turned back to his work. "Oh yes, Mr. St. Gi' in kitchen," he added over his shoulder.

Minikin supposed she had better look in on the Splendid One, and slowly went down the final flight of stairs into the kitchen.

St. Giles, in bright yellow overalls — with characteristic drama — was leading three men in an assault on the kitchen wall, and he waved her back. Jackhammers began their chattering, and the room filled with plaster dust. She closed the door and went back upstairs in the elevator. She was bathed in sweat by the time she reached Max's room and tumbled weakly into bed. I've created a monster, she thought feverishly, and it's consuming me.

For three more days, Minikin stayed in bed with chills and fever. She dreamed of her father, and Jean-Louis, and death. In her dreams, in some confused way, she became responsible for their lives; the full weight of their existence rested with her. In one particularly vivid dream, she knew if she removed a deeply embedded knife from a carved wooden chest they would all die instantly. But the position of the knife was intolerable to her, and she had to fight against an overwhelming compulsion to remove it.

Between dreams, Li C. Fu bobbed in and out of the bedroom with steaming bowls of soup or cereal and alarming news about the demolition of the kitchen. To confirm his dire reports, the entire house would occasionally shudder and reverberate as if it were the scene of some violent battle. Minikin incorporated the noise into her dreams; it became the splintering collapse of a great wall that was restraining a bloodthirsty Mongol horde. She woke several times in terror, her heart pounding.

Once, Li C. Fu brought her news that her presence was immediately required at police headquarters for further questioning. When it was made clear to them that she was confined to her bed, they agreed to postpone her visit for one day only. The following day they telephoned to say she wasn't needed after all.

To Minikin, there was a continual aura of unreality about everything.

On Friday, Lacy came to visit and brought a picnic lunch from the Brasserie. Li C. Fu asked her to wait in the living room while he announced her.

"Great lady to see you, Mees Smawr, name Racy Rammero."

"Where is she?" Minikin asked, sitting up.

"She downstairs."

"Oh, no she not," Lacy called wickedly, through the door. "She waiting right outside."

Minikin shouted back, "Come in, Lacy!"

The door opened and Lacy entered, swathed in shimmering aqua silk, and carrying a picnic basket. She and Li C. Fu circled each other like wary Siamese cats, and Li C. Fu retreated and shut the door.

Lacy stared after him, "Good heavens, it's like being announced by a tame cheetah. Who *is* that? That's your new domestic? Good heavens!"

Minikin laughed delightedly. "Lacy, am I glad to see you! I've eaten nothing but cereal and soup for days."

Lacy turned her attention to Minikin. "You poor thing! For a gorgeous young girl you look simply dreadful. I'll bet you're starved — but don't worry, I've got everything we need right here."

Smiling proudly, she sat down at the foot of the bed and shook out a table cloth. She passed Minikin a napkin and an egg stuffed with truffles and then began to uncork a bottle of Piper-Heidsieck. "The house looks marvelous. You're going to make a fortune, you clever girl; seven figures, at the very least. You must let me guide you when you invest it."

The cork made a well-bred pop and Lacy poured two glasses, passed one to Minikin, and sampled hers. "Ah, still nicely chilled," she purred. She set her glass deftly on a stack of plates and wedged the bottle into a corner of the basket, then began unwrapping a tiny parcel. A six carat aquamarine flashed on her finger.

"I must tell you, I'm simply *mad* about the new living room. Wherever did you put all that dreary old furniture? Do you know I never really noticed the lovely fireplace in all that clutter? Chalfonte said the room was quite passable. Quite passable, indeed! It's beautiful." She leaned toward Minikin, "Confidentially, you have to keep an eye on that one. I mean, the man is a scandal. Though I *do* adore him, literally no one is safe from his clutches; neither *femme* nor *homme*. There was an ambassador *and* his wife, well, that's a long story. Clearly, the man has a brilliant career ahead of him. Have a foie gras sandwich, dear," she said, and passed the dainty thing on a plate. "I confess to a real passion for foie gras."

"Um," said Minikin, biting into the sandwich with gusto.

Lacy gave her a satisfied look. "I simply can't get over the house," she gushed. "On my way upstairs, I noticed the withdrawing room is completely bare — the halls actually echo. It's so different from before. Have a stuffed tomato, dear; vegetables make one beautiful and give long life."

Minikin took a stuffed tomato.

Lacy went on, "Chalfonte showed me the sketches for the new kitchen. It's stunning. Really stunning. And yet, spacious and simple. He said he couldn't *wait* to get his hands on it. And frankly, knowing him as I do, I was rather alarmed for you. But when he told me all about your trouble with the police, and that you were bedridden with fever and fatigue, I knew you were all right. I mean, safe. I mean from him. Oh, you know what I mean." She laughed musically, and bit into her foie gras.

Her mouth full, Minikin smiled and nodded.

"Which reminds me, you really must be more careful to whom you open the door," Lacy scolded her mildly. "These days the barbarians are clanking at the gates, I mean literally *clanking.*"

Minikin nodded again, dutifully. She swallowed, sipped her champagne, and sighed with contentment.

"Try a little capon, dear. Just a small piece. You must try to keep up your strength, you know." Lacy passed her another tiny plate, then helped herself to a small portion. "Oh, so *moist,*" she said, chewing daintily, as she freshened their glasses.

"Um," Minikin agreed.

"I was going to look in on the kitchen to see how it was progressing, but the entire thing seems enveloped in a plastic bag. It's completely inaccessible. Oh, and by the way, do you know I believe that Oriental has been cooking on a hot plate in the powder room? Well, now I think of it, it's as good a place as any. More capon? I will, too. It *is* good, isn't it? Here's the salt.

"I told Chalfonte to see that the front door was properly mended, but he said he had already ordered a new one. If you don't like it, make him send it back and get one that suits you. He has wonderful taste, but sometimes it's a little *outre,* if you know what I mean. I'm going to take one more tomato; they are quite delicious. Here, help yourself. Um." She paused a moment to swallow and dab at her mouth with her napkin.

"And *now*, for some peach ice cream," she said, like a magician about to produce a rabbit. "Isn't this fun! I told myself I was only buying it to keep the champagne cold," Lacy laughed her becoming laugh, and the aquamarines at her ears twinkled. "I only have time for the barest mouthful, before dashing back to work. There you are. And some for me. Ohhh, this is just heaven. Eat, dear, eat — it's good for you. It's apparent to me you've been over-doing. Do you take any vitamin supplements? I'll send you some. Very important for stamina. When there's more time you must tell me all about the knifing incident. I read in the paper, this morning, the poor man died. I feel terrible for you. The whole thing must have been a *real nightmare*.

"Oh, just *look* at the time! I really must fly. I'll send whatshisname up to take care of the basket. Minikin, I enjoyed our little chat so much — it was quite charming. I'll call you," and without giving Minikin a chance to thank her, she gave her a peck on the cheek and vanished out the door: a bright flash of silk, trailing a cloud of Joy perfume.

# 12

# ST. SINNER

HOMER ROHM AND GEORGE ZENGO stood waiting in the outer office of the National Security Advisor while his attractive secretary announced them over the phone. She put down the receiver, smiled, and without further ado ushered them inside and closed the door firmly behind them.

Sanford Baddash told them to be seated.

It was a large, sunny corner office with built-in bookcases, model sailing ships, and many photographs of Sanford Baddash with other political notables — including three United States presidents. In a place of honor on his desk stood a large jar of jellybeans with a personalized inscription.

The dark, slanted eyes of Sanford Baddash looked knowingly at them from beneath drooping lids. His black widow's peak and pointed eyebrows lent a demonic air to the already arresting presence. With great deliberation, he began to speak.

"I regret having to bring you all the way to Washington, this morning," he said, "but, due to the extreme gravity of this matter, the man in the Oval Office down the hall deemed it imperative that I work more closely with you." He paused to let the impact of his words sink in. "I don't need to tell you that I'm acutely disappointed at the way things have been handled to date." He rose from behind the large desk, walked slowly to the bank of windows, and then turned to face them.

"Rohm, we're going to have to bend every effort to salvage this disaster. I will tell you in confidence that the President has thrown his full support behind the development of this weapon — as a peaceful deterrent to war, naturally. He even suggested its code name: the Velvet Fist. Therefore, it is inconceivable that we should lose the secret of its manufacture at the very outset of its implementation. Quite simply, we must retrieve the missing specifications at whatever the cost." He strode purposefully back to his desk and reseated himself in the custom-made leather chair. "Now. I've already read your reports, but I want to hear it from you, personally. I want all the facts, deductions, and even your hunches. Give me everything you've got. Rohm?"

"Yes, sir." The pale gray-brown eyes met his, levelly. "Let's look at the evidence, first. The name, Harry Balding, was obviously an alias and not surprisingly led nowhere. As we expected, the effort to match his voice print with the cassette has proved negative. And of course there were no retrievable fingerprints on anything. The people at Federal Express were very cooperative but drew a complete blank; no one remembers how the package containing the antidote came to be delivered into their hands, and the information on their paid receipt is worthless — another dead end.

"However, early this morning Dr. Grow's motor scooter turned up in Harlem. It had been stripped and was barely recognizable. It's a wonder we got it back at all. Usually an abandoned motor scooter would be stolen outright, but this time the street people broke it up for parts instead. We made the ID by means of the Vehicle Identification Number on the frame. If the homing device was still on it when it was abandoned, some fence somewhere may still be trying to figure out what it is, hoping to get a good price for it. I don't expect much, but we've got our people out asking questions. Something may turn up."

He paused and consulted his notes. "That brings us to the medical report. The testimony of Miss Small seemed to indicate that Dr. Grow was drugged or very emotionally disturbed just prior to the stabbing. The tests showed no drugs of any kind in his system. However, there *was* evidence that he had been tied up. 'Bound with cord,' the report says. Remember he was missing for seven days. If the people that caught him used some other form of interrogation to cause his dementia, it left no mark on his body."

Sanford Baddash interrupted. "I understood your first report to say that his fingernails had been tampered with."

"Yes, sir. That was our belief in the beginning, but his wife told us he was a compulsive nail biter and, in times of stress, he actually did that to himself."

"I see."

"Therefore," Rohm continued, "we believe his mental condition was either the result of psychological torture of some kind or due to the extreme pressure he was under. Given the high-strung nature of the man, I'd say it was the latter. Which would mean that gibberish he kept babbling was just that — gibberish."

"Yes, a curious phrase," Baddash murmured. "How did it go? 'Under the bridge in the light of the moon'?"

George Zengo spoke for the first time, "I believe it was 'Behind the bridge in the shadow of the sun,' sir."

Rohm smiled thinly. "It might as well have been, 'Over Niagara in a shower of stars.' It tells us nothing. Even the computers couldn't relate to it."

Baddash nodded. "I expect you're right; probably the ravings of an overtaxed mind. What about the Small woman? Any leads there?"

"We have run an extensive check on Minikin Small, and she seems to be exactly as she presented herself. No record of Communist activities or extreme political affiliations of any kind. Her father is recently deceased from natural causes, and she returned from skiing in Gstaad to attend his funeral. For the past year she had been racing cars on the European circuit and, for a relative newcomer, doing quite well. Then, suddenly, she quit. Probably due to the death of Jean-Louis Remarque, the well-known racing driver, who was apparently her lover. At present she is making arrangements to sell the New York townhouse where her father lived and then will probably return to Europe where she leads a sort of rootless life on a small trust set up by her father. She also inherits The Small Agency, an insurance company dealing in the Excess Liability of rare art objects."

Sanford Baddash nodded his head, "Yes, I've heard of it. So she checks out clean then?"

"I'm afraid so. We're presently checking on the people she sees while she's here. Our only other lead was her description of the two Asians and the laundry van. Unfortunately, Miss Small stated definitely that she would not be able to identify the Asians and finally admitted she wasn't even sure it *was* a laundry van."

There was a long silence. Finally, the National Security Advisor said quietly, "That's hard. That doesn't leave us much."

"It leaves enough," Rohm replied grimly. "The man who identified himself as Harry Balding undeniably had inside information." He paused for a moment. "He knew enough about the Grow family to pass himself off as a friend to the boy, Gerald. He knew about their recent purchase of a picnic hamper, and he even knew the nickname of the laser weapon. You'll recall that on the tape he specifically asked for the plans to 'Rayburn's ray.'"

"You believe it's possible that he or one of his accomplices works at the Labs?"

"I think it's very likely."

"Then, what are we doing about it?" Baddash demanded.

"I have already submitted a new list of wire taps for the members of the lab staff who had knowledge of the project, which I'm sorry to say is quite lengthy. In addition, we have obtained their personal histories and financial records, and they are presently being screened for any likely suspects. Because these people regularly deal with classified information they have already been scrutinized, but now we're going to probe deeper."

"Good."

"We have also instituted surveillance at all the places where they get together for lunch or stop for drinks after work, on the off chance that someone outside the Labs may have learned of the ray in this manner."

"Excellent. I'll authorize all the extra personnel you need."

Homer Rohm moved uncomfortably in his seat. "I should also mention that the leak could have come from one of us."

Sanford Baddash leaned back in his chair and stared at the bland features of Homer Rohm in surprise. "Of course there's always that possibility," he said slowly. "But, in this case, I don't believe it."

Rohm's eyes locked onto his. "Yet on the cassette, Harry Balding told Dr. Grow that his phones were bugged. How did he know that?"

"He could have been guessing, Rohm. These people aren't stupid, you know."

"Just to be safe, I want to run a double-check on the members of our team." There was a long pause.

"Well, that's most commendable. I feel satisfied that you have overlooked nothing." Baddash studied Homer Rohm quietly for a moment. "You've come a long way since Vietnam, Rohm. Your quick advancement has been wholly earned. I have every confidence you'll pull our chestnuts out of the fire and see to it our fingers aren't burned."

"I'll do my best, sir." Rohm hesitated again. "There is one final piece of business I think you should hear about. It comes under the heading of 'hunches.' George, this is your baby; I think you should tell it."

Sanford Baddash turned the full power of his gaze upon George Zengo, who ran a nervous hand through prematurely gray hair and tried to keep his voice steady as he spoke. "Yes, sir. I believe I recognize the enemy agent, sir." He glanced at Rohm for support, then continued tentatively. "From the first appearance of Harry Balding I felt there was something familiar about this M.0. There is an agent, a free-lance, who always disguises himself as a recognizable celebrity. It's a good ruse, too, because people see the resemblance right away and don't remember anything else about him. He does the voice as well; he's a natural mimic. I ran across him the first time when I was stationed in Berlin. We aren't one hundred percent certain, Mr. Baddash, but we believe his name is Leiter d'Arques — the illegitimate son of a German cabaret dancer and the Frenchman on his birth certificate, named Jean d'Arques, rumored to be a priest.

"We do know he's a trained actor with a gift for languages — he speaks four or five like a native. For the few years we've known about him, he has worked with the Chinese Communists."

"The Chinese?" Baddash exclaimed incredulously. "I hope that isn't all you have to go on, Zengo. After all, the man calling himself 'Harry Balding' might have a natural resemblance to Mr. Selleck."

"No, sir. There is another important similarity. This agent, though he works for the other side, sets a very high moral standard. By that I mean he's a very *just* man, and he always tries to do the right thing." George Zengo, obviously ill at ease, groped for the right words.

Baddash pressed him, "For example?"

"Well, sir. Like sending the antidote to the boy *after* he got the plans. Our doctors said the boy would certainly have died, but there was the antidote, right on time. And another thing, that box — the oriental box with the jade on it that the antidote came in — that's a very valuable piece of merchandise. Mr. Rohm's people checked it out and, although we couldn't find any record of it, it's not the kind of thing that's imported casually. That's something that should be in a Chinese museum."

Baddash turned to Rohm. "Why on earth would he send the antidote in a valuable Chinese box?"

Rohm said, "Go on, George, you're doing fine."

The gray-haired man with the Medici eyes continued. "Well, sir, I think it was his way of making it up to Mrs. Grow. I mean, he didn't know that Dr. Grow had put a homing beacon in the plans, and he regretted having to put them through such an ordeal as having their son poisoned. It was sort of a gesture. I noticed the same kind of behavior in Berlin. On that occasion, he sent some evidence to clear a man who was accidentally involved in a messy border crossing. And a few years before that, in Iran under the Shah, an Irani girl who helped him was captured by Savak, their secret police — infamous, as you know, for their cruelty. Well, he risked a lot to free her. It was a dramatic escape, and then they simply disappeared."

Sanford Baddash snorted, derisively. "You make this mythical subversive sound like Robin Hood."

George Zengo shook his head solemnly. "No, sir. He can be absolutely merciless when it serves his ends. And the master he serves with undivided loyalty is Communist China. It's just that he follows his own set of rules. The boys in Records have code named him 'St. Sinner.'"

Baddash said slowly, "This is fantastic; the man is a paradox, a dichotomy, a . . ." his imagination failed him.

"An oxymoron?" Rohm supplied.

"Precisely," he nodded. "Good word. Well?" Baddash looked from one to the other of them. "How does this help us?"

Rohm answered him, "If it *is* the man George knew, it tells us who the enemy is and who he works for. And it gives us a certain insight into his behavior — *if* he really exists at all. Frankly, he sounds a bit mythical for my liking, too."

George Zengo smiled, quietly, "Oh, he exists all right."

Sanford Baddash sighed, "Okay, then, you'd better let me see the file on this 'St. Sinner.'"

# 13

# A MOURNFUL OPTIMIST

THE NIGHT AFTER LACY'S VISIT MINIKIN found herself unable to sleep. She tossed and turned until close to midnight before finally throwing back the covers and getting up.

She didn't understand her restlessness, the latent sense of urgency that nagged at her. In the bathroom, she splashed cold water on her face and brushed her hair. Twisting it into a knot atop her head, she suddenly realized what was bothering her: she needed to know more about what had happened to Dr. Grow — she had to see a newspaper.

As she dressed in blue jeans and pulled on a sweater, she recalled the way he had clung to her as she lowered him to the floor of the foyer. A disturbing memory.

She shook off the recollection and strode out of the house and into the clammy night air. The late-night streets were nearly deserted, colored street lights were reflected in the greasy pavement, and

Manhattan's manhole covers emitted a ghostly steam. Minikin turned down Madison Avenue taking long strides. The exercise felt invigorating after so many days of inactivity.

At a newsstand on the corner of 59th Street she bought several papers and then retraced her steps to the house, moving more slowly on the way back. Climbing the three flights of stairs to her bedroom, she found herself gasping for breath, and smiled at the unaccustomed weakness.

In the bedroom, she spread out the newspapers on the bed and began turning the pages. On an inside page she found a short column entitled: MISSING SCIENTIST FATALLY STABBED.

She scanned the article quickly. The incident had been down-played as an ordinary street mugging, and she had been cited as a quick-thinking good Samaritan. Though misspelled, her name was given and her street, but no exact address. In spite of the enlightened efforts of the paramedic team and hospital staff, it read, Dr. Grow had died without regaining consciousness. The article puzzled briefly over the mystery of his week-long disappearance, recounted his overwrought mental condition, and touched on the grief of his family. And that was all. In the other newspapers the articles were nearly verbatim down to the misspelling of her name.

Minikin thought it seemed odd; unlike poor journalism, it was more as if the writers had all had to use the same news source, and that source had been carefully controlled. And, while it wasn't surprising that nothing was said about Dr. Grow's unintelligible last words, it seemed strange there was no mention made that the assailants had actually broken down her front door to get at him. It was obvious to her that this was no random attack, yet too many things had not been satisfactorily explained. Something was wrong here.

She reviewed the facts as she knew them. A scientist, missing for a week, turns up — not merely overwrought — but literally frightened out of his wits. The people chasing him go to extreme lengths to kill him rather than let him get away. And when someone tries to help him, she is interrogated all night by the police and the CIA.

Why?

Minikin thought an obvious explanation could be that, as a scientist, Dr. Grow had had access to sensitive technical data of some kind. Maybe he had been kidnapped for it, perhaps even tortured, and then escaped. His captors would have been afraid of what he could tell the police, and so they killed him. *That* would explain his death, the presence of the CIA and her lengthy interrogation. And the CIA could have withheld her address from the newspapers and garbled her name in order to protect her.

She shook her head and decided she was letting her imagination run away with her. The whole thing was too fantastic. Anyway, wasn't the FBI supposed to handle kidnappings?

Minikin tried to put aside her nagging sense of unfinished business. Poor Dr. Grow. She had nearly saved him.

She wandered out of the bedroom and prowled up the stairs. For a while she paced the empty attic rooms — empty except for the few personal things in the house she had been unable to bring herself to sell or throw away. After a while she stopped pacing and paused to wonder why, of all the things she had sold and discarded, she had kept these: her father's desk, the pink and cream Persian rug from her old bedroom, and her grandmother's sterling tea service and dining candelabra. She knew it wasn't their intrinsic value or even their beauty; this old house had held many more wondrous things. She had to admit that their sentimental association had compelled her, though as a rule she didn't like to accumulate things that required a lot of care. What was she going to do with all this stuff? She shrugged her shoulders and resumed pacing.

She was also surprised by her recent illness. It was unlike her, and she wondered how much of it had been psychosomatic. Of late there had been too much death in her life; it had altered her view of living. Her own death was no longer an accident to be skillfully avoided — it had become a certainty to be reckoned with. Minikin shivered involuntarily.

Who was it that said, "I don't want to be immortal through my work, I want to live forever."? She smiled to herself. However, she decided perversely, now she didn't *want* to live forever. Not really. She had no strong ties to life, and one got used to the idea of having to die, some time. What she was finding hard to accept was the meaninglessness of all the pain in living. She decided she would welcome oblivion.

She stopped pacing and laughed aloud at herself; what a mournful optimist she was! Who was she fooling? And what would she feel if she had another option? To live with certain death, that's life. A bargain struck. So, okay, she concluded.

She took the elevator down to the kitchen. Distractedly, she emerged and stared in confusion at the gutted room enclosed in plastic sheeting. She turned aside, ascended the steps and opened the door to the garage instead, snapping on the light. The new bulb shone on the recently swept floor and the small, tarpaulin-covered car.

Slowly, Minikin dragged the tarp away and stood admiring the sleek lines of the 1960 MGA. Her father had given it to her when she was still in prep school in Connecticut, and she had gradually refined and honed it till it ran and looked like the pampered thing it was — pristine white with chrome wire wheels and natural leather seats, a wooden racing wheel and matching gear knob. Under the hood it was even more spectacular. A few years ago, it had become a twenty-five year old certified antique.

She had named it "The Slim," from Gide's novel, *Lafcadio's Adventures.* The "slim" were a special breed, she remembered, a law unto themselves. Elegant and praiseworthy, they would achieve in life what the "crusted" could not. And only another member of the "slim" could recognize the "slim." What better name for this limber narrow thing which could pivot on a dime, dart through invisible holes in traffic, and park on a postage stamp? She loved this car.

It would be great to take a drive now, to watch the sun come up over the river. She looked inside; the key was there, but there was no telling when it had been driven last. More than a year, certainly.

She tried to control a thrill of anticipation as she got inside, pumped the accelerator, and turned the ignition. Nothing. The battery was dead.

She got out, folded back the driver's seat and attached the cables from the wall charger to the battery. She got in and tried it again. This time there was a clicking noise like a broken wind-up toy. She got out, opened the hood, and checked the carburetor to see if it was getting gas. Okay. Checked the spark plugs for spark — uh oh.

She replaced all four plugs, then went to the toolbox and found a lady's emery board. She returned to the car, removed the cap, exposed the points, and with a deft hand carefully abraded the contact points. Then she got in and tried it again. The Slim coughed into life and settled down to a feral rumble.

Minikin disconnected the jumper cables from the battery and closed the hood. She walked around the car and opened the garage door; the night sky was shot through with pink. As she backed into the street she wondered, briefly, what she was going to do with The Slim when she sold the house. . . .

Two hours later she stepped into a soapy shower and emerged feeling like Aphrodite, rising from the foam of the sea. She dried off, changed into fresh clothes and went downstairs in search of Li C. Fu. They spent a quiet Saturday doing laundry.

On Sunday, they breakfasted at a coffee shop off Madison Avenue and discussed landscaping the backyard. This seemed to be a topic of some interest to Li C. Fu, for he blinked rapidly as he sketched diagrams for Minikin on his paper place-setting and napkin. He had spent some time cleaning the small green-house at the rear of the yard while she was ill, and apparently had already given the layout some thought.

It sounded over-elaborate to Minikin, especially the part about the goldfish pond and the cherry tree. It had been her idea to pave as much of the yard as possible with gray stone to match the house, then plant a few small evergreens here and there that would be easy to maintain. Somehow, their roles reversed. Li C. Fu accepted the idea of a flagstoned area near the house, but insisted a cherry tree be planted outside the dining room window. There would also be a winding footpath to the greenhouse through an oriental garden with outdoor lighting. They deadlocked on the fishpond.

"Must have goldfish pond, Mees Smawr. Goldfish lucky, will bring prosperity to your house." He was unshakable.

Minikin stifled a mad desire to laugh with the exasperated sense that he was overstepping himself.

They returned to the house in silence. With the workmen absent the house was strangely quiet, but the framework for the greenhouse window was already in place, stretching the length and height of the kitchen wall. Minikin and Li C. Fu stared at it from the backyard. It became clear to her that the garden would become almost a part of the new kitchen. Perhaps Li C. Fu was right about the outdoor lighting, but no fishpond. This renovation was getting out of hand.

For the remainder of the day she consulted with professional landscapers and garden centers. She was lucky enough to hire stonemasons for the following day, and the plants and sod she selected would begin arriving the day after.

The next morning as Minikin paced off an irregularly shaped flagstone area for the stonemasons,

Li C. Fu, with arms folded, waited patiently by the greenhouse for the fishpond.

Unexpectedly, visions of the recent trays of food he had prepared and brought to her sickbed flashed in her memory. With a hollow feeling, Minikin found herself saying, "We have running water and drains in the greenhouse, would it be very costly to build a fishpond nearby?" She indicated the spot where Li C. Fu stood. The location and design were pronounced feasible, and Li C. Fu blinked rapidly and managed, with great dignity, to contain his delight.

Oh well, Minikin thought, maybe the new owners would like it. But, while *she* lived here, that pond would contain no unhappy fish. She had had enough of death for a while.

The next day the flagstones were laid with a circular space left for the tree, and the kidney-shaped fishpond at the center of the garden was nearly completed.

The following day the men delivering the plants and sod also inserted the cherry tree into the space allotted for it outside the dining room window. Then the backbreaking work for Minikin and Li C. Fu began in earnest. Minikin realized she was driving herself — if she kept busy enough she didn't have time to think, and if she worked very hard she slept deeply and didn't dream.

She let Li C. Fu direct her: where to put what, how much fertilizer, how much mulch. They dug holes, grunted, sweated, and slowly the garden took shape. The tiny greenhouse now peeped modestly from behind small pinecone firs. The shrubbery bordering the fence was artfully arranged, and the winding path led the rambling eye and foot gracefully through the lush emerald sod to the fishpond.

For all his delicate appearance, Li C. Fu was tireless, but after two days Minikin had trouble straightening up, her arms and legs and the back of her neck were sunburned, and she felt exhausted. Even Lacy's vitamins made no difference — Minikin thought she would die of Health. However, except for a few odds and ends, the transformation in the garden was complete.

At sundown on Friday they sat in the shade of the cherry tree, leaning back against the fence, and finished their hamburgers to-go. Minikin noticed Li C. Fu watching her with an inscrutable eye.

He spoke suddenly. "Mees Smawr, I have first cousin in New York City, name Luk Tsi. Luk Tsi a graduate of Juliard Music School. She number one violinist." He hesitated and folded his paper napkin neatly.

Minikin rallied with difficulty. "That's nice, Li C. Didn't know you had any family here."

"Oh, yes. Her family move to San Francisco many years ago, and Luk Tsi win scholarship to New York school. *My* family stay in China."

"I see," was all Minikin could muster.

Li C. Fu took a deep breath. "Would be most honored if you would care to hear Luk Tsi play violin tonight in place called Carnegie Hall. She has given me gift of two tickets." He averted his face as he fumbled in his pocket and withdrew a damp envelope containing the two cardboard rectangles.

Minikin was stunned. She was so tired she wasn't sure she wouldn't drown in her bath tonight. If she went, she couldn't even guarantee she would stay awake. But how could she refuse him?

"Thank you, Li C. What time?"

## 14

# SHARP AND FLAT

IT WAS IMPOSSIBLE TO GET A CAB FRIDAY evening in mid-town Manhattan, so Minikin and Li C. Fu set out down Fifth Avenue on foot. Minikin had dressed carefully for the occasion in a jade-green dress with gold sandals. Li C. Fu had also dressed with care. He wore a black silk *cheong sam,* the traditional formal wear of the Chinese; the full sleeves were lined in white, and a black silk cap was perched on the back of his head. His shoes, worn with white socks, resembled ballerina slippers. In his hands he carried a single perfect rose encased in a plastic cylinder, so deep red in color as to nearly match his *cheong sam.*

At 57th Street they turned right; Li C. Fu trotted alongside Minikin, taking two steps to her every one. She had tried shortening her strides to accommodate him, only to have him shorten his — and so they retained a constant ratio of two steps to one, his head bobbing at her shoulder. Minikin felt vaguely ridiculous. At Seventh Avenue they turned into Carnegie Hall and climbed the steps to the entrance. Li C. Fu presented his tickets at the door, and they were seated immediately — third row center.

Minikin glanced around the semi-restored grandeur of Carnegie Hall. The large, baroque auditorium was about nine-tenths full, and she was surprised at the number of Oriental faces in attendance.

The walk had made them late and she just had time for a quick look at the program. It said, "The New York Philharmonic Orchestra, conducted by Zubin Mehta. . . ." She skipped to the section on Luk Tsi and, under a small photograph, read: "Luk Tsi is nineteen years old and resides in San Francisco with her parents and two brothers, who are also musicians. A full-scholarship graduate of the Juliard School of Music and recent winner of the coveted Leventritt Competition, Luk Tsi makes her New York debut tonight and the beginning of her first tour which will include . . ." and the lights dimmed.

People with respiratory problems immediately made their presence known, then the curtain rose on a full orchestra. There was a great round of applause. As it died away the concert master rose to his feet and signaled the oboe player to give concert A, and the orchestra began the discordance of tuning up. Minikin's weary eyes fell on the balding pate of the man in front of her, the careful spiraling of the sparse hairs over his baldspot. Gradually the raucous sound subsided, there was a final bout of coughing, then silence.

A deafening round of applause signaled the entrance of the popular, elegantly attired conductor: a darkly vital man with a handsome aquiline face and a spring to his step. He bowed deeply several times and took his place at the podium. Almost in anticlimax, the child-like figure of a girl appeared in the wings and walked quickly to stand beside the conductor. The applause was more restrained for the relatively unknown newcomer. She wore a white dress, and ribbons of blue-black hair cascaded down her back to her waist. Her resemblance to Li C. Fu was striking; she possessed the same distant expression and the same wing-like brows above thickly fringed cat's eyes. Luk Tsi inclined her head slightly to the audience, and Minikin couldn't help but admire her composure.

The conductor tapped his baton lightly on the music stand and lifted his arms. There was an expectant hush.

Minikin could feel her sleepy eyes beginning to close. Timpani drums rumbled as thunder in the distance. Then the brilliant sound of a violin cut the air sharp and flat like the blade of an assassin's knife. Minikin came fully awake as the familiar strains of the Mendelssohn Violin Concerto swept over her. The haunting, heroic lyric in a minor key rapidly gained momentum and vaulted skyward to circle and swoop like a joyous meadowlark. Minikin stared in fascination as raindrops, waves, floods of sound poured from the flashing white fingers of Luk Tsi. She dominated the orchestra with the glorious sound of her fiddle, the sensuality of her quick fingerplay, and the slash of her bow. Minikin glanced about her; the audience seemed as overwhelmed as she, and sat staring in rapt attention.

A sustained note in the bassoon sounded the first chord of the second movement and without hesitating, gradually, the other instruments returned, beginning the lovely *Andante* — simple and songlike. The eye lingered on the amazing face of the bassoonist — his lips pursed, his nostrils flared, his brows highly arched with eyes popping, myriad tiny corkscrew curls bouncing in time to his music. But the purity of the violin's tone was like a siren-song, calling one back, drawing one into a finale of impish, scherzo-like playfulness.

The *Allegro molto vivace* movement always reminded Minikin of a steeplechase through English countryside, with glimpses of serene rivers winding through sun-dappled trees and the galloping, galloping rhythm of magical tireless horses. Luk Tsi executed the nervous trilling strokes, and severe sweet sustained ones, with gracefully choreographed gestures of her bow arm — using the almost perverse application of cold technique to evoke sensual response. Minikin felt giddy with the flow of adrenalin. Her spirit took wing, soared, and was rejuvenated.

And then, abruptly, it was over.

With the noise of a dam bursting, the audience rose to its feet and cheered the tiny virtuoso. The smiling conductor and orchestra joined the audience in seemingly interminable applause. Luk Tsi bowed and bowed, and then with a sweep of shining blue-black hair she was gone — but not before giving a quick glance at Li C. Fu.

The curtain at last descended, the house lights went up, and it was intermission. Li C. Fu turned to Minikin and said, "Luk Tsi expect us to go to her. She say use exit door on left of stage."

They rose and filed through the milling crowd and
They rose and filed through the milling crowd and
out of the auditorium. A uniformed guard stopped them at a short, blue-carpeted stairway, but Luk Tsi called to him and they were allowed to ascend. As they passed the first door, Minikin saw the handsome conductor, his jacket off, rubbing his face with a towel.

Luk Tsi's dressing room was next door, and she stood waiting for them in the doorway. With the deference of her old-world training she began a low bow to Li C. Fu, but then her Americanization took over, and she threw her arms around his neck and hugged him instead. There was a rapid exchange of Chinese. Then Li C. Fu, struggling to maintain his composure, presented her with the red rose.

Her voice broke. "Oh, Cousin Fu, it's *perfect.*"

There was more hugging and more Chinese. Finally, Li C. Fu sputtered in confusion, "Luk Tsi, I want present you employer of me, Mees Smawr."

She turned and nodded politely, radiating happiness.

Minikin said, "I'm very glad to meet you. I thought you played beautifully."

They moved inside her dressing room, full of flowers and telegrams, and Luk Tsi closed the door.

"In what capacity are you employed by Miss Small, Cousin Fu?" she asked.

He hesitated, and Minikin suddenly sensed he was about to lose face. She spoke up quickly. "He is the *majordomo* of my house," she replied.

Luk Tsi turned glowing eyes upon Li C. Fu.

He inclined his head slightly, then asked, "Will we see your parents tonight, Luk Tsi?"

"Ah no, they are flying out from San Francisco to attend the concert tomorrow night in Washington, D.C., when we will play for the President. It's going to be black-tie and very chic. That's why I'm so glad you could come tonight, to give me moral support." She smiled at both of them.

"The joy was ours, Luk Tsi," he answered simply.

She glanced down at her watch to hide her blush. "There are only a few more minutes before the piano concerto begins. You don't want to miss it; the pianist is wonderful. He will be doing the tour with me. I'll wait here, and perhaps we can meet afterward?"

Minikin smiled and nodded. "I think this evening's triumph calls for a celebration."

There was a timid knock at the door.

Luk Tsi opened it and saw a confused-looking old man with a halo of tousled white hair, a shaggy white moustache, and soulful brown eyes. He clutched a battered violin case to his breast. "Miss Luk Tsi?" he asked in a frail voice.

"Yes?"

For a moment he seemed to be at a loss for words, then he spoke. "I have brought you a gift — something very fine." There was a trace of middle-Europe in his accent.

She started to protest, but he raised a shaking hand and she allowed him to continue. "My doctors have told me that I am drawing to the end of my days. I have put all my affairs in order with one exception — this violin. Though I am a professor of mathematics, this violin has always been my most prized possession. Through the years it has given me comfort in times of sorrow and multiplied all my joys. It was made in 1739 by Giuseppe Guarneri."

There was a quick intake of breath from Luk Tsi.

"That's right, little one," he confirmed with a nod. "It's a 'del Gesù,' the only violin maker acknowledged to rival, or even excel, the work of Stradivari. And also very much more rare."

Firmly Luk Tsi shook her head, but he went on stubbornly.

"You must see that it is a great responsibility I lay before you, for this violin will *own* you. It will live after you, as it does me." He paused. "I give it to you to be held in trust. To care for in your lifetime and then, finally, to entrust to someone else that you know is worthy." Slowly, carefully, he put the case into her arms.

"But, Maestro, why should you give such a thing to me?"

"Why, for the touch of a master's hand," he answered.

She stared at him blankly, and then to their amazement he began to recite a poem:

Twas battered and scarred, and the auctioneer
Thought it scarcely worth his while
To waste much time on the old violin,
But held it up with a smile:
"What am I bidden, good folks," he cried,
"Who'll start the bidding for me?"
"A dollar, a dollar"; then, "Two!" "Only two?
Two dollars, and who'll make it three?
Three dollars, once, three dollars, twice;
Going for three. . ." But no,
From the room, far back, a gray-haired man
Came forward and picked up the bow;
Then, wiping the dust from the old violin,
And tightening the loose strings,

He played a melody pure and sweet
As a caroling angel sings.

The music ceased, and the auctioneer,
With a voice that was quiet and low,
Said: "What am I bid for the old violin?"
And he held it up with the bow.
"A thousand dollars, and who'll make it two?
Two thousand! And who'll make it three?
Three thousand, once, three thousand, twice,
And going, and gone," said he.
The people cheered, but some of them cried,
"We do not quite understand
What changed its worth." Swift came the reply:
"The touch of a master's hand."

There was a long silence while the old man paused to catch his breath. From her place just inside the door, Minikin could see the tears streaming down Luk Tsi's face. She altered position slightly so that she could see the old man's reflection in the dressing table mirror — he bore a startling resemblance to Albert Einstein! Their eyes met in the mirror, and just for a moment she thought she saw a flicker of recognition.

He continued to Luk Tsi, "Now do you understand? As wonderful as this violin is, *you* will enhance its value. The papers are in the case. I have already signed them."

Luk Tsi bowed low. *"Toh che,* Maestro. *Toh che."*

"There is only one way you can thank me, little one. Make our violin sing." And he turned slowly and walked away.

They were all a little shaken. In the distance Minikin could hear the sound of applause that signaled the curtain was going up in the auditorium. Luk Tsi closed the door and then turned to them in chagrin.

"I forgot to ask his *name.*"

Minikin said, "It will be on the papers inside the case."

Luk Tsi wiped the tears from her eyes and moved to her dressing table. She set down the battered old case, unfastened the clasps, and slowly opened the lid. Then she lifted the gleaming instrument from its faded velvet bed with the reverence of a young mother taking her child into her arms for the first time.

Minikin took a thick envelope from the bottom of the case. She opened it and quickly scanned the contents. "It's not a Wurlizter authentication, but it may be better, if that's possible." She read further. "I'd say it's a genuine del Gesù, all right. And the last owner signed himself 'Professor Topper Bottham.'"

# 15

# SOLEMN REVELRY

MINIKIN AND LI C. FU WAITED OUTSIDE the dressing room door while Luk Tsi changed her clothes. In the distance Minikin could hear the sound of the opening theme of the Tchaikovsky Piano Concerto filling the great hall, but they had delayed too long to be readmitted. At last Luk Tsi emerged, and the three slipped out a side door and set off up the street like happy truants.

On this special night Luk Tsi seemed to radiate with the joy of living, and her mood infected the other two. Gaily, they entered the Plaza Hotel and took a table in the Palm Court. Li C. Fu held a chair for Luk Tsi, and then one for Minikin.

Minikin glanced around. For as long as she could remember very little had changed at the Plaza. In the midst of the frantic city outside, there was a gracious comfortable aura about the old hotel, where the tempo was noticeably slower and one paused to savor the richly flavored atmosphere of yesterday.

The circular cluster of tables in the Palm Court was surrounded by graceful palms and massive electrified candelabra, and in its center a piano player and violinist filled the vaulted space with semi-classical music. The headwaiter wore white tie and tails and spoke with old-world courtesy. The happy trio ordered complex little pastries from a multi-tiered table and selected from a large assortment of coffees.

Minikin sampled the sweet pastry, sipped her bitter espresso and then turned to Luk Tsi. "I am very curious to know what it was like to perform with the New York Philharmonic Orchestra."

"Oh!" Luk Tsi rolled her eyes, set down her demitasse with a clink, and her words bubbled out over one another. "On the first day of rehearsal I was very nervous; they seemed such a formidable group! When I took my place beside the conductor my knees were knocking together. Well, the first violins began the introduction, I whipped the fiddle under my chin ready for the attack, and then I realized they were playing the *wrong* concerto. I couldn't believe it; I stopped and stamped my foot, and then I started to giggle, and they all began to laugh. It was a trick, and they had nearly taken me in! I was amazed that the whole orchestra would do such a thing just to tease me. But afterward there were no more nerves. We laughed and joked a lot, and it was truly an inspiration to have the privilege of working with them."

Minikin was fascinated; Luk Tsi was as outgoing as Li C. Fu was reserved. "Have you always wanted to be a violinist?" she asked her.

Luk Tsi nodded. "My mother started me on the piano when I was four, but as soon as I heard the first sound of a bow on the string I knew that was my instrument. I gave my first violin concert when I was seven."

"Doesn't performing in front of such large crowds make you nervous?"

Luk Tsi laughed and her eyes danced. "No, I have always loved audiences, and the more people there are the more exciting it is."

Li C. Fu stirred his coffee thoughtfully, then raised his eyes to her, "I think perhaps you will be famous, Luk Tsi."

Suddenly she was very serious. "Who can say what the future holds, Cousin Fu. Yesterday I thought only of tonight's concert and the tour, but now the gift of the wonderful violin has seemed to eclipse all that." She hesitated. "In honesty, I do feel singled out. This is the proudest night of my life."

"Is old violin so valuable, then?" he asked.

Luk Tsi replied, "I do not know what it is worth in money, but . . ."

Minikin interrupted gently. "I do. I'd say it's worth, conservatively, about half of Pittsburgh."

Luk Tsi brushed this information aside. "It is above all price to me."

Li C. Fu shook his head in bewilderment. "Name of violin not familiar to me. Have heard of Stradivarius."

With her fingertip, Minikin wrote the name for him on the shiny, marble table top. "It's Latin, so the G is pronounced like an H: del Gesù, accent on the U."

Luk Tsi's face shown, and she spoke with deep feeling. "Let me tell you of the wonder of these fiddles. You have heard of Paganini? He practically created the solo violin performance. Fritz Kreisler? Probably everyone's favorite violinist. And Jascha Heifetz? Technically, the king of virtuosos. Each of these men owned many violins — Strads, Amatis, Stainers and so on. Yet the favorite of each was their own Guarnerius del Gesù. Paganini so loved his that he named it the 'Cannon' because of its rich, booming tone. Paganini was also a terrible gambler and once gambled away his Amati violin before an important performance and had to *borrow* one to play on. But when he nearly lost his 'Cannon' because of gambling debts it so frightened him that he gave up gambling altogether. When he died he left *fifteen* master fiddles to be sold, but he bequeathed his 'Cannon' to the museum in Genoa where he was born. After nearly one hundred and fifty years, it's still there."

She looked from one to the other of them. "Don't you see? These men knew the best, and they all felt nothing could compare with the tone of a del

Ges violin." Ironically, she grinned. "However, I have heard they are difficult to play."

Amused and interested, Minikin thought that conversation would never be a problem with Luk Tsi around.

Gazing into her coffee, Luk Tsi murmured, "Somehow, it all seems too good to be true." But then she brightened.

"Ah, I have another violin story for you. It happened that Fritz Kreisler was browsing through an antique store in Belgium, before the first World War, and he took out his priceless del Gesù and showed it to the dealer. The dealer admired it and then mentioned he had an Amati violin at home which his customer might like to see. He left the shop and returned with a policeman, shouting, 'Arrest him! That man is a thief; he's stolen Fritz Kreisler's violin.' "

They laughed together, delightedly, and she went on.

"It turned out poor Kreisler had no identification with him, and he had to establish who he was by playing 'Schon Rosmarin' on the violin for the dealer and the policeman."

"I hope they decided not to arrest him," Minikin said in mock horror.

"They did," Luk Tsi laughingly assured her. "The dealer said it must be he, for no one else could play 'Schon Rosmarin' with so much feeling."

"Violin more famous than owner," observed Li C. Fu.

"And what the professor said was true," Minikin noted. "The violin will own *you.*"

There was a moment's silence. Then Luk Tsi said, "I did not know I could feel such *solemn* revelry."

Minikin decided it was time to change the subject. "Will someone please tell me what '*toh che*' means?"

Luk Tsi quickly answered, "It means 'thank you' in Chinese. Why do you ask?"

"It's only that I couldn't help noticing how perceptive the old professor was — he understood you immediately." She added, "And did you see how much he resembled Albert Einstein?"

Luk Tsi exclaimed in surprise, "Do you know, I noticed that too!"

The Palm Court violinist had approached their table and now bent politely over Luk Tsi. "Excuse me. Don't I recognize Miss Luk Tsi?"

She turned to him, smiling, and nodded. He offered her his shiny yellow fiddle, saying, "We would be very pleased if you would care to honor us with a tune or two."

Luk Tsi only hesitated for an instant. "Why, thank you. I'd love to." She put down her napkin and, taking the violin from his outstretched hands, strode to the piano. After a brief whispered conference with the pianist, Luk Tsi began to play

Fritz Kreisler's "Schon Rosmarin," her eyes partly closed like a cat dreaming in front of a fire.

Minikin reflected that, for all her deceptive fragility, Luk Tsi was a highly-disciplined powerhouse of energy, with an extrovert's love of performing. The lilting bagatelle drew to an end, and there was an absentminded smattering of applause for the unknown guest musician.

Luk Tsi registered this and returned to their table for the violin case beside her chair. "Let's see if a del Ges, wakes them up," she said. She winked at them mischievously and returned to the tiny stage.

She tuned the instrument quickly, spoke again to the accompanist, and began to play the "Devil's Trill" sonata. Gradually the mundane sounds in the Palm Court faded away, and the penetrating notes of the violin danced upon a perfect silence. The hairs at the back of Minikin's neck prickled as the *terzi tuoni,* or third sound, was clearly heard — though not played — as Luk Tsi double-stopped in perfect intonation. The acoustical phenomenon continued eerily and, as she listened, Minikin recalled the story of its composer Tartini dreaming he sold his soul to the devil in return for the most exquisite sonata imaginable. When he woke, he wrote it down: the "Devil's Trill." And with it he discovered the "differential" note — the *terzi tuoni.*

Minikin noticed a change in Luk Tsi. Gone was the cat-like trance; instead there were the twin lines of concentration across the bridge of her nose that Minikin had seen in Li C. Fu. Her full lips were firmed into a thin line, and a gleam of perspiration shone on her forehead. She finished the sonata to enthusiastic applause, replaced the violin in its case, and returned smiling to the table. But as the sounds of the room returned to normal, Luk Tsi quietly mopped her face with her napkin.

Minikin asked, "Is something wrong?"

"It's true what they say about del Gesùs," she replied weakly. "They don't meet you anything like halfway. You must be very sure of yourself to go in after the rich strong tone, and get it out without breathiness or scratch." She drew a shaky breath. "It was like riding a spirited horse. I will have to practice with it so I can use it on the tour."

The headwaiter bowed over the table. "There will be no check for Miss Luk Tsi and her friends. The management wants you to know we are delighted to have you with us anytime."

They murmured their surprised thanks, and he turned smoothly away. Luk Tsi chuckled, "I guess I sang for our supper."

"Where will you go on tour?" asked Li C. Fu.

"It's part of a cultural exchange program, Cousin Fu. After the concert tomorrow, we're scheduled for Hong Kong, then Shanghai, Tel Aviv, Milan, Budapeste, Vienna, Moscow, Stockholm, Munich, Paris and London." She thought a moment. "I don't think I left anything out."

Li C. Fu was impressed. "It sound like world cruise."

"Yes," she answered gravely. "But we had a lot of trouble with the visas, and I probably won't get to see more than just a lot of drafty auditoriums because there will be so little time." She frowned. "I don't have much time before I leave, either, and I must do something about insuring the new violin."

Minikin hesitated. "Perhaps I could help you. I am connected with The Small Agency. We insure excess liability items in situations like this."

Luk Tsi narrowed her cat's eyes. "*The* Small Agency?"

"I think we're the only one."

"Why, this is wonderful. My brother insures his cello with your agency when *he* travels. Can you do this for me right away?"

"Yes, I'm sure we can. Of course, the violin must be authenticated by an expert first. It could probably be done in half a day while the policy was being written."

Luk Tsi groaned aloud. "But I leave for Washington first thing tomorrow morning. We don't return till late the following day, Sunday. Then, Monday afternoon we depart from Kennedy Airport to begin the first leg of the tour." She looked anxiously at Minikin. "What can I do?"

"Well, if you want to leave the violin with me, I could have it authenticated tomorrow and the policy written up, and then return it to you on Monday. Naturally, I'd give you a receipt for it."

"Ohhh, I *hate* to part with it," Luk Tsi moaned in anguish. "I need to practice on it." She thought a moment, then exhaled in exasperation. "I must have it insured. I'll do it."

Later, in the reception area of the hotel, they obtained stationery, and Minikin composed the receipt standing at the counter:

> Received on this date violin purported to be a Guarnerius del Ges with historical documents of sale, in good condition. Taken to be authenticated for purpose of insurance with The Small Agency. Said violin and documents to be returned to owner, Luk Tsi, no later than three days hence, in the same condition in which they were received.
>
> Signed and dated by, Minikin Small
> Witnessed by Li C. Fu

With some pride Minikin handed the paper to Luk Tsi who took it and folded it carefully.

# 16

# TINY TOWER

THEY PAUSED FOR A TIME OUTSIDE THE entrance to the Plaza Hotel, savoring the mild spring evening. Luk Tsi, especially, seemed reluctant to say good night. But when a rare taxi pulled to the curb in front of them and unloaded its passengers, she handed the violin case to Li C. Fu and got inside.

"I am very sorry this evening had to end," she said. "Perhaps we can have lunch together on Monday when I return?"

A date was set, farewells said, and the cabbie dropped his flag and pulled away.

Minikin and Li C. Fu ignored the horse-drawn hansom cabs parked nearby and set off to walk the five short blocks home. Slowly, they circled the fountain in front of the Plaza where Zelda Fitzgerald once bathed, then crossed 59th Street and headed up Fifth Avenue alongside Central Park. The dim street lights along the park cast an intermittent glow on newly green trees, and for a block or more they didn't notice they were being followed.

Minikin glanced uneasily at Li C. Fu, trotting beside her, and at the same exact instant they both turned to look back. She gasped, and her heart beat faster. It *couldn't* be, she told herself, it was only a frightening coincidence. But the two men a few yards behind them looked like the same two Asians who had assaulted Dr. Grow!

At this late hour the streets were completely deserted. Minikin and Li C. Fu began to accelerate their pace, and the two men behind them immediately accelerated theirs. Minikin quickly realized there was no mistake — whoever they were they intended to catch them, and they were closing fast! Li C. Fu glanced up at her, and an unspoken thought passed between them. Minikin stepped out of her shoes, whispered, *"Now!"* and the two of them broke into a run.

One of the men behind them gave a shout, and Minikin could hear footsteps pounding after them. They raced two long blocks in desperate silence — saving all their lung power for speed. They dashed across to the residential side of Fifth Avenue and were nearly to 63rd Street when Minikin knew they weren't going to make it. The men were gaining and would be upon them before they could reach the front door.

At the corner of 63rd Street Minikin whirled around to face them, and Li C. Fu stopped close beside her. The two men chasing them skidded to a halt nearby and separated from each other. The four of them stood there, panting.

Minikin eyed them warily; both men appeared to be in their mid-to-late twenties and had the athletic build and drab clothes of street hoods. The one nearest her bore an ugly scar across his eyebrow. When she could speak she asked breathlessly, "What do you want?"

The one with the scar, nearly as breathless as she, stepped forward and held out his hand. "Give me the violin case and all your valuables."

To Minikin the "valuables" sounded like an afterthought, but how could he know about the master violin? Behind her, Li C. Fu made a subtle movement, and without looking at him she said, "Don't worry, Li C., I'll handle this." She faced the man who had spoken and said earnestly, "You're welcome to what money we have, but this old fiddle has only sentimental value and would be worthless to you."

He responded equally earnestly. "Cut the crap lady, and give me the violin."

The receipt she had given Luk Tsi made The Small Agency liable for the del Gesù, and to Minikin its loss was unthinkable. She began to speak before she knew what she was going to say, "We won't give it to you. If you try to take it by force, I must warn you I'm skilled in the martial arts, I'll hurt you." She thought wildly, this is insane; I could get us both killed!

The two hoodlums glanced at each other and smiled. Li C. Fu put down the violin carefully and stepped away from it. Minikin's heart sank, but she continued to bluff. "My friend also knows karate. His hands are lethal weapons." She did a double-take as Li C. Fu, looking like a Chinese doll in his *cheong sam* and cap, put both heels together and bowed from the waist.

The two ruffians watching him were as surprised as she.

Minikin decided to press her advantage — she hitched up her skirt, took a step forward and kicked the closest one on the point of his chin with her heel. His head snapped back with the impact, but he was otherwise unmoved. For an instant he stood there grinning. Then he rushed her.

Minikin grabbed his hand and spun around, intending to throw him over her head — it had always worked in class. But something went wrong. She found herself being turned, vaulted off her feet, and hurled bodily into the street.

She rolled, lessening the impact of the fall, and quickly regained her feet. She whirled around to see Li C. Fu in karate stance in front of the violin case — a tiny tower of rage — the two attackers coming at him from different sides.

As the first one reached out for him, Li C. Fu gave a terrifying shout, executed a cross frontal kick to the attacker's groin, set down his kicking leg and turned his other hip toward the rush of the second attacker, meeting him with a jump kick to the solar plexus. The first man went down, rolling in agony, but the second man staggered back and then recovered. His eyes fell on the violin case, and he went for it. Li C. Fu stepped in close to block his move; a necessary error on his part that allowed Minikin to reach it first.

She snatched up the violin and dropped it over a small wrought-iron fence into the shrubbery, then spun around and saw the second attacker had Li C. Fu bent over in a headlock. Li C. Fu was trying to free himself by kicking at the other man's knee; the attacker, well braced with legs far apart, began to punch him in the head and face with his fist. Minikin screamed for help at the top of her lungs, and then she stepped behind the attacker and kicked him well and truly between the legs. With a roar of pain he released Li C. Fu who tumbled to the ground an instant before the larger man collapsed on top of him.

As Minikin bent down to help untangle Li C. Fu the first attacker rallied and, with a bloodcurdling cry, jumped her from behind; his momentum — with her help — carried him over her head. She let go of Li C. Fu, stepped aside, and let the sprawling man have it with a roundhouse kick to the jaw. He went down and lay still beside the second man who was still immobilized with pain.

Both men were down — now was the time to get away — but the violin was somewhere over the fence in the shrubbery. Li C. Fu struggled to his feet, his eyes dazed, as Minikin climbed the fence and dropped to the grass. In the distance she could hear a police siren, and she gritted her teeth in frustration. She retrieved the case from beneath a bush and was astride the fence when she realized the siren was coming closer. The loudly wailing squad car came roaring off Madison Avenue and rounded the corner onto 63rd Street making right for them. The two hooligans scrambled to their feet and started to run.

With a look of pure hatred the man with the scar paused, drew a knife from beneath his jacket, and with a deft movement sent it flying straight at Minikin. She just managed to get the case up in time to deflect the blade then, off balance, fell over backward from the fence into the tiny yard.

The two hoods crossed Fifth Avenue in a limping run, climbed the low cement wall and dropped into the vast darkness of Central Park.

Minikin got wearily to her feet. Holding the violin case under one arm, she once again climbed astride the wrought iron fence. Lights flashing wildly, the blue and white police car skidded to a stop beside Li C. Fu. Detective Kake and Sergeant Mosshammer burst from the car with guns drawn, ready to do battle, then stopped angrily in their tracks and stared.

Li C. Fu picked up his black silk cap from the sidewalk and slapped it across his palm before resettling it on his head. Minikin climbed down from the fence with the sound of ripping fabric and said with shaky relief, "It's Detective Kake and Sergeant Mosshammer. What a nice surprise."

Detective Kake gave vent to his annoyance by demanding loudly, "Miss Small! What's happening here?"

Minikin suddenly felt foolish, and the sight of him irritated her. "I believe my dress is caught on the fence," she replied coldly. "Otherwise, everything is under control."

Scowling, Detective Kake jammed his gun back into its holster and started across the sidewalk toward her. Her dress was caught high on the fence, and she made a very leggy picture. In spite of himself, a slow grin began at the corners of his mouth, and by the time he reached her it had become a lazy smile.

Really angry now, Minikin shoved the violin case into his arms and snapped, "Be careful with that, it's very valuable!" Then she twisted around and, with hands that still shook, struggled to unfasten the hem of her dress from the fence.

Watching with open amusement, Kake drawled infuriatingly, "Looks like you won't be wearing that one again."

Minikin rejoined heatedly, "War is hell."

His smile faded, and the big Detective studied her in silence for a moment. "We had a radio call about a disturbance on this corner. Am I right in assuming that was you?"

She glanced up at him in exasperation, but there was no trace of ridicule in the sleepy-looking blue eyes.

Minikin turned back to the fence. "I'm afraid so," she admitted, ripping at her skirt impatiently. "The other two guys went thataway," and she nodded toward Central Park.

Free at last from the fence, she took the violin case from Detective Kake and crossed the sidewalk to Li C. Fu who was sitting in the back seat of the squad car. The door was open, and his head lay back against the seat. She asked softly, "Are you all right, Li C.?"

He looked up at her from the shadows. "Sure, Mees Smawr, okay. Just resting."

"You wait there," she said. "I'll be right back." She gave him the violin case to hold and turned and walked away.

Detective Kake was speaking quietly to Sergeant Mosshammer who held a microphone from the dashboard in one ham-like hand. "Hey!" he called after her. "Where are you going?"

"I'm going to get my shoes while they're still there," she replied. "New York City has a lousy reputation for theft."

He quickly fell into step beside her. "Fine, you can tell me what happened while we walk."

They crossed Fifth Avenue and retraced the distance along the park to her shoes.

The golden sandals still lay in place exactly as she had stepped out of them.

The Detective's voice was quietly incredulous, "So you think it was the same two Asians from the other night?"

"I can't swear to it," she answered wearily. "I can only say it *might* have been the same two. However, this time I did get a good look at them, and I would know these two men again anywhere." She stepped into her sandals and began to walk back.

He loosened his tie and unbuttoned his shirt collar before turning to follow her. "Well, we could let you look at some mug shots, but it doesn't make sense that the same two men who murdered Dr. Grow would try to rob you tonight."

Minikin narrowed her eyes and looked up at him in the darkness, "And why not? Maybe this is their 'territory.'"

He hesitated, then shrugged his shoulders. "It's just unlikely, that's all. Anyway, they didn't actually *steal* anything. In fact, it sounds like they got the worst of the skirmish." He glanced down at her and smiled, "You never know, they might even want to press charges against *you.*"

The humor of the thing caught Minikin unawares, and she started to laugh. Her laughter continued, doubling her over, until she was aware of a note of hysteria in it. Detective Kake stopped beside her and watched with concern until she finally pulled herself together. Wiping the tears from her eyes, she said, "Well, that's modern justice for you — everyone's got their rights."

They returned quietly to the corner of 63rd Street. Armed with a flashlight, Detective Kake climbed the wrought iron fence and searched briefly among the bushes before finally recovering the knife. Wordlessly, he wrapped it in his handkerchief, put one hand on the fence and vaulted effortlessly back onto the sidewalk.

Once again Minikin found herself locked in the upholstered prison of the back seat. She and Li C. Fu were driven home in the now silent squad car, and the two police officers escorted them inside her house.

In the light of the foyer she watched the sleepy eyes of Detective Kake widen in surprise as he looked from her to Li C. Fu. Minikin knew her dress was badly torn and both elbows and one knee scraped, but she was shocked to see that Li C. Fu had a black eye that was already swollen shut and a rip in the back of his *cheong sam* that revealed an immodest amount of white undergarment. Tactfully, no mention was made of it, and they went into the living room and turned on the light.

Minikin placed the violin case on the coffee table, opened it and removed the del Gesù. She examined it closely; there appeared to be no damage. Relieved, she returned it to its case and reclosed it.

Taking out a leather pad and pencil, Sergeant Mosshammer observed pleasantly, "Nice fiddle you've got there, Miss Small." Minikin had to smile at the understatement.

Detective Kake lifted the violin case from the coffee table and turned it over in his hands. Across the back stretched a four inch gash where the knife had turned from its intended path into the shrubbery.

Minikin's smile vanished, and she drew in her breath with a quiet hissing sound.

The Detective replaced the case on the coffee table and moved away. For a moment a thoughtful expression lingered on his face, but then he shook away the idea.

They took seats on the white modular sofas as Sergeant Mosshammer, with a gentle good humor very different from their first meeting, began to take their official statement. Detective Kake leaned against the doorway with arms folded and watched the proceedings with sleepy eyes.

When Minikin tried to describe the two Asians, Li C. Fu spoke for the only time.

"Not Asian, Mees Smawr. Chinese."

"Are you sure, Li C.?" she asked in surprise.

He nodded just once, "Chinese. And I have seen man with scar before, when I worked in Chinatown."

# 17

# SINFULLY GOOD

MINIKIN WOKE EARLY THE NEXT MORNING, showered, and dressed hurriedly in a cranberry linen Dior dress and matching shoes. From her window she could see Li C. Fu already at work in the garden. His black eye was evident, even from this distance. As she put in a call to Everett Orson Stallworthy, she reflected dryly that New York City got more exciting all the time. "A nice place to visit . . ."

"Morning, Rhett," she said into the receiver. "I hope I'm not disturbing you too early on your day of rest."

"Minikin, dear girl! Of course not. As it happens, I'm baking bread."

"I've got a surprise for you. Can I see you this morning?"

"How delightful! Why don't you join me for breakfast; I'll make something special."

"Fine. Is twenty minutes too soon?"

"It's perfect. I'll let you set the table."

She hung up the receiver and bent to retrieve the violin case from beneath the bed. Stopping on the way out, she told Li C. Fu where she was going and a few moments later let herself out the front door.

It was only four short blocks up Fifth Avenue to Everett Orson's co-op apartment, and it was a glorious spring morning, perfect for walking. Minikin turned right off 64th Street onto Fifth Avenue, swinging the violin case and savoring the early morning air. Behind her, a nondescript man got out of a parked car and slowly turned up Fifth Avenue, following her.

At nine-fifteen in the morning, the events of the previous evening seemed unreal to her and as distant as a thriller on The Late Show. Minikin reflected that Monday or Tuesday she would have to take time to go over the mug shots with Detective Kake. A boring and probably fruitless task. Nevertheless, as she rubbed her sore elbow and thought of Li C. Fu's black eye, she resolved to do it. On this sunny Saturday morning the only thing that really bothered her about last night's attack was the unnerving coincidence that the two attackers had again been Asians. Chinese, she corrected herself. But it was stretching things to automatically assume they were the same two men who had assaulted Dr. Grow. The world just wasn't that small, she told herself. Detective Kake was right; the two events were probably unrelated.

Between 67th and 68th Streets, she turned under an awning and into the building. A uniformed doorman touched his cap and held the door open for her. A security guard announced her over the intercom to Mr. Stallworthy's apartment, and the elevator man took her up to the twelfth floor.

Outside on the sidewalk, the man following her walked casually by, his eyes averted.

Everett Orson opened his front door himself, wearing a vast apron that seemed to have been cut from a French flag. The rich smell of baking bread billowed around him.

"Minikin, dear girl. Welcome."

"Good morning," she replied, smiling. "How's my new partner?"

He chortled with melodious delight as he ushered her inside. "You know, you must cash that check or the sale of the partnership isn't legal. Even if it *is* only for five dollars." Everett Orson was now proud owner of twenty-five percent of The Small Agency.

"Well, if you insist," she told him with pretended disappointment. "But I had planned to have it framed."

As he took the violin case from her and put it on a table in the foyer, Minikin glanced around his "bachelor's digs," as he called them. The cozy apartment, full of books and comfortable overstuffed furniture, boasted a breathtaking overview of Central Park and a large space-age kitchen.

Everett Orson Stallworthy was a gourmet cook of some distinction who did all his own cooking from "scratch," even to growing many of his own herbs and spices under special lights. From past experience Minikin knew that a meal at his table was always a treat.

As she trailed behind him into the gleaming kitchen, she said, "I can see you are burning with curiosity to know my surprise. So, I'll tell you right away."

He nodded and returned to the important business of squeezing orange juice, the electric device whirring pleasantly.

"I've sold my first policy for The Small Agency," she said proudly. "It's for a violin."

Impressed, he turned to look at her. "Why, that's wonderful. What is it, a Strad?"

"A Guarnerius del Gesù," she replied, the words hissing importantly. "It must be authenticated and a policy written for it by Monday, when the owner leaves for a concert tour."

"That's no problem, we'll just take it over to Jacques' after breakfast. Congratulations," he commended her, lightly. "Now, just *wait* till you see what we're having for breakfast." He kissed his fingertips, delicately, "Mwa!"

Minikin smiled to herself. To Everett Orson, a master violin was still only a fiddle, but breakfast, after all, was *breakfast.* She took a seat on the kitchen stool and told him the story of the old professor, and the reasons he gave for gifting Luk Tsi with the fabulous violin.

Cracking eggs into a massive bowl, Everett Orson glanced up and remarked, "There's something in that, you know. A violin should be *heard,* and some of the most famous lie silent in remote museums around the world and may only be *seen.* They treat them like wood carvings." He cracked the next egg with a vengeance. "What a waste."

"Like Paganini's 'Cannon'?" she asked.

"Yes," he replied. "And others. I was thinking most particularly of the wonderful Stradivarius 'Messiah.' Among connoisseurs, for sheer beauty of tone, the most exciting of all. And it has never been played professionally. I believe it is in the Ashmolean Museum at Oxford, England. Immaculate, and mute. And like the Jewish Messiah, it never comes." He began to whip the eggs with a wire whisk, using a quick expert rhythm.

Minikin watched him as he turned and snipped fresh dill from the living plant, chopped it finely, and sprinkled it into the eggs. Then he put her to work setting the table.

"I think we'll use the Limoges, this morning," he directed her. "And the crystal stemware for the orange juice. There is a bowl of roses on the coffee table, and the linen is in the buffet. Pick whatever color pleases you." He called after her, "When you finish that, I'd like you to grind the coffee beans for me. You still remember how, I hope."

"Of course I do," she called over her shoulder.

Minikin hopped to it, creating a charming table setting for two by a window overlooking the spring-time park. What a perfect day, she thought, and paused to admire the pretty scene before hurrying back to the coffee grinder.

At last, Everett Orson removed his apron and donned his jacket. For him, dining was always an elegant occasion. A few minutes later they sat down to a breakfast of piping hot pumpernickel bread, fresh from the oven; sour cream and dill omelets; and — with appropriate fanfare — Everett Orson's best beluga caviar served in a silver icer with minced onions.

Minikin placed the Irish linen napkin across her knees, tore a bite-sized piece from a thick slice of hot pumpernickel, and spread the cold caviar onto it. She popped it into her mouth and chewed in silence. Then, she sipped the sweet orange juice. Ahh. Life is but a long series of physical sensations, she mused to herself; some pleasant, some painful, and a few worthy of seconds.

Dessert — for there was always dessert at Everett Orson's table — was hot apple strudel and freshly ground coffee with heavy cream. The pastry was crisp and paper thin, the apple filling generously laced with black walnuts. Minikin sighed with contentment and thought elevated thoughts.

They lingered lazily over their coffee, savoring all the good things of the morning, but at last rose reluctantly from the table as Everett Orson went to telephone his chauffeur.

"We'll be needing the car in about half an hour, Omar. We're just going to Jacques' for an appraisal. I'll see you downstairs."

He hung up, donned his apron, and together they began to clear away the breakfast things. Wrapping the remainder of the strudel in aluminum foil, he presented it to Minikin who accepted it with pleasure, thinking it would be good medicine for Li C. Fu.

While Everett Orson tidied up the kitchen and loaded the dishwasher, Minikin washed and dried the crystal stemware and Limoges china.

"Rhett, who do you think made the best violins?"

"Why, old Andrea Amati, I suppose. His was the first great design, and he taught all the rest of them. It was the Renaissance, remember, and what we call 'classical' music was just coming into being. These violin makers were carpenters and, for the most part, they all lived in Cremona. After they had been apprenticed to 'old Amati' for a while, and truly learned their craft, they frequently set up shops of their own nearby. In fact, they were all on the same street — if memory serves: the Piazza San Domenico. They called it the 'violin makers' quarters.'"

"There were whole families of violin makers, weren't there?"

"That's right; regular dynasties. Andrea Amati had two sons and a grandson, all highly skilled artisans. Andrea *Guarneri* learned from the 'old Amati,' and taught his own two sons and a grandson to make violins. *Giuseppe* Guarneri — or 'del Gesù as he is now known — was his nephew.

"But the Amatis' most celebrated pupil was Antonio Stradivari. He learned to make violins from 'old Amati's' grandson, Niccolo. Antonio Stradivari had been a woodcarver before he came to them. Eventually he sired two sons, Francesco and Omobono, who were also fine craftsmen — although none were as gifted as he. By the way, most people aren't aware that all these men also made cellos, violas, mandolins and even guitars."

Minikin smiled at the history lesson; she was always impressed by Everett Orson's knowledge of antiques. "Why can't we duplicate their work today?" she wanted to know.

Everett Orson straightened up, clutching his back, and groaned slightly, "They just don't make things the way they used to."

"No, seriously," she insisted.

"Well, the exact process was lost. We know they used to hang the unvarnished violins with selected pieces of seasoning wood in the open attics of their houses, exposed on all sides to the Italian sun. There the women also hung their dried fruits and the washed clothes alongside the maturing violins. You see the problem? It could have been the climate, the fruit, or something in the wash. Or all three. And then there was the varnish: a special formula as unknown today as the glaze on Ming china. They simply no longer know how to make it. It might have been a delicate blend of rosin and rancid spaghetti sauce. We'll never know. Whatever it was, it gave their creations an enduring beauty and tone that continues to last after hundreds of years, while newer instruments begin to look worn and fall apart. You see," he closed the dishwasher and turned it on, "they really don't make things the way they used to."

Minikin took the strudel, Everett Orson the violin case, and they turned out the lights and went out the door.

Downstairs on the sidewalk, Omar handed them into the back seat of the limousine, started the car and pulled smoothly away from the curb.

At the same time nearby, a nondescript man flagged a taxi, got quickly inside, and the taxi moved unobtrusively into the flow of traffic behind them.

Her thoughts on violins, Minikin said, "I visualize Giuseppe Guarneri as a devout young man with dark hair and long esthetic hands, perhaps a poor relation, who came to live with his uncle's family and worked hard to please them."

Everett Orson chuckled happily. "He was a scoundrel and a rogue."

Minikin burst out laughing. "Really?"

He nodded. "A drunken ruffian who regularly scandalized his family and died young. That's why Guarnerius del Gesù violins are so rare. Antonio Stradivari lived to be ninety-three and produced over a thousand instruments. He frequently received commissions from noblemen and kings, sometimes for whole sets of matching instruments. In his time, he was regarded as a refined aristocrat."

"Then why in heaven's name do they call Giuseppe Guarneri 'del Gesù? Isn't that Latin for 'of Jesus'?"

"One of the ironies of fate, my dear," he answered. "You see, probably because he was such a hellion, he signed all his work with a cross and the letters 'IHS', which in Latin stands for: *Jesus Hominum Salvator* — or Jesus, Savior of Mankind. Like so many people he was a paradox, a goodly blend of many things. Our del Gesù was also a true genius and the only one of all those men from Cremona whose work rivals — some say excels — the work of Antonio Stradivari." He chuckled again and patted her hand. "I guess you could say he was sinfully good."

# 18

# SILENT DEATH KNELL

Omar handed them onto the curb on West 57th Street, just a few doors away from Carnegie Hall, and they went inside the building and up in the elevator. Everett Orson was quite winded from his exertions by the time they reached the end of a short hallway and entered the spacious, sunlit room that overlooked 57th Street.

Violins were everywhere: hanging in wall displays, mounted in glass cabinets and resting on countertops and gilt tables. There was even a cello or two in evidence. Customers and sales people bustled about and, in a corner, a young man with a bow tie and a carnation in his buttonhole was trying to decide between the tonal quality of two violins; discordant trills and musical scales erupted startlingly.

A white-haired gentleman in a pearl gray suit looked up and, smiling, came forward to welcome them. The youthful blue eyes in the aged face shone with pleasure.

"Mr. Stallworthy, what a nice surprise."

"Charles, delighted to see you. Is Jacques here?"

"He's on a buy in London; something very special is at auction. But perhaps I can help you?"

"Yes, we've brought a violin that needs your expert appraisal before we insure it. Oh, Charles, allow me to introduce Miss Small, Max's daughter. Minikin, my dear, Charles Grenoble."

The twinkling eyes clouded for a moment, and he took her hand into his own and said, "I heard about your father, Miss Small. I am so sorry. We shall all miss him very much."

She took a deep breath. "Thank you, Mr. Grenoble."

He led them over to a table near the windows and invited them to be seated on the French gilt chairs. Everett Orson lowered himself gingerly onto the flimsy thing and slowly leaned back. It took his weight, and he sighed cautiously.

Grenoble rubbed his hands together and looked at them expectantly, "Well, shall we take a look?"

Minikin passed him the violin case, and he put it on the gilt table between them and opened it. Suddenly, Minikin felt apprehensive — the busy room around them seemed suspended in time, and there was neither movement nor sound.

Then Grenoble drew a deep breath and softly sighed, "Ah, a real beauty."

She exhaled in relief and told him, "There are documents of sale in the bottom of the case. They seem to verify its history."

He smiled at her, chiding gently, "I'm sure they will be interesting to read, Miss Small, but these old eyes still recognize a del Gesù when they see one." He lifted the instrument from its case, and the gleaming wood finish flashed in the sunlight. He peered inside at the signature and date, then turned it over several times in his hands. A puzzled look came over his face. Finally he said, "I must confess this one is quite new to me, and I thought I knew them all." He put down the fiddle, took up the papers and began to read.

Minikin thought she detected a look of surprise forming in the bright blue eyes.

Slowly, Grenoble began to nod his head. "Now I understand," he said. "This del Gesù has been missing for generations." He glanced first at Minikin and then Everett Orson. "According to these documents, in 1921 it was sold by a Russian Prince Alexei Piotr Kutozov to a Chinese mandarin named Shih Tsung. Then, at the close of World War II, it was resold to one Captain Topper Bottham who, nearly forty years later as *Professor* Topper Bottham, has presented it as a gift to Miss Luk Tsi. There is probably quite an epic behind these few sheets of paper — a journey through history. I'm glad to see the violin has survived its journey and been relocated. So many of them become damaged or lost and their value forgotten." He refolded the documents and placed them on the table nodding toward the violin. "Obviously, this is a work of del Ges's best period."

Minikin said, "Mr. Grenoble, it sounds like you may be able to tell us something about this violin before it was lost.,,

He twinkled at her, "Yes, I believe I can. As you may know, many famous violins have special names. If I am right, *this* violin was named for its beauty. I believe it once belonged to Count Cosio di Salabue, in the early 1800s the first great collector of the Cremonese instruments. In his papers, the Count described the luminous beauty of the del Gesù finish — ambered woodgrain, as you see, with a transluscent red overlay — as being like 'the shadow of the evening sun on the waves of the sea.' When a king's ransom tempted him to sell one of his prized del Gesùs to a Russian diplomat, he was amused to note that the Russian gave it a shortened version of that description for its name. Then, for over a hundred years, it belonged to various Russian nobles. However, during their revolution the violin was lost and it was assumed to have been destroyed. At that time many White Russians crossed over into China to escape the Bolsheviks, taking whatever valuables they could carry." He reached over and tapped the documents on the table. "The deed of sale from Prince Kutozov is in French, of course, the language of the Russian aristocrats. In it, he cites the name of this del Gesù as *'L'onere du Soleil'* — the same name the Italian Count Salabue recorded so long ago. You see, *L'onere du Soleil* translates roughly as 'The Shadow of the Sun.' Therefore, the two violins are probably one and the same."

The words tolled a silent death knell in Minikin's head: *the shadow of the sun.* "What did you say?"

"The Shadow of the Sun. I am only assuming, of course. Naturally I will verify its history for you as part of the appraisal."

Minikin didn't doubt its veracity for an instant. "Tell me, Mr. Grenoble," she urged in a low voice, "is there anything unusual about this violin behind the bridge?"

"Well, let's see." He picked up the violin and examined it closely. "No, not really. The E tuner is a little ornate. It has been inlaid with a tortoise-shell 'eye'. Interesting. I'm sure it's not the original tuner, but that's not surprising after several hundred years." He put the violin down again. "Now, if you will excuse me a moment, I'll just get the forms you need." And he hurried away.

Everett Orson looked at her, oddly. But then his chair creaked, and he shifted his weight carefully and thought thin.

Minikin felt as if she were stifling; her mind reeled, and she made a conscious effort to breathe deeply. She needed time to think. The name of the violin couldn't be mere coincidence, and that had to mean the two Chinese last night weren't a co-incidence either. There was something terribly important about "The Shadow of the Sun." What were Dr. Grow's exact words? The awful night came back to her with frightening clarity. She needed time to think it through.

Grenoble returned to their table. While he worked on the forms, Everett Orson recounted for him the story of Professor Bottham presenting the del Ges to Luk Tsi on the night of her debut at Carnegie Hall. Grenoble was suitably impressed and in return regaled Everett Orson with yet another violin anecdote.

Minikin was too distracted to follow their conversation and instead watched the man in the bow tie trying to decide between two violins of equal quality, the racket he made registered only dimly.

At last Grenoble folded the appraisal, placed it in an envelope and passed it to Everett Orson, saying, "I hope nothing happens to that del Gesù — it would cost The Small Agency a pretty penny."

Everett Orson chuckled as he placed the envelope in his breast pocket, "That's what we're in business for, Charles — to protect our clients. Please send us the bill, as usual."

Grenoble smiled and nodded. "If you don't mind, I'll hold on to these documents, temporarily. They will help me in my historical verification."

Everett Orson rose nervously from his chair. "Of course you may, Charles. Of course you may."

Grenoble gallantly escorted them to the elevator, and while they waited he spoke pleasantly to

Minikin. "I enjoyed meeting you, Miss Small. I hope we'll be seeing more of you here at Jacques'."

Preoccupied with her thoughts, Minikin had to make an effort to respond. "Thank you, Mr. Grenoble. You certainly know a great deal about violins."

The bright eyes in the old face studied her for a moment. "You seem very interested in this particular violin. I predict that in future years *L'onere du Soleil* will become known as the 'Luk Tsi del Gesù.' Her review in the *New York Times* this morning is quite a rave. If nothing unforeseen happens, posterity will remember her."

The antiquated elevator arrived with a gust of cool air, and the door rattled open.

Minikin shivered and then replied, "I hope you're right, sir. I hope posterity will be as kind as you are."

# 19

# ALONE IN A CROWD

DOWNSTAIRS ON THE STREET, OMAR stepped from the limousine and came around the car to open the rear door. As he reached out to take the violin case from Minikin, she drew back and turned to Everett Orson.

"Wait, Rhett. It's such a beautiful day, I think I'll walk home."

Everett Orson looked disappointed. "I had hoped to give you lunch, Minikin," he said. "Couldn't I persuade you?"

She smiled and shook her head.

He sighed, "Very well. I could probably use a short walk myself, but I have some lamb marinating at home that needs my prompt attention. How about dinner?"

"No really, I can't. We're starting work in the drawing room today; that awful wallpaper must come down. We'll probably be up half the night working."

He shrugged. "Very well. The policy for the del Gesù will be ready for you in the office first thing Monday morning."

"Okay," she replied.

"See you then."

With Omar's help he climbed ponderously into the back seat where he discovered the small foil wrapped package.

"Minikin," he called to her, "don't forget the strudel. I only give it away to those I love."

She took it from him, laughing.

Omar closed the car door. His white teeth flashed as he touched his cap to Minikin, and a moment later they pulled away into the traffic. Minikin waved after them, then turned to join the bustling throng of sidewalk shoppers. She needed time alone to think — alone in a crowd.

A nondescript man got out of a waiting taxi and joined the busy flow of people behind her. He carefully watched her.

Preoccupied, Minikin strolled along slowly, swinging the violin case. She decided to start at the beginning and try to recall Dr. Grow's exact words to her on that rainy night not so long ago. Did he say, "Behind the bridge in the shadow of the sun"? Or were his words, "*It's* behind the bridge in the shadow of the sun"? Until a few minutes ago she hadn't really considered that he had known what he was saying. When she was being interrogated she had repeated the first phrase over and over again to the men questioning her. But now she knew there was actually something named, The Shadow of the Sun, and that thing incorporated a *bridge*. She began to feel certain Dr. Grow had said, "It's behind the bridge, in The Shadow of the Sun." Now *that* made perfect sense! Overwrought he may have been, but it seemed possible he knew exactly what he was saying. Okay. So, *what* was behind the bridge? And exactly *where* was it?

On the corner of 57th and Fifth, Minikin stopped and gazed unseeing at the diamond display in the window of Tiffany's. She knew the bridge on a violin was the erect piece of wood between the f holes, over which the strings passed to be attached at each end. When she had asked Grenoble to look behind the bridge, he had looked at the widest end of the fiddle, the end with the chin rest. As soon as she got home she would examine it herself.

Slowly, she began to walk again and continued on past Fifth Avenue toward Madison. Fine so far, she thought. Now to return to the question of what might be hidden behind that bridge; it would have to be pretty small for Grenoble to have missed it. The other night she had reasoned that, as a scientist, Dr. Grow could have had valuable technical information. She supposed with the latest hi-tech equipment any document could be shrunken down to an insignificant size and then hidden inside something else. So perhaps that was it: something reduced in size and hidden in the violin. Now, what kind of data might it be? She remembered the newspapers had said Dr. Grow was a *nuclear* scientist — and she had been questioned all night by the CIA. That combination could add up to . . .

She walked blindly into a matronly woman carrying several shopping bags, stopped to untangle herself and apologize profusely. Then she continued on.

So! she told herself excitedly, these people could be after something of real importance — actually playing cloak and dagger games for the highest kind of stakes! This much she knew: Dr. Grow had been intentionally *murdered.* He had told her about The Shadow of the Sun and then lay dying in her foyer. And last night, when she had walked home carrying The Shadow of the Sun, the same two men had tried to take it from her and been ready to kill her, too. Whatever the violin represented, at least two men wanted it badly enough to kill for it. But then, given their bloodthirsty determination, why had they let her carry it all over midtown today without touching her?

Minikin stopped dead in her tracks and looked around. The sidewalk was full of normal, everyday people; normal for New York City, anyway. They jostled against her, impatiently, and she relaxed and let them carry her forward again.

No, she thought, she was letting her imagination carry her away. The whole scenario was just too incredible — nuclear plans hidden in a fiddle. Doubtless the balance of world power rested with *her.* What an imagination she had! Feeling a little foolish, she turned up Madison Avenue and headed toward home.

However, she told herself finally, it wasn't *all* imagination. There *was* something very dangerous connected with the violin — it was indisputable. Okay, so for argument's sake, say that something was hidden in it. Now, why would anyone want to hide something in someone else's fiddle? She walked on shaking her head. She couldn't think of a single reason.

Minikin decided that before she told anyone else about this, she would have to have a story that made sense. So far it was mere conjecture, and it all seemed so fantastic. She had better things to do, she told herself, than spend time at the Nineteenth Precinct being interrogated and insulted.

She stopped at the corner of 59th Street to buy a *New York Times;* when she got home she wanted to read Luk Tsi's review. As she waited for her change she glanced casually about her — there still appeared to be no one suspicious watching her that she could see. She took her change and stuffed it with the strudel into her handbag, juggling the newspaper and the violin case. Then she continued slowly up Madison Avenue, pausing frequently to gaze at the opulent window displays of the many smart boutiques.

As she turned onto 64th Street and approached her house, she saw Chalfonte St. Giles in a mauve three-piece suit and matching candy-stripe shirt, directing two sweating workmen on the installation of her new front door. The door was a glossy black affair with a small inset casement window. It seemed to weigh a ton, and there was a gaping hole in the building where the new frame had been installed.

Closer, she could overhear St. Giles encouraging the men with patient, careful words while at the same time, in French, making quiet observations about their physical defects that exhibited real pornographic flair. The uncensored remarks rocked Minikin back on her heels and faced her around the other way to hide her laughter. When she had regained her composure, she greeted them politely and they moved aside to let her pass inside the house.

She went into the living room and put down her things, glancing through the open doorway into the dining room. The transformation there was so complete she could hardly believe her eyes. Overhead, the afternoon sun struck flame from the old crystal chandelier; she moved through the doorway into the dining room. The Victorian table and sideboard shone with polish, as did the silver candelabra and tea service they supported — she recognized Li C. Fu's fine hand there. But the great surprise was the white Austrian curtain which partway descended the broad rear window in billowing waves, framing the new tree outside. Her pink and cream Persian rug blended perfectly with the pink marble fireplace and the pink cherry blossoms on the tree.

Minikin walked slowly around the table shaking her head. It had never looked lovelier. She turned to see St. Giles leaning against the doorway watching her.

"Pretty, isn't it?" he observed casually.

"It's just lovely," she stammered. "I didn't expect it to come together this way. I . . . thank you, Chalfonte."

He smiled and waved his hand dismissively. "Li C. Fu and I hoped you'd be pleased. I've added the curtain to my bill — it's silk, you know." And he turned away and rejoined the workmen at the front door.

The man knew his business, Minikin acknowledged to herself gratefully. He had even seen to the repair of the dumbwaiter. She walked to the mahogany panelling, pressed it, and it popped open to reveal the miniature elevator to the kitchen below. She reclosed it and glanced around a final time. Soon the restoration of the house would be complete and she could go back to her life, wherever *that* might be.

She returned to the living room feeling distracted and depressed. What was wrong with her? She sat down and opened the newspaper to Luk Tsi's review. The venerable music critic began:

> A young girl, a child in years and person, but a sublimely accomplished musician, debuted last night before the audience at Carnegie Hall. Miss Luk Tsi, 19 years old, a graduate of Juliard, and recent winner of the Leventritt Competition, is a Chinese-born American who resides in San Francisco.
>
> When she made her entrance I was struck by her sphinx-like expression, but throughout her performance of the Mendelssohn Violin Concerto I found it refreshing. She doesn't allow herself the luxury of grimacing or moving around which would distract from all the emotions which are in her music. And the mechanism of a highly trained musician is beautiful to behold; the pure performance gratifying beyond mere words. Her tone, her execution, especially with the bow hand, were all perfect — the latter in particular: her graceful, limber wrist produced some of the most sparkling staccatos by and up and down bowing that I have ever heard.
>
> Luk Tsi's music is of remarkable purity and is accurate in all sorts of technical difficulties. I predict the beginning of a notable virtuoso career. She doesn't ask you to listen, she demands your ears. When Luk Tsi returns from her world tour, hers is a name that will become familiar to us all.

It was well-deserved praise, Minikin thought as she closed the paper. She smiled to herself irreverently: boy, if I had known I was hearing all that I would have enjoyed it more.

Then, gradually, it dawned on her — a world tour.

That was it! she thought. That was the missing piece! Now it began to make sense. What were some of the cities Luk Tsi had mentioned? Shanghai, Moscow, Munich . . . once again, that incredible violin would make a journey through history. Only this time it would carry a value apart from itself — something *nuclear.* Whatever insidious thing it was, to be delivered by special messenger: Luk Tsi. No wonder such an incomparably valuable del Gesù had been given *away* — Luk Tsi would be sure to take it with her on her first concert tour. And — somewhere — they would be waiting for her.

Now Minikin understood why no one had tried to get it away from her today. If they had, Luk Tsi wouldn't have it for her tour.

Somehow, they must have discovered that she, Minikin, was merely the agent insuring a priceless *objet d'art.* As long as they thought she didn't know the secret of what it contained, the violin was safe with her.

Minikin stood up and opened the case with hands that shook. She lifted out the gleaming instrument and turned it this way and that. She looked inside it. It appeared to be empty, but now she knew she wasn't imagining it; the terrible thing was there.

Outside on 64th Street, an average-looking man crossed to the other side and got into a parked car. Absently, his eyes watched the workmen in front of the building nearby. He could hear the polite directions and the insulting French asides. He thought, amused, the over-dressed decorator is creative in many things. Then, his thoughts returned to the problem before him.

He decided his men had acted hastily last night. He had instructed them merely to *watch* the violin. The fools. In their confusion they had nearly ruined all his careful planning. The girl seemed unconscious of the importance of the thing she carried around so carelessly today. Her mind appeared to be on the many luxuries she wanted to buy. An empty, self-absorbed type of mind, he thought; the typical American consumer, oblivious to anything beyond her own creature comfort.

Still, it would be a pity to have to kill her. The world was overcrowded with people, but there was always room for one more long-legged, athletic young woman — provided she showed no further sign of getting in his way.

He decided, just to be sure, he would watch a while longer.

# 20

# SLEEPY VIGILANCE

MINIKIN GRABBED THE VIOLIN CASE, took the stairs two at a time up to Max's bedroom, and closed the door. What should she do first? She would call the CIA, of course. She picked up the receiver and thought: How do I reach them? What do I say? First, I'll ask for Information in Arlington, Virginia. Then, when I've got CIA headquarters, I'll ask for Homer Rohm and they'll tell me where I can reach him. Hmmmm, she thought. Sure they would.

Slowly, she replaced the receiver. That might prove to be rather awkward, she decided. They might even pretend never to have heard of Homer Rohm. Either way, they would certainly require endless information from her first. Perhaps that wasn't the best way to approach it.

How, then? Well, she had reached them the first time through the Nineteenth Precinct; she could do it again. She picked up the receiver and dialed. As the phone rang, she decided she'd better ask for Detective Kake or she'd end up explaining everything over and over till the wee hours of the morning — again. The ringing stopped.

"Nineteenth Precinct, Sergeant Coffey."

She thought, Coffey and Kake — this can't be real. She said, "Er, may I speak to Detective Kake, please?"

"I'm sorry, he's on the night shift and not due in until seven o'clock. May I help you?"

Minikin glanced at her watch: one-thirty. She didn't think she could wait that long. "This is very important, could you possibly give me his home number?"

"I'm sorry, Miss, that's against the rules. Anything I can do for you?" The voice sounded friendly.

"No, no thanks. I'll try back later." She replaced the receiver and sat drumming her fingernails on the bedside table. Now what? She got to her feet and began to pace the floor. It was impossible to be casual about this. On the other hand, she had to keep her head. She began to change into blue jeans and her blue "Foat Wuth" sweater.

She could try to get in touch with Sergeant Mosshammer. No, that's no good. Obviously he's on the night shift, too. Anyway, she preferred Detective Kake. He seemed alert. And there was something about his hardworking dishevelment and the sleepy vigilance in his eyes.

She tried to tell herself it would be all right to wait until he came on duty to speak to him, but she felt herself trembling with urgency. She tied her second sneaker, then walked over and sat down again by the phone. She rubbed her palms across her knees, once again lifted the receiver, and dialed.

"Nineteenth Precinct, Sergeant Coffey."

"Hello, Sergeant. This is the same lady who was trying to reach Detective Kake. I wonder if I've got his name right; it *is* Detective Edward Kake, isn't it?"

"No, I believe his first name is Paddy," he replied helpfully.

She faltered, "Paddy Kake? Oh, dear. I wonder if I've got the wrong man. Well, thank you anyway." She replaced the instrument, then immediately lifted it again, and dialed Information. Paddy Kake! she thought. *Merde!* His name was nearly as foolish as her own.

"Information, may I help you?"

"Operator, may I have the telephone number of Detective Paddy Kake?"

The voice came back, suspiciously, "Are you kidding, lady?"

Minikin sighed; one always knew when one was in New York. She answered, patiently, "No, that's the name. I think it's spelled K A K E. Would you try it, please?"

There was a moment's pause, then, "Sorry, we have no one listed by that name."

"Oh. Thanks." Minikin spent the next few minutes calling information in all the nearby burroughs of New York. Finally, she slammed down the receiver and thought to herself, angrily, I believe Sergeant Coffey was having me on.

Well, she would just have to wait until seven o'clock for Detective Kake, that was all. She rose and started downstairs in search of Li C. Fu; it was time to get going in the drawing room. But suddenly, midway down the stairs, she made an about-face and returned to the phone in the bedroom. She sat down, took a deep breath, picked up the receiver once again and dialed.

"Nineteenth Precinct, Sergeant Coffey."

"Hello, Sergeant. It's me, again."

"Yes?" he acknowledged, warily.

"Listen, darlin'," she cooed, dropping her voice down in her socks, "I'm a go-go dancer in a club over on Eighth Avenue, and Detective Kake comes in every once in a while to see me. He gave me his number and told me to call him if ever I'm in the mood. And, baby, *now* I'm in the mood. But I've lost his number."

"Well, why didn't you say so, doll? Hold on a sec, I'll get it for you." The friendly voice chuckled, and she could hear papers rustling over the phone. "Here it is," he said, and read the number off to her, happily.

Minikin jotted it down feeling a queer mixture of elated irritation. "Thanks," she said. "I'm sure he'd do as much for you." She hesitated a moment, then asked wickedly, "Tell me something, Sergeant, could your first name be 'Mocha'?"

"Naw," he answered, delightedly. "That's my wife. My given name is Cole!" and he hung up laughing.

Minikin growled to herself softly, then put through the call to Detective Kake. It rang several times before a heavy hand lifted the receiver. There was a long pause, then a gruff voice said, "Detective Kake."

"I'm sorry to disturb your rest, Detective Kake. This is Minikin Small, but I've got something very important to tell you." She hesitated, "By the way, what *is* your first name?"

"Well," he began sleepily, "my Polish father named me Pasquale, but my Irish mother calls me Paddy. And so does nearly ev . . ." There was a long pause, and Minikin could visualize those sleepy eyes coming fully awake.

"Say, what is this?" he boomed, incredulously. "Did you wake me out of a sound sleep to ask me that?"

Good grief, she realized, his name really was Paddy Kake! "No, no," she hurried to reassure him, "I just had a little trouble reaching you, that's all." She paused to reorganize her thoughts. "Listen, you're not going to believe what I've found out about the violin that was nearly stolen from me last night. Our company is going to insure it, and I had it appraised this morning and discovered its historic name is *L'onere du Soleil* — in French that means 'The Shadow of the Sun'!" She waited expectantly for his response.

Gruffly, "So?"

Minikin tried to contain her excitement, "Don't you remember? That's what Dr. Grow said to me just before he was stabbed. He said, 'It's behind the bridge, in The Shadow of the Sun.'"

He cleared his throat, "Yeah. So?"

Completely exasperated, she thought: sharp as a tack in the morning, he's *not.* "It means the two incidents have to be related," she said. "Don't you see? A violin has a bridge on it, and this particular violin is known as 'The Shadow of the Sun.' It makes sense out of Dr. Grow's words. I'm sure he was murdered because of something he knew about this violin. And last night the same two men tried to steal it from me!"

There was a long pause, then he asked slowly, "*What's* behind the bridge?"

Minikin sighed, impatiently. "Actually, I don't know, but I'm guessing it's something like a microdot. The newspapers said Dr. Grow was a nuclear scientist and, you'll recall, the CIA was very interested. I bet you even money they know what's behind the bridge. I should also mention that this violin is scheduled for a world tour: China, The

Soviet Union, Germany . . ."

"Okay, okay, I'm beginning to get the picture. Hold on a minute and let me think."

She heard him bounce out of bed, walk heavily across the floor, and then silence. Finally, he returned to the phone.

"Miss Small," he began, his voice sounding skeptical, "I must tell you frankly, this sounds like you've left your jet stream." She clamped her jaw shut and waited. He continued slowly, "However, the CIA doesn't confide in us the way they should, and maybe they'd like to know about this. So, just in case — and at the price of looking ridiculous — I'll make a couple of phone calls for you."

"I assure you, Detective Kake, this is no figment of my imagina —"

"Yeah. We'll see. Okay, now give me that bit again about L'honor do. . . something-or-other. How do you spell it?"

She spelled the French name of the violin carefully for him.

"Fine. Where are you now?" he asked.

"At home."

"Good. Stay there. And put the violin someplace safe." He hesitated a moment. "And for the time being, Miss Small, I advise you not to tell anyone else about this. I'll get back to you as soon as I can." She agreed immediately, and he rang off.

Minikin hung up the phone and gave a whoop of excitement. Well, all right! *Now* they were getting somewhere. Minikin Small, girl detective. The President, himself, would probably invite her to dinner. Very hush-hush, of course.

She grabbed the violin case and thought to herself, okay, now where's a really safe place? Might as well be clever about this. She opened the case, removed the violin and wrapped it in her ice-blue quilted robe. She started to close the empty case, but decided it needed a little more weight to be realistic. She glanced around a moment, then sat down and removed her sneakers. She placed them neatly inside, closed the case, gathered up everything and padded downstairs into the dining room.

Not every house comes equipped with its own secret panel, she thought smugly. Only she and her decorator would know for sure. She pressed the wooden panel, and the door to the dumbwaiter popped open. Minikin placed the carefully wrapped violin inside and reclosed it. Now that the violin was well hidden, she would put the *case* someplace obvious; someplace easier to find.

She wandered into the living room and thought a minute. Aha, she had it! She opened the bottom doors of the black lacquer armoire, placed the case inside, and closed and locked the doors with the fancy brass key. Then she put the key behind the mantle clock. There, that ought to do it, she thought, satisfied.

She returned to her bedroom for another pair of shoes. As she descended the stairs once again into the foyer, she noticed the new front door beginning to open slowly. She caught her breath and froze.

Chalfonte St. Giles backed in, still talking pleasantly to the workmen outside, then turned gracefully to face her.

"Oh, Chalfonte!" she breathed in relief.

"Ah, Minikin dear girl," he drawled, languidly. "We are actually finished here for the nonce. If you will only discourage your lustful suitors from battering in your door for a day or two, to give the masonry a chance to harden, your fortress will be virtually impregnable." He touched his mouth in mock horror, "Egad, what a *bleak* prospect. Oh well, never fear," he said, withdrawing a ring of shiny brass keys from one pocket. "You can still pass out lots of these and save all the wear and tear on the door." He raised one eyebrow suggestively and shook the keys at her.

Minikin smiled, came the rest of the way down into the foyer and took the key ring from him. "Thank you, Chalfonte. It's a beautiful door and a good choice. I'll try to take care of it."

"I'm glad you approve," he murmured adjusting his pocket handkerchief slightly. "And now, alas, I fear you shan't feast eyes on me again till Monday." He turned back toward the open door. *"Au revoir, mon petit chou."*

*"Ciao, bello,"* she replied, and closed the door behind him and locked it, feeling suddenly alone and quite vulnerable. Anyway, she told herself, the

door *looked* good and solid. She opened the small casement window and peered through the wrought iron grill out into the street. For a moment she watched a fashionable woman walking her dog, but she failed to notice the man parked in the tan Ford across the street; he replaced the telephone receiver in the cradle beside his seat, started the car quickly, and drove away.

# 21

# WISE FOLLY

MINIKIN HAD SEARCHED THE HOUSE and garden for Li C. Fu and realized he was nowhere to be found when the new doorbell chimed. On her way to the front door she glanced at her watch; it had only been about forty minutes since she had spoken to Paddy Kake. It seemed too soon to be him, perhaps it was Li C. Fu.

She paused at the door, then cautiously opened the casement window and stared in surprise. She was face to face with Jacqueline Onassis.

The woman spoke quietly in a breathy little-girl voice. "I'm from *The Agency* I believe you're expecting me. May I come in?"

Minikin opened the door and took a step backward as the tall, elegant woman swept inside. She wore a stylish trenchcoat with the broad collar turned up and dark sunglasses. The resemblance was overwhelming: the red-brown, tousled bouffant hair; the square-jawed, slightly masculine face, the short straight nose. She smiled a Mona Lisa smile and removed her sunglasses. Minikin noticed the resemblance was less pronounced with the glasses off — something not quite right about the shape of the eyebrows, and the brown eyes set not quite so far apart. Even so, the impression lingered.

"I'm special agent Angela Devlin," she continued softly, flashing the CIA identification and then replacing it in a black alligator bag slung from one shoulder.

Minikin recovered herself quickly. "Please come in. I must say, that was fast service." She followed her guest into the living room and gestured for her to be seated.

The woman took a seat on the sofa and her raincoat spilled open to reveal a man's three-piece gray suit, complete with white shirt, and red and gray striped tie. The long, aristocratic feet were encased in black opaque stockings and shod in black alligator pumps. Slowly, she crossed her legs and peeled off long, black leather gloves.

Minikin tried not to stare while she thought how perfectly the latest fashion suited her. She said, "I suppose everyone tells you how much you look like Jackie Onassis?"

The woman lowered her carefully made-up eyes modestly. "Of course one would rather be an original, you know. Still it is a flattering comparison." She lifted her eyes and looked directly at Minikin. "I've come for the violin. Where is it?"

With a sinking feeling, Minikin remembered her childish efforts at hiding it. The woman would think she was a complete fool.

"Oh, yes," she said, reluctantly. "I've got it right here." She moved to the mantlepiece and took the key from behind the clock. "I just thought it would be a good idea to hide it," she said. "One can't be too careful."

"Quite right," the woman agreed.

With a feeling of anticlimax, Minikin went to the armoire and unlocked it, removed the case and reclosed the doors. She put the case on the sofa opposite her visitor and started toward the dumbwaiter. This wasn't what she had expected, at all. Now she was dreading the moment when she would have to open the violin case and expose those well-worn sneakers to the woman's fastidious gaze.

She tried to mask her chagrin, saying over her shoulder, "I'm afraid I'll have to ask for a receipt for the violin, and I must specify that it be returned by Monday. You see, it's a very valuable antique, and the owner plans to take it with her on a concert tour."

"Of course," the woman said in the distance.

Minikin reached the other end of the dining room and pressed the wooden panel of the dumbwaiter. It opened and she lifted out the bundle and turned back toward her visitor. She walked into the living room and stood, holding the violin wrapped in her robe, and looked around. She couldn't believe her eyes — the woman had simply vanished. And so had the violin case.

The idea took a long moment to penetrate — it seemed impossible — but if the woman calling herself Angela Devlin was who she had claimed to be, there would have been no need for her to grab the case and run. She must have been in quite a hurry to give herself away like that. Minikin Small, girl detective, had been neatly bamboozled. Fortunately, and just by accident, she still had the violin.

As she stood there feeling fatuous, Minikin began to realize that as soon as whoever-they-were discovered they didn't have the violin, they would be back. She doubted they would be so subtle about it the next time. She had a fleeting vision of the unreliable new door toppling inward with a resounding crash and decided she had about three minutes to get out of there!

She tucked the bundle under one arm, grabbed her handbag and turned and ran downstairs to the garage. She dragged the tarp off The Slim, put the violin carefully in the trunk, opened the garage door and was backing into the street when she caught sight of Li C. Fu. He was walking along the sidewalk carrying two bags of groceries. His small bruised face looked like a battered child's. She thought quickly, I can't leave him here — they might suspect he knows where the violin is.

She called to him, "Li C., come on. Let's take a drive! Just put those bags in the garage, we'll get them later."

At first he protested, but then with great deliberation he did as he was asked, carefully closing the garage door and then getting into the passenger seat beside her. Before his door was properly shut, Minikin laid three feet of rubber on the street in front of her house.

She sped crosstown, used the 62nd Street access to FDR Drive and turned north to follow the river, as if pursued by rabid hounds. She drove with skill, weaving gracefully in and out of traffic, her eyes constantly on the reflection in the rearview mirror. This time, she was sure no one was following her.

She glanced at Li C. Fu; his face was pale, his body rigid, the wind whipping the hair around his face. She decided for the time being, for his own protection, not to confide in him. She nudged him gently and shouted over the sports car's roar, "Isn't this fun?" He didn't answer, and her thoughts quickly turned to other things.

She couldn't help marvelling to herself. What a lucky fluke! It was only the merest chance that she still had the del Gesù. Minikin thought her efforts to hide the violin would have looked foolish in the eyes of a bona fide CIA agent, but as it had turned out — that foolishness was now revealed as wise folly. And the woman calling herself Angela Devlin had been too quick for her own good.

Minikin was stunned by what had nearly happened. How could they have acted so swiftly? Perhaps they had just been waiting for the workmen outside her house to leave. But it would have been far easier to simply take the violin away from her in the street this morning. Anything was possible, she knew, but why had this happened so quickly after her phone call to Detective Kake? There was something very wrong there; something almost *sinister.* She would have to give the Detective time to contact the CIA, then she would call him again. But *this* time she would demand to speak to Homer Rohm.

Minikin didn't question the fact that she felt obligated to place the violin in the proper hands as soon as possible; Dr. Grow had entrusted that responsibility to her, and she accepted his charge readily. The challenge was how to accomplish that feat without getting herself and Li C. Fu killed in the bargain. It didn't seem incredible to her anymore.

Now, she thought, her first priority was to put the violin someplace where it would be completely safe until she could figure out exactly what must be done — that someplace befitting a Guarnerius del Gesù, and worthy of the daughter of Max Small. I probably should have left it in the dumbwaiter, she told herself, but perhaps a thorough search would have uncovered it.

She turned onto Harlem River Drive and began a counterclockwise circuit of Manhattan Island. Suddenly, she knew just the place.

On a terrace in Georgetown a hand reached out to answer a ringing telephone.

"Mr. Baddash, this is Homer Rohm speaking. I regret having to disturb you at home, but I knew you would want me to keep you apprised of the latest developments regarding the Velvet Fist."

The National Security Advisor replied immediately, "Yes, quite right. What's happened?"

"The wiretap we had on Miss Small turned up something quite interesting. I think the quickest way to communicate it to you is simply to play the tape for you. This is the gist of their conversation; Miss Small is speaking to Detective Kake of New York's Nineteenth Precinct. Ready?"

"Yes. Go ahead."

From a tinny distance, Minikin Small's voice said, "Listen, you're not going to believe what I've found out about the violin that was nearly stolen from me last night. Our company is going to insure it, and I had it appraised this morning and discovered its historic name is *L'onere du Soleil* — in French that means 'The Shadow of the Sun'!"

The recording stopped, and Sanford Baddash's voice exploded into the phone, "You don't mean, 'Behind the bridge, in The Shadow of the Sun'?"

"You said it," Homer Rohm agreed, trying to keep the excitement out of his voice. "Apparently Dr. Grow was trying to tell us the document — it must have been reduced in size — has been hidden behind the bridge in that particular violin. Somehow, the girl must have stumbled onto it, and was trying to report it to. . ."

Baddash interrupted, angrily, "But why hide it there in the first place?"

"For a very good reason," Rohm answered quietly. "Listen." There was a whirring noise as the tape was rapidly advanced.

Minikin's tinny voice continued, "I should also mention that this violin is scheduled for a world tour: China, The Soviet Union, Germany . . ."

"God in Heaven!" Baddash bellowed. "What is it, a paper route? How many countries were they planning to sell it to?"

Rohm answered calmly, "Don't worry, sir, they aren't going to sell it to anyone. We'll get the violin back for you."

"What do you mean," the National Security Advisor said between clenched teeth, "is it lost, already?"

In spite of himself, Rohm flinched. "No, sir. We never had it. You see, Detective Kake instructed Miss Small to remain at home and to put the violin somewhere safe until we could get there."

"What went wrong?" the words dropped like weights from a great height.

"The wiretap was reported to me even before the police could contact us. I directed Zengo and Gonzales — who were the closest to her — to take both the girl and the violin into custody and wait for me. When I arrived at her house they were there, but she had already gone. We're searching the house now, but it appears she took the violin with her."

Rohm paused, but Baddash remained silent so he went on. "Up to now she has behaved rationally. I can only think something must have spooked her. We're in close touch with the Nineteenth Precinct, in case she calls in, and we have every reason to expect she will. She seems to have taken her car, and there is an All Points Bulletin out, with a full description. Don't worry, sir. It's just a matter of time. We'll get her."

"Rohm," Baddash growled, "I don't care how you do it, but *get me that fiddle.*"

"Yes, sir!" he replied. When he hung up the phone he was sweating. He turned and called angrily to his men, "Zengo, Gonzales, face it. The violin is not here! Put all that stuff back. We don't need a suit for property damage on top of everything else. Which reminds me. For Christsake, George, what happened to her garage door?"

George Zengo spoke apologetically, "Well, when she didn't answer the bell, we took one look at her front door and decided to break in through the garage, instead."

Rohm tried unsuccessfully to keep his voice steady, "What did you use, *dynamite?*"

"No," confessed the man with the Medici eyes. "Gonzales' truck."

## 22

# A GENUINE PHONY

MINIKIN PARKED IN FRONT OF A FIRE HYdrant on West 57th Street and asked Li C. Fu to wait for her. She explained she had a quick errand to run, then she removed the bundle from the trunk of her car. On her way inside the building, she retrieved a somewhat battered Bloomingdale's shopping bag from a trash basket and placed the wrapped violin carefully inside. Carrying the master fiddle around without the protection of its case worried her.

Charles Grenoble met her at the locked front door of Jacques', and his kindly face looked bewildered. "Your call caught me just as I was leaving — we close early on Saturdays. Tell me what I can do for you, and I'll be happy to be of service."

Minikin decided to tell him just enough to elicit his aid. "Thank you, Mr. Grenoble. I'm sorry to have to bother you, but I had a theft at my house this afternoon, and just by accident they didn't get the violin." She gestured toward the shopping bag.

"In fact, they stole the case."

Concern shone in the blue eyes, and he clucked like an old hen. "Good heavens, did they take anything else?"

"No, I don't think so. But I'd like to leave the violin with you where I know it will be safe.

"His response was immediate. "Of course, Miss Small, of course." He took the shopping bag from her and carried it through the main room back toward the vault. At the massive door of the safe, he turned to her and asked curiously, "How did they happen to steal just the case?"

Minikin floundered for an instant.

"We-ell, you see, I'm having some alterations done on the house. And workmen are in and out all the time. They must have heard about the value of the del Gesù." She shrugged awkwardly. "The case just happened to be empty at the time it was stolen."

Charles Grenoble turned back to the safe, visibly upset. His old voice quavered, "Isn't it awful about all the crime these days? When I was a boy, people were safe on the streets at any hour of the day or night. Today, one is threatened in one's own home in broad daylight. It's all very distressing."

Minikin felt uncomfortable lying to the old gentleman, and his quick sympathy only increased her feeling of guilt. But she was glad she hadn't burdened him with the whole story of what had happened — the poor man might have fainted dead away. She wondered how old he was; over seventy, certainly.

With trembling arms he swung wide the heavy door and switched on the light. The small, hermetically sealed room was lined with shelves containing valuable musical instruments of every description, mostly violins, many of them in cases. Grenoble picked up the shopping bag, set it carefully in one corner of the vault, swung the door shut and spun the dial. His fine white hair was tousled by all his exertions.

"There, now we both can breathe easier," he said, taking Minikin by the arm and walking her back toward the front door. "It occurs to me that Miss Luk Tsi might like to purchase a new case for her del Gesù. A violin like that deserves the very best, and we have an extremely fine selection here at Jacques' that she might like to choose from."

"I'll mention it to her, Mr. Grenoble. And thank you for waiting for me."

Outside on the street, Minikin climbed into the driver's seat next to Li C. Fu. The violin was safe now, and she could relax. She decided to give Detective Kake plenty of time to reach the right people at the CIA before phoning him again, so they had some time to kill. As it seemed unwise to go home just yet, she turned to Li C. Fu, saying, "Listen, Li C., it's Saturday and we've been working very hard. What do you say we take the afternoon off and see the sights? Have you been to the top of the Empire State Building yet? Or ridden the Staten Island Ferry?"

He shook his head solemnly.

She started the car and shifted into gear, smiling, "Also, I think it's time we had some lunch."

They paid a quick call to the Empire State Building; no longer the tallest building in the world, but still providing a breathtaking view. From the top, outside on the windy terrace, the spectacle of the mighty city stretched in all directions. Looking uptown, they could see skyscrapers clustered around the long green rectangle of Central Park — its lakes and reservoir glittering in the sun. They turned to the right and watched as a helicopter lifted from the heliport on the East River, and darted away like a dragonfly toward Long Island. On their left, a pleasure cruiser was docking at one of the long line of piers that fringe Manhattan's Hudson River, and in the distance they heard its mournful hoot. Far below, on the crowded midtown streets, tiny people scurried about their monumental tasks, while horns honked impatiently and a police siren wailed. It was like watching the many various movements of a busy machine at work. Their ears popped in the elevator on the way down.

Back in the car they headed down the Westside Highway toward the tip of the island and Wall Street. Minikin continued to watch the rear view mirror. The weekend highway was uncrowded, and The Slim easily outdistanced the sparse flow of traffic. The afternoon sun shone brightly on the Hudson River, and the trees along its banks were swollen with the feathery green of early spring.

In the bustling Wall Street area — the oldest section of the great city — Minikin drove slowly through streets so narrow they could only be one-way and skyscrapers so tall and close together that it was always dark below, even on the brightest day. She turned The Slim into the driveway of a garage, and watched an attendant take the car up to the floors above in a rattling, antiquated elevator.

They left the cool shadows of the streets and emerged into the warm sunlight of the park by the ferry. Minikin and Li C. Fu bought hotdogs from a street vendor with a brightly-colored umbrella over his cart and chomped away contentedly while they waited for the ferry to return from Staten Island. It no longer cost a nickel to ride, but for a quarter she thought it was still a bargain.

Finally, they sat on a wooden bench on top of the old ferry with the wind pulling frantically at their hair. Seagulls screamed lazily overhead, and the game little ferry bucked the swirling currents. Minikin pointed at the Statue of Liberty on nearby Liberty Island, and Li C. Fu nodded. The old girl was swathed in scaffolding today, as the process of her restoration continued. It seemed slightly embarrassing to Minikin, like catching a great beauty in a mudpack. Still, even thus, the lady had the heroic presence to quicken the pulse and raise a lump in the throat. Minikin felt her sense of urgency draining away. The world seemed so enormous and so normal. The important things would endure. What difference could the efforts of one individual make?

She remembered she had the rest of Everett Orson's strudel in her handbag. On the return trip across New York Bay, she and Li C. Fu bought coffees and split it, tasting the salt air with the sweet pastry.

Back in the cool canyons of Wall Street, Minikin told Li C. Fu she had a phone call to make. It was too noisy on the street, so they ducked into a quiet bar. Taking a small table in a corner, she told him to order whatever he wanted; she would be right back.

Minikin sat down in the old-fashioned wooden phone booth and closed the door. She tried to organize her thoughts, and then glanced at her watch: five-thirty. The afternoon had vanished as quickly as Angela Devlin. She deposited a coin and dialed.

"Nineteenth Precinct."

She recognized the voice. "Hello, Sergeant Coffey, this is Minikin Small. Is Detective Kake there, by any chance?"

He wasted no time on snappy repartee. Instead, she heard the line ringing, then Paddy Kake's anxious voice answered.

"Miss Small, Minikin! Where are you? Where did you go? I told you to —"

"Wait a minute," she interrupted him quietly. "Hold on. I don't plan to talk long. Were you able to contact the people at the CIA?"

"Yes, they want to see you right away, and they want that violin! Tell me where you are. We're coming to get you."

So! she thought, perhaps she wasn't such a bad detective after all. Her pulse quickened in spite of herself, but she answered calmly, "I'm afraid not. I'll call again in half an hour, and then I'll want to speak to Homer Rohm. No one else."

"What?" the big Detective's deep voice rose nearly an octave. "Are you crazy? Listen to me, Minikin. You could get hurt. We've had to put out an All Points Bulletin on you."

She was quietly incredulous, "Why?"

"The CIA insisted!" His booming voice moderated and took on a more persuasive tone. "Minikin, for your own safety, let us bring you in. We're trying to help you."

She was silent a moment as she thought it over, then she shook her head. She was going to decide this based on the facts she had, and her own best judgement. She sighed, "Detective Kake, if you're trying so hard to help me, what happened the first time? I might remind you how much help you were to me then."

"What are you talking about?"

"I'm referring to the fact that less than one hour after I told you what was in that violin, a genuine phony calling herself Angela Devlin came to collect it. It was just pure luck that she didn't. In fact, she stole the empty case. I can't trust you anymore, Pasquale," she added with regret. "There appears to be a leak in your pipeline."

The silence on the line seemed interminable. At last he said, "I see. What do you want me to do?"

"Just let me speak to Homer Rohm. I have the impression he knows what this is all about, and he'll know how to handle it. I'll call back in thirty minutes."

As she replaced the receiver, she heard him saying, "Minikin? Minikin, wait. . . ." And someone else in the background, shouting, "Did you get that?"

She sat there trembling. It was obvious she was out of her depth. An All Points Bulletin? Great horny toads. She ran long, nervous fingers through her hair. What a mess! And the police and CIA were in such a flap they would surely rattle poor old Mr. Grenoble. She was sorry now she had ever thought to put the violin in his vault and wondered if she could get it back without involving him in all the brouhaha.

Luckily, Charles Grenoble's home number was listed, and she put through a call to him. Her face burned as she tried to explain to the kindly old gent — without actually lying to him again — why he had to return to Jacques' and give the violin back to her.

"I'm terribly sorry to have to inconvenience you this way, Mr. Grenoble, but I'm afraid something rather urgent has come up and I must have the del Gesù back today."

His agitation was only thinly disguised as he told her the earliest he could manage would be eight o'clock; his wife would be serving dinner soon, and then it would take him some time to get back uptown. He hoped Minikin would be able to wait until then.

Humbled, Minikin readily agreed. They would meet at Jacques' at eight.

She stumbled back to the table and sat down across from Li C. Fu. There were two drinks on the table.

"Oh, good," she breathed in relief, "you ordered one for me, too. I can use it." She lifted the dark, frosty highball and took a big swallow; it was cold and sweet, and there was something unusual about it. She lowered it to the table and tried to glance inconspicuously around the bar. An All Points Bulletin, she thought to herself nervously; an APB, as they said on television. She guessed that meant the police had her description — along with those of all their other fugitives — and, if they weren't completely occupied with fighting crime, they would try to keep an eye out for her. She thought that over and decided she was probably safe from arrest for the time being. However, she grinned to herself, this probably meant dinner at the White House was off.

Minikin felt the adrenalin pumping through her and noticed the drink trembling in her hand. No doubt there was an APB on her car, too. Oh God, she groaned inwardly. They were both rather conspicuous — maybe she just ought to call Detective Kake back and let them come and get her. But she was afraid to risk it. Someone else might show up first, someone affiliated with Angela Devlin. She took another sip from her drink, then glanced at it curiously; it was different, something she didn't recognize. Distracted, Minikin set it down again.

She had to ask herself, did she really believe Paddy Kake was in league with the bad guys? No, she finally decided, but one thing for sure; she wasn't looking forward to her next interview at the Nineteenth Precinct — she had an uneasy foreboding that, this time, it would prove to be more dangerous than exhausting. Minikin told herself she had come this far, she would see it through, but it would have to be on her own terms. There was just no dignity in being dragged somewhere you were prepared to go of your own free will.

Minikin sipped again from the frosty drink; it tasted peculiar and this time it registered, and she examined the half-empty glass closely before transferring her gaze to the inscrutable Oriental. Li C. Fu was calmly eating peanuts — one eye heavily discolored, even in the dim light of the bar.

She was unable to keep from asking, "Li C., what is this drink?"

He blinked rapidly. "Chivas and Coke, Mees Smawr, you like?"

"Mmmf," shrugged Minikin.

23

# MILITARY INTELLIGENCE

IN THE TOP OF A NEW OFFICE BUILDING on the Eastside of Manhattan, a shadowy figure opened the exit door and stepped noiselessly into the darkened firewell. The lofty stair landing was musty with the smell of new cement. The man didn't have long to wait — the whisper of ascending footsteps was already audible. He stepped back into the shadows.

A well-dressed, well-rounded Chinese gentleman fastidiously spread his pocket handkerchief and, quite winded, sat down on the bottom step of the final landing.

"Ah, these meetings keep me from attaining a really honorable girth." He breathed deeply and tugged at the bottom of his vest. "What has happened? We are both taking a terrible chance here."

The figure in the shadows spoke softly. "I'm afraid it was unavoidable, Zhao Ping. We have a problem."

"Go on," the seated man prompted.

"The CIA has discovered the secret of the del Gesù."

The little man squinted into the shadows. "How can such a thing have happened?"

The shadowy figure replied, "I take full responsibility. I underestimated the Small woman."

Zhao Ping waved this aside with a quick, impatient gesture of his hand. "I know there are always good reasons for the things you do, my friend. Tell me what this means. How bad is it? We have other copies of the plans, do we not?"

"Regretfully, no. Dr. Grow destroyed them all before making his escape; only the microfiche in the violin remained. There was no time to make more." He switched to Mandarin Chinese, "I want you to know that the Ch'an brothers acted without my instructions. Will Grow's death was a shameful waste of a valuable human being. He was to have been released when the film was safely delivered in Shanghai."

Zhao Ping answered in kind. "I see that you are upset. I realize you are handicapped by the criminal element we are forced to use; the Ghost Shadows of Chinatown understand the importance of what we do, without being able to grasp the spirit in which it is to be done. Console yourself with the knowledge it was out of your hands when Dr. Grow escaped. He could not be allowed to tell what he knew."

The man known to the CIA as "St. Sinner" bowed his head and was silent.

"We must return to the problem before us," Zhao Ping continued in English. "When you first proposed this plan, you promised us the X-ray laser in exchange for the del Gesù violin. In your own words, the violin was to be liberated from the hush of our People's Museum and given voice in the hands of a true daughter of China. I confess I admired the subtle way it was to be the instrument used to carry the film back to us. You know we were happy to do this for you; one of many such gifts expressing our esteem. But you have yet to deliver the laser plans to us."

The shadowy figure answered, "This is why we had to meet. The CIA does not yet have the violin with the microfiche. They expect to get it today, and it is still possible that I may find a way to get the film back for you. However," he hesitated, "if I make the attempt, there is a good chance I will expose my real identity. I could not make this decision — it is for you to decide."

"Ah, I see." There was a long silence. Zhao Ping twisted a heavy gold ring around his finger while he thought. At last he spoke. "It is very difficult to have to make such a decision — you are most valuable to us here in your present capacity. Even so, I am informed by our Military Intelligence that the X-ray laser is essential to the present welfare and future supremacy of The People's Republic of

China. Therefore, I must say, if it is necessary to give up your position here to secure it, that is what you must do."

The man in the shadows inclined his head obediently.

Zhao Ping glanced up at him. "You may be interested to know that President Li Xiannian has lately developed a taste for the fiction of Buck Rogers. An amusing facet of this otherwise cultured man, don't you think?"

The shadowy figure did not answer, and Zhao Ping continued to mull over his dilemma while he went on, distractedly, "In fact, Captain Rogers has become a vogue among the senior members of the Communist Party Politboro. Without doubt, this is owing to you and your secret ray." He nodded his head once emphatically. "Yes, I am convinced this is the correct decision; it is of *primary* importance that you retrieve that film. In the event your cover is blown — and you are still at liberty — you will be provided with a new identity and a safe means of returning to Shanghai."

The soft voice said, "With a little luck, perhaps that won't be necessary and I will continue to be of service here."

Zhao Ping registered the dedication implicit in the other man's words and studied his agent thoughtfully. "You are a strange man, my friend. I know you would rather stay here and continue with your work." He peered at him in the uncertain light.

"Why do you risk so much for us in the unhappy charade you have chosen for your life?"

The answer was a quick one. "I suggest you do not look too closely at this fallible human."

The seated man sensed the threat behind the other man's words, but was unable to refrain from pressing him. "I already know that you are obsessed with oxymorons and the dualities of life, *Leiter d'Arques.*"

The other man replied, "I believe that is not uncommon. You, an armchair adventurer, have chosen an alias that sounds like a ricocheting bullet, Zhao Ping."

The rotund little gentleman shifted his weight uncomfortably on the stairs; the enigmatic figure continually fascinated and perplexed him. Against his better judgement, he insisted, "For once do not evade my questions. What impels you? You have no roots, no home and few friends. Even though you excel at what you do, it can't sustain you forever. In your place I would return gladly to China, where you will be honored and enabled to live in safety and comfort."

After a moment, the man in the shadows answered him. "I enjoy my playacting, it's the thing I do best. But by itself what meaning does it have? It's a game for children. What I do with it gives it meaning, and this is what impels me." He went on quietly. "Americans today are so drunk with comfort that they have few great men to recommend them, but Adlai Stevenson understood. He said, 'Those lives do not count who do not know what they are living for. The test of a human being is: what cause do you serve with heart and soul?'"

Zhao Ping rose slowly to his feet and looked at him sadly. "You make me ashamed, my friend." He folded his handkerchief, adding gravely, "I hope this isn't goodbye."

## 24

# UNVOICED SCREAM

AT SIX O'CLOCK, MINIKIN SMALL PUT through a call to the Nineteenth Precinct and waited while they patched her through to Homer Rohm. A pulse throbbed in her throat and her palms sweated; she was surprised to realize she was frightened. She thought irritably, couldn't these people see she was trying to do them a service? It was infuriating to be treated with so much suspicion. She heard a click and instantly recognized the bland voice of Homer Rohm.

"Hello, Miss Small?"

"Yes, I'm here." She tried to keep the anger out of her words, "I suppose you are trying to trace this call, but I assure you it isn't necessary. I have every intention of turning the violin over to you so it can be examined. I believe it contains whatever it was you were looking for, 'behind the bridge'."

Rohm answered brusquely, "Detective Kake has relayed that information to us and made it clear you are trying to cooperate. We are grateful for your efforts, Miss Small. However, matters of such extreme importance can't be left to your judgement."

Minikin took a deep breath and tried to calm down. "I understand."

"Tell me, do you have the violin with you at this moment?"

"I regret to say, I do not. However, I can guarantee its safety. In fact, my company The Small Agency has undertaken to insure it."

Rohm said urgently, "You must tell me where it is."

Minikin rubbed a trembling hand across her knee. "I. . . I'm not going to do that." His quick protests exploded in her ear, but she cut across the words saying, "And I refuse to argue about it. I will be able to get the violin for you at eight o'clock tonight. No sooner."

There was a strained silence from his end.

Trying to keep the trembling from her voice, Minikin went on reasonably, "At that time, I'll be happy to just bring it to you, if you like."

"No, It can't be done like that. You have to do things *our* way."

"Then what do you suggest?"

"We must pick a public place, with plenty of lights and people, to meet. This is for your own protection. Is there such a place close to where the violin is?"

She thought a moment. Yes, of course there was; it was practically next door. She asked, "What about Carnegie Hall?"

"Perfect," Rohm replied without hesitation. "You will bring the violin, and we'll meet on the steps of Carnegie Hall at precisely eight o'clock."

"Better make it a few minutes after," she suggested, allowing Mr. Grenoble a few minutes of grace.

"Very well," he agreed slowly, a noticeable edge to his voice. "Shall we say, eight-fifteen?"

"Eight-fifteen will be fine," Minikin told him, unable to keep from smiling at the exactitude. She thought, they certainly do enjoy their intrigue. Next, he'll ask to synchronize our watches.

Rohm seemed to read her thoughts, "I hope you are taking the safety of the violin seriously, Miss Small. I can't impress upon you strongly enough that this is no laughing matter."

Minikin thought her actions had already demonstrated her concern, and her temper flared. "I assure you, Mr. Rohm, I take it very seriously, indeed. It's the cloak and dagger attitude I find so amusing."

The wire fairly crackled with his angry silence.

At last he spoke quietly. "Miss Small, as an officer of the CIA and a guardian of the national security, I need your assurance that the violin will be safe until we have it."

She decided their conversation had gone on long enough. She said, "It's as safe as a book in a library or a grain of sand on the beach. See you at eight-fifteen, Mr. Rohm," and replaced the receiver on its hook.

Minikin found her way back to the table and sat down shakily. Bureaucrats! she fumed. She noticed Li C. Fu watching her and tried to gather her thoughts; she hadn't made up her mind what to tell him yet, but she was going to have to decide pretty quick. If she took him with her, and it was as dangerous as everyone seemed to think, he might get hurt. On the other hand, sending him home wasn't the best idea either. She cleared her throat nervously, "Uh, Li C. Fu?"

He placed both palms flat on the table in front of him and answered quietly, "Yes, Mees Smawr?"

She lifted her eyes from the strong, square little hands and made up her mind. "I have to tell you that Luk Tsi's del Gesù was nearly stolen again today. The person that tried to steal it only got the empty case by mistake." She thought, I hope he doesn't get frightened and give notice, and went on doggedly, "I have just spoken to the police, and they believe that something very valuable may be hidden inside it — something to do with smuggling. At eight-fifteen tonight, I have to give them the violin to examine. If you come with me, Li C., you will only become involved yourself. Since I can't let you go home until I know it's safe, I've decided it would be better if you took a room at a hotel while I —" She broke off in surprise as he lifted one hand imperiously from the table and began speaking earnestly.

"Mees Smawr, for over two years I live and work in this country. Frankly, I am disappointed, is nothing like American books I read or movies I see before I come. In few weeks with you I have seen more of real USA than whole rest of time. You meet trouble like a Chinese warrior. As *majordomo* of your house, is my responsibility to join you in danger."

Minikin stared at him — she suspected it was the Chivas and Coke speaking. However, she couldn't offend such loyalty. She focused on his good eye and told him gently, "Listen, Li C., I appreciate your offer, I really do. But this time there is nothing for you to do. It's just a matter of giving the violin to the authorities and getting a receipt from them to protect Luk Tsi and The Small Agency. Tomorrow we can go back to our decorating, and Monday we'll have lunch with Luk Tsi and return her violin."

His hands disappeared from the top of the table and he was silent. Minikin could sense his let down, though his face betrayed nothing. They finished their second Chivas and Coke in silence, left the bar, and returned to the garage for The Slim. As they got in the car, Minikin began to worry about the All Points Bulletin again. She decided as soon as she dropped Li C. Fu at a hotel, she would park the conspicuous Slim in another garage and take a cab.

At ten minutes to eight, in the darkened hallway of the building on West 57th Street, Charles Grenoble put his key in the pick-proof lock of the door to Jacques', opened it and stepped inside. As he snapped on the lights, he heard the sound of clothes rustling behind him. The next instant he was propelled across the shining wood floor on his belly, coming up short against a glass display counter. He sat up and turned around, and to his horror saw two oriental thugs cross the threshold behind him and close the front door.

"See here, what do you think you're doing?" he piped furiously. "Get out of here, there's nothing for you here!"

"Quiet," the man with a jagged scar across one eyebrow told him softly. He gestured to his brother and spoke in Chinese, "Ssu, check the other rooms. See if anyone else is here." He strode to Charles Grenoble, lifted him effortlessly to his feet by his lapels, and started moving him back away from the front door.

The second man reentered quickly. "The place is empty, Tsin. There's a big vault in the next room — it must be inside."

The three men converged immediately on the safe, Grenoble's feet barely allowed to touch the floor. They released him with a jerk, and he staggered to regain his balance.

"Open it," the scarred man ordered him in English and shoved him toward the vault door.

Grenoble smoothed his jacket with dignity and straightened his tie. "There is no money in there," he told them in a firm voice. "Nothing but musical instruments. No use to you at all."

Tsin Ch'an grabbed the neat tie, tightened it, then slowly brought Grenoble's face close to his own. Grenoble could see the perspiration on the other man's upper lip and smell his fetid breath. He watched the cruel mouth in fascination as it said, "Open the safe, old man, if you want to get any older."

Grenoble hastily turned to the safe, loosening his tie with hands that shook, and began to spin the dial. In his anxiety he fumbled the combination and had to start again.

Close to his ear, the quiet voice said, "You better get it right this time, *old man.*"

The last tumbler fell into place with an audible click. Grenoble turned the handle with both hands, and the heavy door swung wide.

Ssu Ch'an felt for the light switch and illuminated the dizzying array of a fortune in antique musical instruments. Then he turned to his brother in confusion, saying, "Oh shit, look at that. How do we know which is the right one?"

Tsin shoved them both aside and stepped into the vault. "I don't see it," he admitted. "They all look alike."

Peering over his shoulder, Grenoble asked incredulously, "You're looking for a *violin?*"

Tsin Ch'an turned back to him, angrily, "Not just any violin, you old fool. One you got this afternoon. The girl left it here, Minikin Small."

"Oh," Grenoble said, his eyes straying inadvertently to the shopping bag in the corner.

Tsin saw the quick look, reached out of the vault and took Grenoble by the lapel. "Which one is it, old man? Come and show me."

Grenoble let himself be pulled into the vault, his shrewd mind thinking quickly. Obviously, he could give them one less valuable and they wouldn't know the difference. He lifted a rich mahogany-brown Stainer from the shelf beside the shopping bag and handed it to the hoodlum with the scar.

Tsin took it by the neck and, pushing Grenoble backward out of the vault, stepped into the room. He held the violin up to the light, examining the face of it behind the bridge.

Calmly, he placed the fiddle on the counter beside him, then spun back toward Grenoble — his vicious backhanded slap catching the old man across the mouth. The sheer strength of the blow knocked Grenoble down, and his momentum carried him into the main room on his back.

The two brothers sauntered after him. Tsin lifted a cello from a nearby stand, put one foot on the fallen man's chest, and placed the sharply pointed end pin in the hollow of the old man's throat.

"I can kill you now," he said quietly, "or I can take the right violin and leave. You decide."

Desperately, Charles Grenoble put both hands against the bottom of the cello and struggled to lift the weight of its point from his windpipe. He nodded his head violently to the man standing over him.

Suddenly there was a gentle tapping at the front door.

The two brothers exchanged a startled look, and Tsin signaled Grenoble to be quiet. They waited in silence. Again, there was a gentle rapping at the door, and this time it opened and Minikin Small stepped into the room. She took in the scene with a single glance and in that instant poised for flight.

"Stand still or I'll kill him," Tsin Ch'an told her. "Now, come inside and shut the door."

Reluctantly, she came forward into the large, shadowy room and closed the door slowly behind her.

Ssu Ch'an looked her up and down with pleasure and licked his lips. "So, big momma, we meet again." He strolled across the floor, stopped in front of her, and stood grinning at her.

With an effort Minikin tore her gaze away from Grenoble, faced Ssu Ch'an and held her ground.

"Don't hurt him," she said with outward calm. "The violin is in there. I'll get it for you." Quickly, she started across the room, but Ssu Ch'an grabbed her by the arm and spun her around against a glass display cabinet.

"Not so fast," he told her, reproachfully. "You should've given us the violin last night. Now, we got some unfinished business between us — a little score to settle." His eyes crawled hungrily over her blue sweater. He gestured toward the oily black letters scrawled across the front, "You really love Ft. Worth, big momma? Foat Wuth Ah Luv Yew? Is that how they say it in Texas?" He laughed quietly, and his brother joined him in the laughter. Still smiling, Ssu Ch'an put his reptilian face close to hers, "You *luv* it, hey?"

Minikin tried to meet his eyes without flinching. "I can take it or leave it," she answered.

"Oh, so this is just a *lie?* Well, then I think I ought to erase it." Deliberately, he put both palms on her breasts and began rubbing at the letters with opposing circular motions — leering into her face, watching her reaction. His brother's laughter became a strange, high-pitched giggle.

Near panic, Minikin struggled to get away, but Ssu Ch'an grabbed the front of her sweater with one hand and pulled her to him; at the same time bringing his other hand high up the inside of her thigh, lifting her up on her toes.

"Stop it!" Charles Grenoble demanded in a strangled voice. "This is an outrage, let go of her at once!" He struggled to rise from the floor, his attention turning to Tsin Ch'an. "And take your filthy hands off this Amati —"

Excited by his brother's actions, Tsin turned to Grenoble impatiently. "Oh, be *still,*" he said, taking the neck of the cello in both hands and pushing him back on the floor with all his strength.

In one stroke, the endpin punctured the carotid artery and jugular vein of the frail throat, cracked the sixth cervical vertibra and punctured the spinal cord. Death was nearly instantaneous. The old man's blue eyes bulged, and his mouth popped open in an unvoiced scream. Bright red blood spilled out of his mouth and down either side of the withered face, spreading quickly into a gorey halo around the white head.

Angered by his unintentional act, Tsin Ch'an let go of the cello in disgust; it tilted to one side, but remained standing. Grenoble's body turned slightly under its weight, his arm extended in the grotesque parody of a fiddler with an out-sized violin tucked beneath his chin.

For a moment they all stared in horrible fascination, then Minikin seemed to go mad. She seized a violin from the counter beside her and slammed it hard against the head of Ssu Ch'an with all her might. It shattered in her hands, and she let go of it as Tsin Ch'an leapt Grenoble's body and came for her. She braced herself and met his headlong lunge with both arms outstretched toward him, her palm shoving the sharp bone of his nose back into his brain. He dropped like a brainshot buffalo and lay quivering on the floor beside Grenoble.

Minikin glanced around the room in shock. On the floor beside her, Ssu Ch'an stirred and began to groan. Someone else, somewhere, was whimpering in fear. She stumbled blindly across the floor, retrieved the shopping bag from the open vault, then turned and fled.

## 25

# SWEET SORROW

OH GOD OH GOD OH GOD, SHE THOUGHT, what had she done? In the hallway, she turned toward the red exit sign in the rear of the building and began to run, down the stairs, down the stairs, down the stairs, out a back door and into a dark alley. She tripped headlong over a garbage can, went sprawling, and before she hit the ground felt a dull blow to her right temple. Tangled in the trash and debris, she rolled over and tried to get to her feet. Her head spun — it was like the last unwinding frenzy before the rubber tire swing stopped turning and slowly began to gather momentum and spin in the opposite direction. She closed her eyes and held on — centrifical force seemed to pull at her — and she lost consciousness.

Sometime later, voices nearby woke her. In her mind, she was in another place wrapped in warmth and security, but curiosity prompted her to listen. The footsteps of two people were coming toward her.

"Look at that, mon. What is that, some kind new type bag-lady?" The footsteps stopped.

"Let her alone, Ramon. She's probably just sleeping it off."

Hesitantly, one of them moved closer to her. He stopped beside her, and his voice sounded frightened, "Like, wow. Look at the cut on her head."

The other voice answered quickly, "Yeah. She's been mugged. Let's get outta here."

Minikin heard their rapid footsteps moving away. She knew they had been talking about her and, with difficulty, she opened her eyes. What was that awful smell? She was enveloped in it. She struggled dizzily to her feet and began to brush the garbage from her clothes. The smell was suffocating. Why was she all covered in garbage? What was she doing here? Suddenly she was overwhelmed with nausea. She felt hot, steaming, and her stomach contracted violently. She placed one hand against the brick wall to steady herself, and then she vomited. And vomited again.

She stood there for some time, her head resting on her arm, until the sickness passed. She was exhausted and covered in cold sweat; she had to get away from here. Where was her purse? Blindly, she searched the debris at her feet. She picked her shoulder bag out of the trash and slowly turned and began to follow the narrow alley toward the lighted street. She paused in confusion and wiped the cold sweat from her face with her sleeve. Which way?

She turned right and began walking. She wanted to go somewhere safe, have a bath and climb into bed. She needed the car, it was around here someplace. Where was it? Oh yes, she remembered she had put it in an all-night garage. She tried to walk a little faster; it was agonizing, like the old nightmare of wading through waist-high water. Steady, she told herself, one foot in front of the other. One step at a time would get her there, eventually. She walked until she recognized the bright lights of Broadway, then she turned left and started down the Great White Way.

Masses of people jarred against her, hordes of night-people. Too many people, she thought. It was like a parade — an unsmiling military parade. She needed a taxi. She moved to the curb and waited patiently. No taxis. Amidst all the traffic a bus roared by, a large poster across the back of it asked, DO YOU JOU JOU? She wondered dimly what that meant. She didn't know if she did or not.

She joined the teeming jostle on the sidewalk and moved forward. She kept moving. SIZZLER! the blazing sign said. SIZZLER! She needed a taxi. DO YOU JOU JOU? She stopped watching for taxis and kept walking.

The blinding lights of LA CAGE AUX FOLIES flashed before her face. HOWARD JOHNSON 28 FLAVORS. ROY ROGERS — ROAST BEEF —

CHICKEN BURGERS. COOKIE ODYSSEY. Thousands and thousands of lights; they were unbearably bright and hurt her eyes. She kept walking, endlessly walking. She would be there soon, she told herself.

Minikin started across 43rd Street and a *New York Times* truck narrowly missed her. The furious driver yelled, "You stupid bitch! Watch where you're going!" She had a brief but satisfying vision of vomiting on him.

At 42nd Street she turned right and started to cross Broadway. She watched all the people coming toward her from the opposite side — waves of people — they closed around her, and she walked forward onto 42nd Street. A man, dressed all in black except for the white sweatband on his snapbrim hat, strutted by trailing a whiff of eau de cologne. She thought, he smells a lot better than I do. She saw a bum lift a can of Pepsi from a trash basket and begin to sip from the bent straw, the Adam's apple bobbing in his scrawny neck. Her own neck prickled, and she put a hand to her throat and swallowed convulsively. She didn't want to think about *that,* now. She *couldn't* think about it.

Faces, leering moving faces everywhere; a laughing man with a gold earring and a missing front tooth; a garrishly made-up youth with carrot-yellow hair and theatrical clothes; gliding beside her, a thin blade of a face with impenetrable black sunglasses and earphones. Invisible hands snatched at her shoulder bag, and she turned and fought back against a suddenly invisible thief.

The glaring lights of the theatre marquees overhead dazzled her — they were brighter than day and warm to her skin. APHRODESIA'S DIARY . . . FANTASEX ISLAND . . . XXX RATED. People shoved by her, and she moved forward through the crowd; shoulder to shoulder, front to back. She stared at the swinging shoulders of the man moving ahead of her and the deep lines on the back of his neck. He stepped quickly aside, and she bumped head-on into a fat girl in red satin pants, eating pizza. The smell made her sick, and she stumbled out of the moving throng and leaned against the glass window of a seedy arcade. The sign above said ONE STOP SEX SHOPPE — VIDEO PEEP 25¢. She gazed in dizzy amazement at a full-sized mannequin in the window wearing a leather vest with crisscrossing ammo belts across its chest and, below the waist, only a woman's spangled G-string. A sign at its feet read SEX AIDS. She felt a hand slide around her waist.

"Looking for a little action, pussy?" an ingratiating voice purred in her ear. "You lonesome, hmmm?"

She turned to look into the dilated pupils of a pimplefaced body builder. A tan T-shirt with "Gucci" written in gold stretched tautly across his muscular chest. He pulled her toward him in an iron grip, saying pleasantly, "Come on, pussy, let's get acquainted. I can make you feel good. *Real* good."

She pushed away from him with all her strength. "No," she whispered. "Leave me alone."

"Well, look at you," he smiled at her with bad teeth. "Do you love Ft. Worth, pussy? Do you really?"

She felt the muscles bunch in his shoulders as he pulled her closer. She felt trapped, helpless. She looked into his blurry face and told him with hatred, "I can kill you."

His smile froze, and his eyes widened slightly. "Aw, that's no way to talk, puss. Are you on a bad trip?"

She pushed him back and turned and walked away.

"Don't leave me, puss," he called after her. "Do you love Ft. Worth? Do you really love it, pussy?"

Her stomach clinched and bile rose in the back of her throat. She wouldn't think about *that,* now. What was she doing here, anyway? She must be lost. Where was the garage? She hurried across Eighth Avenue and a bus eased by, lifting her hair around her face. DO YOU JOU JOU? it asked in passing. The insinuating intimacy of the question was insulting.

The next block was emptier and darker. Ahead, on the corner across the street, she saw the bright lights illuminating Al Jolson's Restaurant. YOU AIN'T SEEN NOTHING YET it told her ominously, in giant letters. One more block, she thought; the garage is on the next block. She crossed Ninth Avenue, craning her neck to see. Yes, there was the sign: PARK & LOCK.

She turned into the entrance and followed the painted yellow arrows up the ramp toward her car. The Slim was a welcome sight. She walked to it quickly and bent to open the driver's door.

A heavy hand fell on her shoulder. "Miss Small?"

She turned to see a police officer in a blue open-necked shirt, dark trousers and holster-belt. He carried a billy club, and he looked as surprised to see her as she was to see him.

"Yes?" she answered.

"Miss Small, you're under arrest."

The incredible words took a moment to penetrate, then Minikin began to laugh; softly at first, but her laughter grew — echoing eerily through the garage — until the sound of it began to remind her of Dr. Grow. The thought of Dr. Grow saddened her, and so at last she stopped laughing and hung her head. She stared at the dirty pavement beneath her feet, and gradually she began to cry — amazing, how simple to cry — until now she had been unable: for her father, for Jean-Louis, for Mr. Grenoble. Sweet sorrow, welcome tears. Behind her back, she felt the handcuffs on her wrists.

# 26

# ORDERED MAYHEM

THE YOUNG PATROLMAN TOOK MINIKIN by the arm and started walking her down the drafty garage ramp. They retraced the painted yellow arrows nearly to the entrance and stopped beside the glass cashier's booth. The officer set down her shoulder bag, fastened his night stick to his belt and removed a compact walky-talky. Minikin licked a salty tear from her top lip and gazed at him dully, registering only the snubnosed face, fair hair beneath the visored cap, and careful blue-gray eyes.

He began to speak into the walky-talky, "Midtown South Patrolpost number 6 to Central K."

A female voice from the walky-talky answered, "Go ahead South Patrolpost 6."

"Holding one for transportation. Request Sergeant with transportation for myself and other to station house. I am in Park & Lock Garage on 42nd Street, between Ninth and Tenth."

Through her apathy Minikin could hear the woman's voice calling, "Available South Unit with

Sergeant respond to request for transportation, area 42nd Street between Ninth and Tenth Avenues, Park & Lock Garage. Pick up Patrolman and one in custody."

For a few moments there was only static and garbled voices from the walky-talky. Minikin blinked away her tears and noticed the pitying eyes of the black cashier in the booth watching her. She glanced away and wished she could blow her nose.

The woman's voice from the walky-talky spoke again, "South Patrolpost 6, Midtown South George is responding."

The young policeman answered, "South Patrolpost 6, 10-4 Central."

Minikin wondered vaguely if all that really made sense to anyone. The officer calmly refastened the walky-talky to his belt, picked up Minikin's purse and took her by the shoulder. They moved past the red and white gate arm, the blue ticket machine, and stopped outside the entrance. Minikin felt the night breeze on her face. She was actually being arrested. They would fingerprint her and photograph her with a number hung around her neck for their criminal records. Why did she feel nothing?

"Look, Stanley."

The shrill voice distracted her, and Minikin noticed that a tiny blue-haired matron in a mink coat had stopped in the entrance to the garage and was gesturing to her husband.

"Look at the cut on the girl's forehead — it's bleeding. Obviously that officer hit her with his club. That's police brutality if ever I saw it! Can't we do something, Stanley?"

The embarrassed little man answered in hushed tones, "Now, Ivy, it's none of our business. Come on, let's get our car."

"No," she stamped her foot emphatically. "I'll not move from this spot until you do something. This isn't a police state. I insist you help her."

The little man sighed with resignation; he knew from experience there was no use arguing with her once she had taken a stand. He said, "Oh very well, Ivy," and turned and approached.

Minikin felt as if she were watching from a great distance. The young patrolman beside her narrowed his eyes and stuck out his jaw.

Stanley stopped in front of Minikin and spoke firmly, "Young lady, if you require any assistance at all I want you to know that Stanley P. Twickersham is solidly behind you." Mrs. Twickersham toddled over to stand beside her husband, and a few people began to gather around them on the sidewalk. Minikin tried to think of anything he could do to help her and found she had nothing to say.

Stanley Twickersham withdrew a leather case from the breast pocket of his overcoat and removed his business card. "Please feel free to call me at any time. Fugett & Twickersham Associates. Tax law's Our Specialty. New Rochelle, New York." He held out the card to her. Out of politeness Minikin moved to take the card and found herself struggling with the handcuffs behind her back.

"What's happening?" someone asked.

Ivy Twickersham piped up, "The officer attacked this defenseless young girl with his stick."

The crowd murmured angrily, and the flustered patrolman tried to speak with authority, "You're jumping to conclusions, lady. You and your husband better go on about your business or you'll be joining us at the station house."

Her eyes widened in surprise. "Don't you threaten me, young man," she said, the blue curls trembling with outrage. "Stanley, did you hear what he said to me?"

"Just a moment, my dear," he said patiently, continuing to offer his card to Minikin. "Go on, Miss, take it. Don't be afraid."

Minikin slowly turned her back and reached out with manacled hands. He pressed the business card carefully in her palm. On her other side, Ivy Twickersham took a lace handkerchief from her purse, reached up and began dabbing at the wound on Minikin's forehead.

"You poor thing, you've been crying, too," she murmured, now scrubbing at her face energetically.

Minikin winced. "He really didn't hurt me. I hit my head."

"Of course you'd have to say that, wouldn't you, dear." She radiated understanding.

Stung by the continued injustice, the young patrolman protested loudly, "I'm warning you, lady! Leave my prisoner alone or I'm going to run you in."

Ivy Twickersham shot him a withering look and returned the scrap of lace to her purse. "Will you hit me with your club, Officer?" she inquired, archly.

"Go ahead, arrest her," someone urged.

"Yeah, but let Miss Fort Worth go," demanded another.

The crowd began to chant, "Oink! Oink! Oink!"

Someone pushed someone else, and Ivy Twickersham started to scream, "Help! Help! Someone has hold of my handbag!"

Her husband sprang to her aid, while the patrolman elbowed Minikin back against the wall and unfastened his billyclub. Minikin gazed with peaceful detachment at the onset of a riot.

Noiselessly, a blue and white patrol car pulled to a stop at the curb. The driver touched the siren once, and the crowd immediately began to disperse.

Stanley Twickersham grabbed his wife by the arm and shook a pink finger under the snub nose of the patrolman, "In future you better watch your step, young man. We taxpayers have our eyes on you. Come, Ivy." He turned with dignity and marched back inside the garage and up the ramp.

Her voice echoed out to them, "You were wonderful, Stanley."

Leisurely, two uniformed policemen opened their doors and stepped out of the car. Full-bodied and barrel-chested, they strolled across the suddenly empty sidewalk, exuding a masculine aura of creaking leather and authority. Thumbs in their belts, they stood there grinning at the young patrolman.

He flushed and said, "Evening, Delaney. Sarge."

The Sergeant, with graying hair and deep laugh lines, replied, "Evening, Bonaventure. Having a little excitement for yourself?"

Bonaventure stuck out his jaw. "Nothing I couldn't handle, Sarge."

Delaney murmured sweetly, "I was hoping you'd hit one with your purse. I *love* your purse."

Bonaventure glowered back at him.

The Sergeant's smiling eyes flickered over Minikin. "Well, what have you got for us?"

"This is Minikin Small," Bonaventure answered. "She's acting kinda strange. Looks like she's been in a fight and smells like she's been sick."

Delaney tugged at his ear in amusement. "You can't arrest her for that, rookie."

Bonaventure drew himself up, "I told you, she's that APB from the Nineteenth Precinct: Minikin Small. I spotted her white MG inside. I watched it for over an hour before she showed up."

The older man's smile faded, "Oh, yes. Minikin Small and the 1960 MG." He looked her over more carefully this time. Minikin stared back at him impassively. He said slowly, "She's an important collar; they want her yesterday. That's heads-up police work, Bonaventure."

The young patrolman swelled with pride.

The Sergeant was all business now, turning to the officer next to him. "Delaney, get on the radio and request Central to notify the Nineteenth Detective Unit that their suspect on APB has been apprehended. We're taking her to Midtown South." He turned back to Bonaventure, "Anything else, Patrolman?"

"Her car is parked just up that ramp, Sarge. I think we ought to take it in for safekeeping."

"Right, let's go." The Sergeant took her car keys from the patrolman, turned and headed up the ramp.

Minikin found herself in the back seat of the patrol car with Patrolman Bonaventure. She was getting a lot of free transportation at the city's expense, she thought. This time it looked like she was also going to get free room and board. For a confused moment she wondered if she would meet Barney Miller at Midtown South. Her head ached, and the ride downtown made her sick to her stomach.

West 35th Street was a narrow, dingy block crowded with diagonally-parked squad cars and lined with derelict tenement houses. Rusty, barely functional fire escapes clung to the brownstone faces like ashamed hands. In the center of the block was an unexpectedly modern three-story office building, with Midtown Precinct South written above the twin glass doors in three-dimensional block letters.

There were no parking places left, and their squad car inched bumper-to-bumper along the one-way street toward the station house. Up ahead, a paddy wagon began to off-load a sizable drug bust from a massage parlor. One scantily-clad lady was carrying a well-worn teddy bear and steadfastly refusing to surrender it. At the wheel, Delaney swore quietly; Saturday night was the busiest night of the week.

Minikin leaned forward in the seat to ease her aching shoulders and rested her temple against the cool glass of the window. What chaos, she thought, peering out at the law enforcement efforts of New York's finest. Somehow she had joined life's busy throng of lawbreakers, and now she was caught in the ordered mayhem of detention. Last month she was skiing in Gstaad.

She was mildly surprised to see Detective Kake hurrying past on the sidewalk, up the steps of the station house, and into the teeming building. Sergeant Mosshammer and another policeman she didn't recognize followed closely on his heels. A few minutes later he pushed out through the doors and stood looking worriedly up and down the street. Minikin marvelled to herself at the handsome face — those sleepy eyes and that pointed, cleft chin. Boy, he looked like Robert Mitchum. And he looked dangerous.

From the other direction up the street, she watched Homer Rohm and a slender, graceful Latino approach at the run. The five men faced each other on the steps of the station house and began to gesticulate wildly and yell. From a distance, to Minikin, it was like watching a French farce — mildly diverting. They separated and began to run from squad car to squad car. She guessed they were looking for her.

Suddenly, something clicked. Minikin leaned back in the shadows and began to breathe quickly. Oh God, she thought. Oh, God. She would have to confront them! They would demand to know what had happened. She had to deal with it now.

The door beside her was wrenched open, and Paddy Kake's iron grip lifted her from the rear seat up and out onto the sidewalk. "Jesus Christ," he said, looking her over.

Patrolman Bonaventure scrambled out of the back seat after her. "Just a moment, there. What are you doing with my prisoner?"

The Detective turned to him. "I'm from the Nineteenth. Detective Kake. What happened to her?"

"I don't know. That's how she was when I apprehended . . ."

Kake turned back to her. "Minikin, are you all right? What happened? Where's the violin?"

Minikin blanched, and her knees seemed to give way. "The violin?" she faltered. The violin! she thought in panic; she had *forgotten* the violin. Where was it? she tried to remember. She had gone to Jacques' to get it. It was at Jacques'. No. . . . She had taken it from the vault before she ran away. . . down the stairs and into the alley. She must have left it in that alley. Oh God, she'd *left* the violin! She stared at Paddy Kake in horror. And her look was reflected in his.

She stammered, "I left it there. They were *waiting* for me, and . . . I left it there."

Homer Rohm moved between them. "That will do, Detective Kake. I'll take her now." He took hold of Minikin's arm, "You're coming with me, Miss Small."

Paddy Kake pushed him away. "Leave her alone. Can't you see she's in shock? She needs medical attention. Leave her alone."

The towering Sergeant Mosshammer stepped forward, saying, "Paddy, let her go. Federal takes precedence over us. You know that." He struggled with him briefly. "Let her go."

Minikin felt herself being jerked back and forth.

Rohm said, "What do you take me for, Kake? I'll see to it she gets proper medical care."

For a moment Kake and Rohm faced each other across her, then Detective Kake dropped his hands and stepped back.

Rohm and Gonzales took Minikin by the arms, turned around and began to walk her up the block past the brightly-lighted station house and into the darkness beyond.

Minikin glanced back once and saw Paddy Kake in earnest conversation with Patrolman Bonaventure. The young patrolman was still holding her handbag. Minikin's head spun. What was happening? She glanced in confusion at the faces of the two men holding her.

# 27

# MANDATORY OPTION

AT THE CORNER OF 35TH STREET AND Ninth Avenue, Rohm held the rear door of their car open for Minikin. She got inside and, easing her shackled hands to one side, leaned back against the seat. Rohm opened the front passenger door and removed a flashlight from the glove compartment. He squatted on the sidewalk beside her and shined the dim light into her pupils, lifting first one eyelid, then the other.

"It appears you've got a mild concussion, Miss Small. It doesn't look too serious, but it *will* be tended to directly." His words were so unemotional, she was surprised at the gentleness of his touch. "Besides the bump on your head, are you hurt anywhere else?"

She answered, "No, I don't think so."

He sat back on his heels and drew a long breath, "Good. Now, what happened to the violin?"

Minikin closed her eyes; she didn't think she could bear this. A part of her conscious mind went somewhere else, and she began to speak in a quiet monotone, "I left the del Gesù with Mr. Grenoble at Jacques', the violin appraisers. He put it in the vault. When I returned for it, around eight o'clock, they were waiting for me."

"Who?" he asked.

"The two Chinese who killed Dr. Grow."

Rohm exchanged a startled look with Gonzales, and swore softly to himself.

"What happened?"

Tears escaped from her closed eyes and began to run down her cheeks; the scalding drops seemed to sear her flesh. She choked and was unable to speak.

Homer Rohm leaned forward and gently took her face in his hands. "Miss Small. This is *vitally* important; you must tell me what happened."

Minikin swallowed with difficulty, opened her eyes and gazed unseeing into his. "He murdered Mr. Grenoble, there on the floor. The one with the scar. We fought, and . . . I killed him. Afterward, I took the violin and ran away."

"Santa Maria," breathed Gonzales.

Rohm let go of her and sat back on his heels.

He glanced quickly at Gonzales in disbelief before asking her, "You're sure you *killed* him?"

"Yes."

Her head dropped forward, and she began to sob. "Mr. Grenoble was my father's friend. I'm also responsible that he is dead."

Rohm patted her shoulder.

"No. No, Miss Small. You're not to blame." He ran a nervous hand over his closely cropped hair and then glanced at his watch. Finally, he turned back to her. "Listen to me. I am very sorry, but we don't have time for feelings right now. We must get that violin. Do you know where it is?"

Minikin nodded and tried to pull herself together. "I know where it is," she responded numbly. "I . . . I need to blow my nose."

Rohm stood, groped through his pockets for a handkerchief, and held it out to her. She struggled helplessly with the handcuffs behind her back. Impatiently, he turned and demanded, "For Christ's sake, Gonzales, get those cuffs off her."

They helped her out of the car, and Gonzales bent in the uncertain light and unfastened the regulation Smith & Wesson cuffs with his keys. Rohm passed her his handkerchief, and she wiped her face and blew her nose. Then she took a deep breath and began to describe what had happened in the alley.

Rohm cut her story short, his voice at last incredulous. "Are you telling me that violin has been lying in an alley in a pile of garbage since eight o'clock tonight?"

Minikin nodded miserably. It had occurred to her that The Small Agency was liable for the loss of the del Gesù.

Gonzales glanced at his watch and grimaced. "It's nearly three a.m., Mr. Rohm."

To Minikin, the ride back uptown was a dizzy blur. Apparently their tan Ford was not equipped with a siren, but Gonzales drove as if it were, while Rohm sat beside her in the back seat quietly snapping his fingers. They went up Eighth Avenue to 56th Street and turned right, crossed Seventh Avenue against the light and passed behind Carnegie Hall.

They parked in front of one of the many chic restaurants — now closed — that lined the block. Outside on the sidewalk, Minikin had some difficulty locating the alley. The narrow dog leg was used primarily by vans delivering food and was cluttered with trash and overflowing garbage cans. Even in the shadowy light it was clear the brick walls along its sides were covered with graffiti. The rancid smell of rotting garbage was overwhelming. Minikin gagged and leaned dizzily against a wall, while Rohm and Gonzales kicked and pawed through the debris in the darkness at the rear of the alley.

She heard them calling to each other: "I don't see it." "It isn't over here, either."

Minikin swallowed with difficulty and said, "It's in a brown Bloomingdale's shopping bag, and the violin is wrapped in my blue quilted bathrobe."

There was a very long silence. She raised her head to see Rohm standing in the light from the flashlight in Gonzales' hand, holding the Bloomingdale's shopping bag, and Gonzales pointing a very long gun at him. Minikin tried to focus more clearly and realized her eyes were not playing tricks on her.

Rohm said angrily, "You'll never get away with this, Gonzales."

Minikin made an effort to stand upright, thinking to herself in amazement, they actually do say things like that.

The slim Latino smiled without humor. "I think I will, Mr. Rohm." He motioned to the other man to turn around and face the wall. "You know the position, I believe."

Rohm placed his palms against the brick wall, and Gonzales kicked his feet back away from it until Rohm was standing off-balance and helpless.

Minikin looked from one to the other of them in confusion. Is everyone here crazy? she wondered and began to ease backward out of the alley.

Instantly, Gonzales glanced over at her. "That's a no-no, Miss Small. Come over here where I can see you."

She walked slowly over to stand beside Homer Rohm in the circle of light from the flashlight and faced the wall.

With a single graceful motion Gonzales bent quickly, placed the flashlight on the ground, and rose. Then, expertly, he began to frisk the other man; removing a gun from Homer Rohm's shoulder holster, and another one from the small of his back. He dropped them in the trash at his feet and kicked them away. Carefully alert, he withdrew the shiny handcuffs from his pocket.

Minikin watched as Gonzales handcuffed Rohm with the same cuffs that had been used on her, and flinched involuntarily as she heard him tighten the cruel bracelets around the other man's wrists.

Gonzales left the flashlight lying on the ground and picked up the shopping bag standing next to him by the handles. "Okay, you two," he ordered, "now we go back to the car." He waggled the gun at them.

As Minikin stepped back from the wall and turned around, she caught a dull glint from the trash at her feet. She leaned forward, put her hands on her knees and said weakly, "The smell is nauseating; I think I'm going to be sick."

Following Rohm toward the entrance of the alley, Gonzales could only give her a sharp look over one shoulder. In the moment his back was to her, she stooped quickly and reached into the trash. It was the smaller of Rohm's two guns. She stuffed it in the waistband of her blue jeans, covering it hastily with her sweater. In the next instant, Gonzales caught hold of Rohm by the handcuffs and turned back toward her, saying savagely, "Throw up out here, Miss Small!"

Minikin groaned and followed them out of the alley. She was covered in sweat and shaking; she leaned against a corner of the building and rubbed her sleeve across her forehead. She told herself she wouldn't be ready to kill anyone else for at least a day or two. But she was responsible for that violin, and it was beginning to look like every man for himself. She straightened up to find the two men standing beside the car watching her.

"Hurry up, Miss Small," Gonzales said impatiently. "If you're finished being sick, I want you to drive. If you're not yet finished, then hurry up."

Minikin walked unsteadily over to Gonzales. "I can't drive," she told him feebly. "I'm not feeling well."

Gonzales opened the rear door of the car for Homer Rohm, who climbed inside, then slammed it behind him. He turned back to her, saying with grim humor, "You do have another choice, Miss Small. However, in your shoes, I would understand that getting behind the wheel *right now* is a mandatory option."

# 28

# ESSENTIALLY UNIMPORTANT

MINIKIN GOT BEHIND THE WHEEL, AND Gonzales took the precaution of seeing that all the doors were locked. She started the car, and they pulled away from the curb, made two left turns and went crosstown to the Westside Highway. Gonzales directed her to turn north, and they entered the sparse flow of late-night traffic heading up the Hudson River toward the George Washington Bridge. Minikin reflected moodily that she had spent the whole day and half the night touring the city.

At Gonzales' direction, Rohm had moved over in the rear seat to sit behind Minikin. Now he watched Gonzales, warily. Gonzales sat in the front with his back to the door, the shopping bag at his knee. His gun rested on the back of his seat, pointing first at Rohm and then at Minikin.

From the corner of her eye, Minikin studied him in the random lights. Gonzales was slender and finely made, with handsome Latin features and a graceful bearing. It was hard to guess his age, for while there were a few flecks of silver in his dark hair, there was also a youthful vulnerability about his mouth. Most evident was the fact that here was a highly-trained professional.

Rohm said, "You're out of your mind, Gonzales. The Company will track you down and squash you like a bug."

Minikin glanced at Rohm in the rearview mirror and felt like a spectator at The Late Show.

Gonzales smiled thinly, "The Russians are going to pay me enough to make the risk worthwhile, Mr. Rohm. If you're interested, this is how it will work. Tonight, you and the violin are going to vanish without a trace, and I'll wake up in that alley tomorrow morning with a large bump on my head. They'll find this car at Kennedy Airport. Your disappearance will be damning — they will think you were in league with St. Sinner. They're so paranoid maybe they'll even believe you *are* St. Sinner, and you've succeeded in getting away with the violin and the plans. For a time I'll just sit tight, with my nice numbered account safe in Switzerland. Then one day in the near future, *I* will disappear. Perhaps I'll stage it to look like I died heroically in the line of duty." He paused to savor the irony. "Yes, I like that. It really helps to talk things over, doesn't it?" He smiled and continued conversationally, "Then I will retire quietly somewhere and enjoy all the fruits of my ill-gotten gain."

His voice emotionless, Rohm asked, "How did the Russians find out about the ray?"

Gonzales grinned cynically. "In our business there are leaks all over the place, you know how it is, Mr. Rohm. Sometimes I think that's our main function; leaking information."

"Sure, I know how it is," Rohm said quietly. "How long have you been doing business with them?"

For a moment Gonzales looked surprised. "Actually," he replied, and his candor seemed genuine, "they just approached me. They already knew about the x-ray laser, and they made me a very generous offer for the film. Tonight, you might say, I acted on impulse."

It was Rohm's turn to look surprised, and he was silent while he digested this.

Minikin was listening with interest. An x-ray laser! she thought, fascinating! So *that* was what all the fuss was about. However, she reminded herself excitedly, the film was Rohm's responsibility — hers was the violin. She had to protect it. She glanced at Gonzales and asked, "Just out of curiosity, may I inquire what you plan to do with the del Gesù?"

He appeared startled by her question, but he answered, "I realize it's valuable, Miss Small, but it would be too dangerous to try to sell it — they might be able to trace it back to me." He shrugged, "Anyway, I won't need the money. Once I have removed the film, I'm afraid the violin will have to be destroyed."

Minikin winced at the thought of such a monstrous act, but managed to ask politely, "May I make a suggestion?"

"Certainly," he smiled expansively. "Why not?"

She drew a deep breath. "You might find it convenient to deal with The Small Agency. As the insuring party they would be the most generous because they have the most to lose. Naturally, you could rely on their discretion."

The dark brows drew together in his pale face, and he studied her for a moment.

She asked pleasantly "Can one really ever have enough money, Mr. Gonzales?"

Unexpectedly he smiled, and then his smile broadened into laughter. He took his time laughing and thoroughly enjoyed the humor. "It's the violin you're concerned about, is it?" He laughed some more and shook his head, "You know, Miss Small, you've been a pain from the very beginning. You know that? In fact, you're a real headache. And you know something else? You ought to quit worrying about the *violin.*"

For the first time it dawned on Minikin that he intended to kill her. The knowledge surged through her like a powerful electric charge — and the steering wheel lurched involuntarily in her hands. In the fast lane, the left front tire climbed the curb. She corrected violently to avoid the wall in the center isle, and the car fish-tailed wildly for a hair-raising moment until she again brought it under control.

There was silence throughout the car. She waited for Gonzales' wrath, but he said nothing. Gradually, she realized words were unnecessary. He couldn't threaten to kill her if it happened again, because he was going to kill her anyway. And he knew there was no point in her committing suicide in the car just to get even, because she would still be dead — alive, at least there was still hope. This was quiet reality, and it was eloquent. She began to tremble and tried not to think about what lay ahead. The gun in her waistband dug into her stomach.

At last Rohm said, "This isn't like you, Gonzales. You have an impressive record behind you; nearly eighteen years of impeccable service. Why are you doing this?"

In the darkness of the front seat, Gonzales' eyes slid away from the other man's direct question, but then he glanced back defiantly, "*Why not?* I'm wasting my life, and what's it all for?"

Gonzales was quiet for so long that Minikin jumped when he began to speak again.

He directed his words to Rohm, his tone reflective, "Do you remember the time we were assigned to protect Kissinger and he kept trying to get us to carry his briefcases? Our job was to defend him with our lives, and he wanted to use us like servants."

Rohm nodded slowly, "How could we defend him if our hands were full carrying his damned papers?"

"Right! And remember when he wanted to go swimming from that beach posted with shark warnings? He actually wanted us to swim with him in the water to guard him from the sharks. Like he expected a shark would come over to take a bite, and we would plug him!" For a moment he relived that outrage in incredulous silence. Then, quietly, he began to speak again, "Every morning for two years, rain or shine, I jogged with President Carter. He never said one word to me. Not one. Even Nixon always said good morning and, when my mother was so sick, he asked how she was doing. Imagine. Nixon!"

Minikin glanced at Rohm in the rearview mirror and saw him listening with something akin to understanding.

Gonzales passed his free hand across his face. "Mr. Rohm, do you remember Martinez? That young Cuban who was so gung-ho?"

Rohm nodded silently.

"The Company was convinced he was a double agent and arranged an 'accident' for him. Did you know that's what happened to him? The accident was arranged. *I* did it . . . and he was my friend."

Minikin looked at Gonzales in horror, as much for what he had done as what he had been asked to do.

The man's voice broke as he asked again, "Tell me, Mr. Rohm, what's it all for, anyway?"

Rohm couldn't look at Gonzales; he glanced away and gazed out of the window as he spoke. "I guess you have to answer that for yourself, *amigo.*"

Gonzales waved the gun in wordless frustration for a moment, then said with ironic understatement, "Well, I think some people deserve a little recognition."

Minikin stared. It was a universal complaint — so essentially unimportant — yet valid cause for more than a few to smash their lives. She almost felt sorry for him.

They drove on in silence; there didn't seem to be anything else to say. Just before they reached the George Washington Bridge, Gonzales ordered Minikin to turn off the highway and onto Riverside Drive. They traveled along the park for a few minutes, then he directed her through a dizzying maze of side street turnings. Finally the car left the paved road, bounced across the grass, through some trees, and came to rest on an embankment at the foot of the mighty bridge.

Gonzales told Minikin to shut off the ignition and douse the lights. As their eyes became accustomed to the darkness, they were able to make out the glimmer of the river and, twinkling on the far shore, the tiny lights of Ft. Lee, New Jersey.

Minikin's heart was an agonizing drum in her chest that interfered with her breathing. Gonzales ordered her to leave the keys in the ignition, get out of the car and come around to his door. Nearly paralyzed with fear, Minikin was shaking so badly she could hardly manipulate the lock on her door and once out could barely walk.

Gonzales unlocked the two doors on his side and, when she reached him, got out and opened the rear door for Rohm. His eyes darted quickly between them, as Rohm struggled to get out of the car without the use of his hands or arms. Minikin glanced around helplessly.

Behind them and to the left, the base of the immense suspension bridge rose above them into the starry darkness like a great cliff. Minikin began to shiver violently in the cool breeze from the river.

As soon as Rohm stepped from the car and straightened up, he began to speak quietly to Gonzales. "The Russians will never let you quit, you know. They'll have something on you now. They could make you stay in place and work for them here."

"They'll have to find me first," Gonzales answered, and the gun in his hand waved them down toward the edge of the watery abyss.

Minikin and Rohm drifted half-heartedly ahead of him across the grass. Minikin knew it was up to *her* — she was going to have to use that little gun now. Her palms were sweating, and she kept rubbing them against her trembling thighs.

Rohm said, "It's not too late, Gonzales. We can get back in the car with the violin and nothing will ever be said about tonight. I'll see you get the recognition you deserve. You have my word."

Gonzales ignored him. "Just a little farther, you two. I want you standing right down by the edge." His lips pulled away from his teeth in a horrible grimace, and his next words seemed to hiss at them through the darkness. "The currents are strong and dangerous here. The tides will carry you out to sea, and your bodies will never be recovered."

Trembling at the edge, Minikin thought, *doing as he orders is profoundly stupid.* She suddenly turned around and began to walk the other way, quickly separating from Rohm by the space of a dozen feet.

Gonzales turned toward her with the gun, saying, "Stop where you are, Miss Small," and Rohm rushed him. Gonzales turned back to Rohm, and the little gun seemed to appear magically in Minikin's hand. Rohm hit him with a body block and fell to the ground, as Gonzales fired at him and spun back toward her.

Minikin squeezed the trigger, and a tidy black hole appeared in his forehead above his right eyebrow. She stood staring at him, the smoking gun in her hand. There was no expression on Gonzales' face at all. The dead man pivoted in place like a dancer, then slowly crumpled to the ground and rolled down the embankment into the river.

No one — anywhere — appreciated him.

# 29

# OPEN SECRET

MINIKIN'S LEGS COLLAPSED BENEATH her, and she found herself sitting on the wet grass. The shots still seemed to reverberate in her ears, and there was a sharp smell of gunpowder in the chill air. She knew she couldn't rise, and so she remained shivering in the wet grass until she thought she saw Rohm move. Numbly, she evidenced surprise; she thought Gonzales had . . . She rolled over onto her knees and crawled slowly over to him in the darkness.

"Mr. Rohm? Mr. Rohm," she whispered. He moaned, and very gently she eased him over onto his side. His eyes were open, and he looked up at her.

"What happened to Gonzales?" he asked, dazed.

"He's dead. Are you hurt?"

"I think I'm shot. Either that or I broke my shoulder when I fell on it."

She tried to help him up, but he groaned and protested, "No, don't move me. See if you can unfasten these handcuffs. The key is on the ring in my back pocket."

With trembling fingers she hurried to free him. Then, together, they got him to his feet. Minikin could see the bloodstain spreading darkly across the left shoulder of his jacket. She said helpfully, "You didn't break it, you were shot."

Irritably, he glanced at her. "Thanks a lot." Then he looked around in confusion, "Where is Gonzales' body?"

Minikin said, "He fell into the river."

Rohm stared at her for a moment, then his look softened and he glanced away, shaken. "I can hardly believe it, I honestly thought we were done for. He was a consummate professional, and we took him — a handcuffed man and an untrained girl with a concussion." He looked back to her, and his eyes narrowed. "Where did you get that gun?"

She held it out to him. "From the alley, it's yours."

He took it with his good hand, saying quietly, "And I didn't even suspect. . . . I must be losing my grip. Come on, let's get out of here."

Minikin helped him to the car and opened the passenger door for him. She said, "I think we ought to take a look at your wound. Perhaps we can do something to stop the bleeding."

He sat down and they removed his jacket, unbuckled his shoulder holster, and unbuttoned his shirt. His shoulder was covered with blood. Minikin looked around for something to use, and finally unwrapped the violin and began to tear her satin quilted robe into pieces. Carefully mopping his shoulder, she said, "There's a chunk missing from the muscle above your collarbone. He almost missed you."

Through clinched teeth, Rohm said, "Yeah, the bastard was slipping. If he wasn't already dead, I'd fire him."

Minikin folded the sleeve from her robe neatly and tied it over the wound with his necktie. She said, "If you press on the bandage it will help to stop the bleeding."

Rohm placed his hand experimentally over the dressing, and winced, "It hurts."

"It's your blood," she shrugged. "You act like this is the first time you've been shot."

Stung, he replied, "As it happens, it is."

Placing his jacket around his shoulders, she stopped to look at him. "Oh, I'm sorry. I guess I thought it was sort of an occupational hazard."

"Nevertheless," he insisted, "it's the first time."

She answered wearily, "Okay, I believe you," and closed his door.

Overhead, the stars were flickering out and the sky was beginning to lighten. As Minikin walked around the car to the driver's side, she noticed the sound of wakening birds in the trees. The river looked greasy and cold, and she shuddered.

She started the car, made a U-turn, and bounced back across the grass. They found the road, and eventually the highway, and decided their first destination should be Emergency Receiving at Lenox Hill Hospital. Minikin stopped shivering as the heater in the car warmed her, and then fatigue began to creep through her like an insidious fog. Involuntarily, her eyes began to close.

"Hey! Watch it!" Rohm's words jerked her awake in time to keep the car from crashing through the guard rail and vaulting out over the river below. She glanced at him guiltily; it would be a fine thing to kill them both, now.

"Are you all right?" he demanded.

She stammered, "I'm sorry, it's . . . been a long day." She shook her head and widened her eyes, but after a moment she felt herself beginning to nod off again. She turned to Rohm, saying, "I think you'd better talk to me; it will help me stay awake."

"Sure," he said, anxiously cradling his arm. "What shall we talk about? Pick a topic."

"Anything that's interesting," she yawned into her hand. "Tell me about St. Sinner."

"Absolutely not," he snapped. "That's Top Secret."

From the depths of her exhaustion Minikin began to laugh quietly. What a world! She wondered if she would ever stop laughing.

"Okay, okay," he agreed quickly. "I suppose it won't make any difference since you know so much of it already. St. Sinner is an agent for the People's Republic of China. We believe his real name is Leiter d'Arques."

"Lighter Dark?"

"No, Leiter d'Arques; he's German-French."

"Oh, I see," she said, hazily. "But he works for the Chinese?"

"Right."

"And you call him 'St. Sinner'?"

"Right again. Actually we don't know very much about him, just his M.O. We thought we recognized him by his M.O."

"By the way he operates?"

"Right."

Minikin yawned again, lingeringly. "Actually," she said, "you're putting me to sleep."

Homer Rohm drew a deep breath before asking cautiously, "What else do you want to know?"

She shrugged, "Tell me about his M.O."

With his good hand Rohm rubbed the back of his neck and then sighed, "Well, according to one of our agents who has run up against him before, St. Sinner always disguises himself as a recognizable celebrity to distract the people that see him, so they won't remember anything else about him. For example, we think the man who blackmailed Will Grow for the plans . . ."

"Oh," Minikin gasped in surprise. "He was being blackmailed?"

Rohm glanced at her quickly and held up his hand. "Before you ask, I must tell you I can't elaborate on that any further. However, I will say that Dr. Grow was a brilliant and courageous man." He hesitated a moment and rubbed a hand over his face, "Where was I? Oh yes, we think the man calling himself Harry Balding was intentionally disguised to look like Magnum, on TV."

With difficulty, Minikin dragged her thoughts away from Dr. Grow and tried to concentrate on what Rohm was saying. "You mean Tom Selleck? And he called himself 'Harry Balding'?" Slowly she chuckled, "St. Sinner has a sense of humor." She thought a minute then added, "He would also have to be quite an actor."

Rohm cleared his throat. "As a matter of fact, we believe he trained professionally as an actor. Anyway, that's about all we know about him."

Minikin was quiet while she pondered this. After a moment she spoke carefully, "Mr. Rohm, I believe I've seen him."

Homer Rohm groaned loudly, "Miss Small, you have an overworked imagination, and my shoulder is killing me."

"Now, listen," she insisted. "Do you happen to know how Luk Tsi got her del Gesù violin?"

"Yes," he replied. "I read the police report. Someone gave it to her. It was a donation."

"That's right. I was there the night of her debut and I saw it — the del Gesù was presented to her by a man named Professor Topper Bottham, and he bore a curious resemblance to *Albert Einstein*. We all remarked about it. He had a German accent, and — this is fantastic — he even mentioned he was a mathematician!"

Rohm said slowly, "You realize this is mere speculation, Miss Small. It might very well have been him, but we can't automatically assume it was. We need hard evidence, something substantial. You're jumping to conclusions."

Minikin smiled tiredly, "I suppose you're right, that's how I got into this mess in the first place. Still, it's most intriguing. Topper Bottham," she mused, "Harry Balding. They sound like different choruses of the same song. But then I guess I'm sensitive to names." She fell silent. In spite of her fatigue she began to feel the excitement coursing through her. Suddenly she hit the rim of the steering wheel with her palm and turned to Rohm, "Aha! I can sing you another chorus of that song . . . Angela Devlin, who just happened to be a ringer for Jackie Onassis! How does that sound? Pretty substantial?"

"Who?" he asked, blankly.

"Angela Devlin, the CIA agent who wasn't a CIA agent. Don't you see? It's the same pattern. The recognizable celebrity disguise, and the crazy nonsensical name. It's not really nonsensical, you know, there is a word for it," she thought a minute, then snapped her fingers sharply . . . "Oxymoron.

The names are oxymorons, all of them! Leiter d'Arques, Harry Balding, Topper Bottham and Angela Devlin. What a remarkable actor he must be. I never once guessed Angela Devlin wasn't female, even though she was wearing a man's suit! Or rather, I should say, *he* was wearing."

Rohm was staring at her, his mouth open. "What are you talking about?"

Minikin shrugged, "Well, I don't suppose it helps you any, but I would bet you lunch at Lutece that the phony agent who stole the empty violin case yesterday was St. Sinner in drag."

"Oh, I see," he said quietly and glanced away out of the window. "Interesting theory. I'll mention it in my report."

Minikin felt very pleased with herself. Now that she had some understanding of her adversary, the pieces of the puzzle had begun to fall into place. She realized she would probably never know the whole truth, but at least now she could try to make some sense out of what had happened:

An agent working for China had blackmailed Dr. Grow into giving him plans for the manufacture of an X-ray laser, and the microfilm had been secreted in a valuable violin. Dr. Grow had known its hiding place and sacrificed his life trying to tell someone. Then, the violin had been given to Luk Tsi before her world concert tour with the certain knowledge she would want to take it with her. To Shanghai? . . . probably, Minikin decided, but then frowned.

"Mr. Rohm, do you think St. Sinner planned to have the del Gesù stolen from Luk Tsi while she was on tour in order to retrieve the plans? I mean, it all seems such a lot of trouble to go to. Surely, there would have been a simpler way."

Distracted, he answered, "I don't know. I suppose so. Or, more likely, the Chinese government could have taken the violin from her at Customs, along with the rest of her things, removed the film in private and then returned everything to her. Such acts aren't uncommon over there."

"Then St. Sinner actually intended Luk Tsi to keep the del Gesù. Why would he want to give away such a valuable thing?"

"You mean, assuming it was up to him?" Rohm scratched his chin before replying, "According to his file he's a contradictory person, like his names. Sometimes in the past, when he has had to use people, he has tried to repay them. It's one of the reasons they call him 'St. Sinner.' I believe it is an egotistical trait."

Minikin shook her head, "I don't understand."

Rohm glanced away. "I don't either."

Her fatigue forgotten, Minikin returned to her thoughts. It seemed natural to her that, after giving the violin to Luk Tsi, St. Sinner would want to keep an eye on it. Hence the two thugs following them along Central Park that night. It must have been a shock to them to discover that the violin had been handed over to the one person who might discover its name translated as 'The Shadow of the Sun,' and then make sense out of Dr. Grow's garbled message. When the two Chinese failed to take it away from her that night, the next afternoon St. Sinner presented himself on her doorstep disguised as Angela Devlin, from the CIA, come to collect the violin.

Minikin stopped and held her breath; she had overlooked something. She suddenly realized that Angela Devlin had *known* she was expected. Minikin had only told one person about *L'onere du Soleil* — Paddy Kake — and there was hardly enough time elapsed between her call to him and Ms. Devlin's appearance to admit the possibility of it being anyone else. It was hard to believe but, come to think of it, Detective Kake did bear a suspicious resemblance to Robert Mitchum.

Minikin shook her head and drummed her fingers on the steering wheel. His name wasn't an oxymoron. Anyway, she didn't want to believe that Paddy Kake had betrayed her. She could think of only one other explanation.

"Mr. Rohm?"

"Now what?"

"Could you tell me if by any chance my phone is tapped?"

For a long moment his pale, expressionless eyes bored into hers. Then he replied, "This is strictly off the record, and I'll deny it if you repeat it but, yes, we did monitor your phone. It was for your own protection."

His words had the impact of a small explosion. Minikin drew a shaky breath and said, "Then you must realize there was a leak from your wiretap. St. Sinner, posing as Angela Devlin, knew that I had telephoned for help and was expecting someone."

Rohm took his time answering, "Yes, I am already aware that we have a security breach. For a while tonight I thought it was Gonzales."

Minikin was aghast. "Do you mean to tell me the CIA has more than one leak?"

Rohm replied bitterly, "Miss Small, the chances of a breach in security are equal to the *square* of the number of people who know about it." His tone became that of a parent explaining to a backward child, "It's an open secret — people aren't trustworthy, and nothing in life is secure."

Minikin turned to stare at him — the man was infuriating. With a straight face she repeated, "Nothing in life is secure?" Then she clutched her forehead, wide-eyed, "Egad, what a revelation!"

There was a moment's pause, then Homer Rohm began to laugh. It was completely silent laughter, only the sound of air being expelled. Watching him and beginning to smile, Minikin wondered whether he had had much practice. Suddenly she felt sorry for him; she suspected life must have shown him a sordid face. At last he sighed and wiped the tears from his eyes with his good hand.

Minikin drove on deep in thought. Though she had pretended to joke about it, it was still a shock to her. Homer Rohm had actually admitted that St. Sinner had a conduit to the CIA! Just how secure was their National Security, anyway? The question made her squirm, and she returned to her conjecture uneasily.

She had presumed there were people listening in on the phone call she had made to Rohm from Wall Street because they had been trying to trace her location. Now, she realized, it was probably from her own mouth that St. Sinner had learned where to send his two goons to search for the violin. What were the words she had used to Rohm? "It's as safe as a book in a library or a grain of sand on the beach." What irony, and what a fool she was! Naturally, a violin would be hidden among other violins, in a place she had indicated was close to Carnegie Hall. Jacques' was internationally known. The only surprise was that the CIA hadn't figured out where she had hidden it first and then beat those two goons to it.

Minikin began to drum on the steering wheel again. What was wrong? Surely the whole CIA had as much initiative as St. Sinner. Why hadn't Homer Rohm —

She stopped drumming and thought suddenly, what an amazing coincidence, Homer Rohm's name was an oxymoron: Homer Roam! She clutched the wheel tightly and looked at Rohm. Slowly, he lifted the gun from his right hand pocket and pointed it directly at her.

"I must say," he remarked quietly, "it's been *mesmerizing* watching you. You're a bright young woman, Miss Small. Now, what am I going to do with you?"

# 30

# STRANGELY INTIMATE

AS THE FULL REALIZATION OF WHAT HAD happened hit her, Minikin's mind swirled. How many times had she met this man in the last few days, and in how many different guises? Now she remembered the recognition in the old professor's eyes when he spotted her at Carnegie Hall. No wonder he was shocked to see her — he had just spent the night interrogating her, as Homer Rohm. But disguised as Angela Devlin, Rohm had been astonishingly convincing. And now, unexpectedly, she could visualize him easily as Harry Balding. Sitting next to her in the car, the violin between them, he suddenly seemed remote, unknowable, almost alien. She could only gasp, "*You* are St. Sinner? But you're an agent for the CIA!"

He shrugged mildly, "So was Gonzales."

"And you're doing this for the money?"

He answered indifferently, "I assure you my reasons are not mercenary."

"Then why *are* you doing this? You are responsible for the loss of all those lives."

He said slowly, "There is no way to explain to you that there are things more important than a few human lives." He looked at her as though a door had closed between them. "Just keep driving, Miss Small. I will tell you where to turn off the highway."

Minikin felt the panic building inside her again. She thought wildly, he's going to kill me because I know his double identity! He has to; what else can he do? The accumulated strain of the past few days began to blot out her reason; she knew in a moment she would be screaming in terror and frustration. She drew a few deep breaths and tried to calm down. Her thoughts raced ahead into the darkness, and then some dim instinct for survival told her to get him to talk to her.

"Look," she said, and grinned sheepishly, "if I was going to shoot you, I would at least feel I owed you an explanation. Tell me, what is more important than my life?"

"To you, nothing. To me, the welfare of China," he answered easily. "It is also more important than *my* life."

"I should be interested to know why you think China is so important."

"This is a waste of time," he said impatiently.

"Try me," she challenged. "Or perhaps it sounds foolish put into words."

He seemed to consider this for a moment. "Perhaps," he agreed. "People aren't always able to explain why they do things. Why does a soldier go to war and shoot at strangers? Why does a bombardier drop bombs on a city full of people?" He paused and then went on slowly, "I believe we are coming of age. Mankind has survived forty years on this planet without destroying himself with nuclear weapons. Technologically, we are on the brink of conquering space and traveling in time. We have reached a point where we are about to mature and to expand our horizons. Our values and priorities must be sound. One looks around for the best philosophy mankind can devise to shape his destiny. For decades the Soviet Communists mindlessly sacrificed everything to the state, from their religions to their creature comforts. Capitalists in the 'free world' believe whoever has the most 'toys' when he dies, wins. It is impossible to decide which is more misguided. Yet one needs something to believe in. The Chinese, as a people, have more wisdom. They have a better appreciation of the elusive joys of living, and they understand the tragedy of death on the smallest scale. They are nobler. It is my judgement that their values should prevail in the world. Not in this century I know, but soon and for ages to come, in the outposts of space that mankind will explore and colonize. I intend to help them get that opportunity."

Minikin let her breath out slowly. Finally she said, "You mentioned the tragedy of death on the smallest scale. It is ironic that in serving these 'noble' people you must sacrifice the very ideals you are trying so hard to preserve."

The man sitting next to her replied, "Unfortunately, in my business, that is the case whichever country one serves." He cocked one eyebrow, "Haven't you noticed? None of them has scruples."

Minikin blinked in surprise and had no answer.

After a while she asked, "Where are we going?"

"To Chinatown," he answered.

At the other end of Manhattan, they turned off the highway onto Canal Street. The already dim glow from the street lights was clouded by an early morning mist. The narrow buildings lining the foggy thoroughfare were two and three stories high with peeling paint and broken panes in the upper windows. At street level the closed oriental shop fronts were barred against vandals by folding metal gates, and the street signs bore their names in both English and Chinese characters.

Minikin watched the exotic scene gliding past her car window with the morbid fascination of one seeing it for the last time. To the left of Canal Street lay Little Italy, an ethnic island of pasta restaurants and coffee houses sleeping uneasily in the China Sea around it.

They turned right onto Mott Street, the tourist-shop section of Chinatown. Minikin felt uncannily transported to an eerie Hong Kong slum: Wing Toy Jade & Jewelry, Hung Fat's Restaurant, Tai Lo's Fine Chinese Furniture, Dinnerware, and Ebony & Ivory Carvings.

With easy familiarity, Rohm directed her through the twisted foggy maze, until at last they paused in front of a closed camera store. Then, slowly, they drove around the corner to an alley in back and parked. He advised her to get out of the car carefully. In the gray predawn, her legs weak with trembling, Minikin stepped out onto the wet pavement.

Leaving his jacket on the front seat, Homer Rohm got out of the car slowly, the small gun unwavering in his good hand. He held the violin loosely by its neck in his other hand. With the gun he waved her toward the rear door of the camera store. It was covered with a heavy grillwork and padlocked. There was a doorbell on the left.

"Ring the bell, twice," he told her.

Minikin did as ordered and heard the shrill bell resonate deep within the house. The wait seemed interminable. She shivered and glanced at her watch; it was nearly five a.m.; whoever was being summoned would be in bed.

"Ring it again," Rohm said, and again she touched the button twice, then glanced curiously around the small alley. Suddenly she realized there was something familiar about the van parked behind the Chinese laundry next door. Thoroughly frightened, she recognized the van they had used to chase Dr. Grow that rainy night.

Her breath came shallow and quick. She saw a light suddenly illuminated behind the dirty glass and heard locks being turned. The inside door was opened and the heavy grillwork unlocked and swung wide. A slender Chinese in a soiled technician's smock nodded once to Rohm, then stepped back to admit them. As soon as they were inside, he quickly refastened the grill and closed and relocked the door.

"Zhao Ping told me I might expect you," he said in a raspy voice, then he began the hacking morning coughing of a heavy smoker. He motioned them through another doorway into what was evidently the shabby office of the camera store in front, while he continued to cough. There was a battered oak desk, some metal files and, on the far wall, a black box-like safe. The Chinese took a pack of cigarettes from the desk, lit one and inhaled deeply. He coughed a final time, then cleared his throat and stood listening as Homer Rohm began to speak to him in rapid Chinese.

Minikin watched as Rohm gestured toward her, his pale face and even features like a blank slate. Under the harsh neon light overhead she could see that the left side of his face looked sunburned, and his brows and eyelashes were singed. With a shock she realized his face was powderburned from Gonzales' shot. The thick bandage on his shoulder bulged beneath his bloody shirt.

The Chinese continued to listen, the cigarette dangling loosely from the corner of his mouth, the slanted eyes nearly closed against a ribbon of smoke.

At last the two men moved together toward the safe. Rohm winced as he laid the violin down on top; his shoulder was obviously hurting him. He waved Minikin over to stand on its other side as the Chinese hunkered down in front of the safe and began to spin the dial. Minikin stepped back as its door swung open beside her, trapping her against the wall. The Chinese placed his cigarette on the edge of a well-filled ashtray on top of the safe and began to search among some papers with nicotine-stained fingers.

Through her fear and fatigue Minikin began to feel a heightened sense of awareness. Each detail in the room seemed to leap out at her with a kind of slow-motion clarity — the light overhead seemed too bright, her nerves recoiled at a sudden cough from the Chinese, and the smoke from the burning cigarette was suffocating.

On the floor in front of the safe, the Chinese located the passports and identity papers he was looking for and extended them to Rohm. Rohm replaced his gun in the clip at the small of his back and bent over him to make his selection.

On impulse, Minikin reached out and lifted the cigarette from the ashtray, intending to stamp it out. The lengthy ash dropped from its tip, leaving a smoldering cone-shaped ember. The violin lay beside her, its chinrest nearly touching her elbow. Almost without thinking, she touched the glowing ash to the tortoiseshell "eye" of the E tuner. After an instant there was an acrid odor of burning plastic. Trembling violently, she mashed the cigarette out in the ashtray as Rohm glanced up suspiciously.

Waving her hand back and forth to disperse the smoke, she said breathlessly, "I put it out, the smoke was getting in my eyes."

His gaze locked onto hers for an endless moment, and then he bent again to his papers.

Minikin's knees could barely support her. Her mouth was dry and she struggled to swallow. What have I done? she thought. If I've actually destroyed the film, he's bound to notice! Now, he's not only going to kill me, he's going to *enjoy* it. She leaned back weakly against the wall and closed her eyes. She heard the door to the safe whisper shut and the dial being spun. There were a few random words exchanged in Chinese. Then, quietly, Rohm began to speak to her.

"In spite of what you may think, Miss Small, it is not my intention to kill you. After careful consideration I have decided to return to China for a rest, while I can still live with myself."

Minikin opened her eyes in surprise and found him watching her.

He continued, "Unfortunately, it will be necessary to keep you here temporarily while I effect my departure. I'm afraid the accommodations aren't up to your usual standard; however, I've discovered you have the ability to endure." His look softened, and his voice became strangely intimate. "We aren't so very different, you know. As I perceive it, we're both solitary misfits who know how to survive and who view the world without reverence. The main difference between us is that I suffer from an excess of commitment, and you from a lack of it."

Perhaps he didn't mean to be unkind, but he hit too close to home. Minikin straightened up and answered sarcastically, "And of course everyone believes their perception is reality."

For a moment it appeared he had been about to say something more, but then he frowned and turned away.

Strangely, Minikin felt disappointed in herself — but why should she care about this man's regard?

The Chinese lifted the violin and began to unscrew the E tuner. He handed it to Rohm who dropped it without a second glance into the envelope containing his travel papers.

When Rohm spoke to her again his voice was carefully expressionless. "The Agency will want to examine the violin, Miss Small. There is nothing in it now, but they will want to examine it anyway. When they have finished with it I know you will see that it is returned to Luk Tsi."

Minikin nodded, and the Chinese thrust the del Gesù into her hands. She wondered fleetingly how Luk Tsi's performance for the President had gone last night. A triumph, probably.

Impatiently the Chinese spoke to Rohm, then turned and left the room. Homer Rohm nodded tiredly and waved Minikin out of the room ahead of him. The Chinese was waiting for them at the foot of a dark stairway, and the three of them ascended two flights of creaking stairs. On the top landing the Chinese unlocked a deadbolt, opened a door, and stepped back to let them enter.

Minikin clutched the violin to her and glanced around the room dejectedly. She had a strong aversion to small enclosed spaces, and evidently this was to be her prison. It was a grim little room with a sagging bed and a rickety table and chair. High overhead, the first pink of dawn was beginning to light a dirty skylight.

Rohm told her, "When my friend and I are safely away, I will let Detective Kake know where you are. This shouldn't take more than a day. Until then, I advise you to be patient and get some sleep."

Wordlessly, Minikin nodded, and Rohm turned to go.

On the landing down the hall another door opened, and Ssu Ch'an emerged, shirtless and disheveled with sleep. A long row of black sutures sprouted along the line of his eyebrow where Minikin had hit him with the violin.

"What is he doing here?" Rohm demanded of the slender Chinese.

"He was injured and wouldn't go home," was the confused reply. "He wanted opium. I gave it to him."

Minikin watched with horror as the expression on the big Oriental's face changed slowly from dazed inquiry to outraged fury. She gasped and took a step backward as Rohm began speaking to him in rapid Chinese, but the urgent words had no effect. Like a locomotive slowly gathering a full head of steam, Ssu Ch'an ignored Rohm and started toward her. He brushed the protesting Chinese aside as if he were a puff of smoke and headed directly for Minikin. She trembled and backed away, still clutching the del Gesù.

Authority rang in Rohm's voice, as he stepped between them and switched to English, "Stop where you are, Ssu Ch'an. Listen to me!"

"She killed my brother," Ch'an growled and kept coming, his eyes never leaving Minikin. "She killed Tsin!" With a grizzly bear swipe of one arm he knocked Rohm to the floor, crossed the room and grabbed Minikin by the throat.

Minikin dropped the violin and clawed at his hands. The pressure around her neck became intolerable, and she began instead to claw at his face. He smiled at her with satisfaction and squeezed tighter. She felt a crunching in her neck and blood thundered in her ears. The need to breathe became more and more urgent. She seemed to hear people yelling. She panicked and began kicking at her attacker's legs and gouging at his eyes. He penned her against the wall. There didn't seem to be any way she could hurt him. In a moment her lungs would explode she had to get air! Time stood still. She thought, this is how I am going to die. Her eyes closed and she began to be swallowed up by darkness. . . there was an echoing silence. Then her eyes opened and she watched — through a nightmare of terror — the face so close to her own beginning to darken, the reptilian eyes bulging. The grip on her neck seemed to be lessening as his color deepened. His entire face appeared to swell. The mad eyes still glared at her in fury, but the whole of his weight began to press her down. Her back slipped sideways across the wall, then her legs collapsed beneath her. She crashed to the floor, and he came down on top of her. He still held her by the throat, but now she began to take in small regular gulps of air. She was unable to tear her gaze from his face and stared with revulsion as his mouth slowly opened, and his tongue began to protrude. In a sudden frenzy she fought her way out from under him and frantically rolled away.

Too exhausted to stand, she remained on the floor, leaning on one elbow and breathing heavily. Uncomprehending, she stared at Ssu Ch'an. He lay unmoving where he had fallen, his eyes open. Gradually she realized he was dead.

The Chinese unwound his wire garrote from about the dead man's neck, wiped it on the tail of his open smock and calmly returned it to the lining of his leather belt. He glanced at Rohm. "We must hurry," he rasped. "We have much to do." He turned quickly and began to drag the dead body from the room by its heels. Rohm nodded to him and returned his gun to its holster. His shoulder was bleeding again, and his eyes were clouded with pain. He said, "We have to go. I. . . I'm very sorry, Miss Small."

She inclined her head once and, through a throat almost too swollen to speak, whispered, "Au revoir, Leiter d'Arques." He nearly smiled. "Auf Wiedersehen, Minikin. Perhaps we'll meet again."

Then he was gone. She heard the door close and the deadbolt slam home.

# 31

# VICTORIOUS DEFEAT

MINIKIN DIDN'T KNOW HOW LONG SHE lay unmoving on the floor, staring at the violin, but finally she sat up, reached out and picked it up. She revolved it slowly in her hands. Magically, it appeared undamaged, and she breathed a sigh of relief.

She got to her feet and looked around. In a corner by the bed was a covered tin pail. Gradually she realized it was intended to serve the function of a chamber pot. Apparently someone else had been imprisoned here before her. Dr. Grow? It was too depressing to think about. She had always hated being shut in. She was tired and wanted to go home. She decided, then, that she had no intention of staying.

Minikin stood the violin upright in a corner and walked over and looked up at the skylight; sometimes, being tall paid off. It was very high — about fifteen feet — but there was an exposed metal bar spanning the area about three feet beneath it. Suddenly, she realized she was exhausted, and her arms and legs felt unreliable. She glanced with longing at the bed, but then her eyes fell on the indignity of that chamber pot. She knew she couldn't face the prospect of staying here for another day — she would give it a try.

She dragged the bed under the skylight, lifted the small wooden table onto its sagging mattress, and then carefully placed the chair on top of the table. She stepped back and gazed up at her handiwork. Whew! It certainly didn't look very stable; it even listed slightly to one side. Minikin estimated that she wouldn't be able to reach the metal bar above without jumping for it, and that was providing she could actually stand on top of that leaning tower. She decided she would have to be crazy to try it; she would probably break her neck. However, she knew she was going to try it and trembled with the flow of adrenalin.

She set the chair back down on the floor and adjusted the table on the bed slightly to allow for the listing. Then she drew a deep breath and stepped up onto the mattress and began to climb carefully onto the table. The mattress bounced unsteadily beneath her. She got to her feet on the table, bent shakily and lifted the chair by its back rung and brought it up slowly. She set it down on the table between her straddling legs and, taking care not to overbalance, gradually got up on her knees onto the chair, then to her feet, and slowly began to stand upright. She felt dizzy and held tightly to the back of the chair for support. Sweat began to run down her face. This was insanity. Her eyes fell on the violin in the far corner. God, she had forgotten the violin! Oh well, she thought frantically, it would be safe until she could come back for it. Right now, she had to let go of the back of the chair and stand erect. But she couldn't move. How could she leave the violin?

Slowly, she reversed the process: kneeling onto the chair, then edging down on the table to straddle the chair, lowering the chair to the floor, and then jumping down to land sitting in the chair, trembling. What was she thinking of? There was no way she could take the violin with her; she would need both hands to climb out of that skylight.

Minikin remained where she was until she stopped shaking. Then she rose and strode over to the del Gesù, picked it up and stubbornly stuffed it up the back of her sweater, tucking the hem of the sweater deep into the waistband of her blue jeans. It felt like a quiver of arrows across her back, the neck of the violin protruding from the top of her sweater to a level with her ear. She extended her arms overhead; it didn't seem to inhibit her movements. Robin Hood had always managed all right. Well, she thought, if I fall I'll try to land on my face and save the violin.

Again, she steadied the table on the sagging bed, stepped up onto the mattress and climbed carefully onto the table. She bent and lifted the chair between her straddling legs, eased slowly onto it on her knees, and then got painfully to her feet. Once again, the room swayed and the mattress rocked with her slightest motion. She caught hold of the back of the chair and, trembling violently, began to straighten up. Very tentatively, she let go of the chair back and stood erect uncertainly in the slanted gray light. Keeping her eyes fixed on a spot on the wall opposite her, Minikin nervously drew a few shallow breaths while she steadied herself. Okay, she decided, you can do it. Now! She gave a deep bounce on the springy bed and rose into the air. She heard the furniture crash to the floor beneath her as she snatched desperately for the bar overhead. One hand slipped from her dusty grip, but she caught on with the other and held tight, kicking herself up to grab hold with the second hand.

For a moment she hung in space, breathing heavily. Then she curled her legs up to her chest, leaned back and slipped one foot over the bar. Quickly, she swung upright, hunching her back to avoid the window above her. Perched precariously astride the bar, Minikin hastily adjusted the violin and retucked her sweater.

She was up, she thought in relief, but in the next instant she immediately froze. Plaster dust was beginning to fall from the places inside the skylight where the bar joined the walls. She held her breath and waited, was it going to support her? Far below, on the floor, the furniture lay in disarray; the mattress had collapsed, and the table and chair were upended. As a possible site for a crash landing it looked singularly uninviting. Minikin closed her eyes and considered the possibility of throwing up, but the feeling gradually passed.

Trapped in the airless confines of the skylight, she felt the sweat begin to pour off her. She turned her attention to the window above. The hasp came unlocked easily, but through years of disuse the window refused to budge. She noticed the glass panes were webbed with fine wire; they would crack but never shatter. Minikin put the top of her head against the glass skylight and began to push upward. She was afraid the bar would collapse beneath her before the window would open. She refused to look down again — there was no going back. Slowly she increased the pressure, dreading to hear the sound of cracking plaster and feel the empty space below her, but the window seemed hopelessly stuck. Desperate now, she gritted her teeth and put all the strength of her back into it. At last — with a metallic groan — it pushed open! Fresh air flowed in and washed over her.

She got to her feet on the bar and opened the skylight fully. Then she grabbed hold of the sides and pulled herself up and out of the opening. Once on the roof, with shaking hands, she tugged the violin from the bottom of her sweater and used her sleeve to wipe her sweat from its gleaming finish.

If she had had any strength left, she would have shouted aloud in triumph, but her mouth was dry and her trembling legs could barely carry her across the dirty tarpaper roof. She leaned heavily against the parapet wall and gazed down into the alley. The sinister atmosphere had evaporated with the first light of day. A cotton bedspread flapped listlessly on a clothesline below. The laundry truck was still there, but the tan Ford was gone. She raised her eyes and for a long while was content to watch the sun rise. It was a moment for philosophical reflection and profound insights, but her exhausted mind could only register dim relief. She was alive. She was free.

Finally, she noticed a fire escape on the building next door. Minikin shook herself out of her reverie and turned and crossed the roof, climbed a low wall separating the two buildings, and then descended the fire escape into the alley below with relative ease.

She emerged wearily from the alley and headed back toward Mott Street. Where to? she asked herself, as she swung the violin onto one shoulder and thrust her other hand deep into the pocket of her jeans. She had lost her handbag and had no money to get home. Once there, she had no keys to get inside her brand new front door anyway. Well, that left the Nineteenth Precinct. The police were probably still interested enough to loan her cab fare. She knew their price would be that she answer a lot of questions. Minikin sighed with resignation. She supposed it was her duty to let them know what had happened. My country tis of thee. . ., but where had all their idealism gone?

Poor Homer Rohm, she thought to herself. Or rather, she should say, poor Leiter d'Arques — if that really was his name. What a victorious defeat; that film would never yield the plans for the x-ray laser. If he could make good his escape, Minikin wondered how the Chinese would reward the failure of their Oxymoron. She kicked a pebble from her path. Gonzales had been a bad good guy, but St. Sinner was a good bad guy, and much more preferable somehow. There was a moral there, she thought. Silently, she almost wished him luck.

Whatever his reasons, St. Sinner had wanted Luk Tsi to have the master fiddle. Well, at least Minikin could see to it that Luk Tsi got it.

On the corner of Mott Street and Canal, Minikin used the violin to hail a taxi. The cabbie was just beginning work for the day and studied her suspiciously before unlocking his rear door and letting her in. Her voice was so hoarse that she had to repeat herself several times before he understood their destination. She fell asleep on the trip uptown. At the Nineteenth Precinct she awoke exhausted and disoriented and tried to explain to the protesting driver that he would have to wait a moment for his money.

Inside, she asked for Paddy Kake and gave her name. Evidently the early shift had never heard of her; their disinterest was overwhelming. However, they assured her, Detective Kake was still around somewhere and would be located. She found him herself, upstairs, asleep on a couch. He looked more tired and disheveled than usual, and she tried not to think about how she looked.

"Paddy?" she croaked. "Paddy, I need to borrow cab fare." She shook him, gently, "Paddy?"

Slowly he opened his eyes, and Minikin never witnessed a more complete transformation in a human being. In quick succession the now alert Detective Kake dispensed with the cabbie, alerted the people from the CIA and summoned police stenographers. In a matter of minutes they had gathered around Minikin and all their questions came at her, rat-a-tat. Her voice somewhere between a whisper and a croak, she managed to get through her story once, then fell asleep with her chin in her hand and couldn't be wakened. She seemed to remember Detective Kake lifting her from the chair and carrying her down the stairs. And that was all.

Minikin slept throughout that entire Sunday, waking in the evening in a bed at Lenox Hill Hospital. Her neck was wrapped with gauze, and she felt a small patch on her right temple. She stretched experimentally and nothing hurt. She felt fine.

After a while they noticed she was awake and asked if she felt up to dinner. She felt ravenous. When the nurse came by later to remove the tray, Minikin was already sleeping again.

She woke early Monday morning to a glorious spring day. Her doctor came by to examine her again and told her the concussion had been minor, but that she would have to stay in the hospital one more day for observation. She began to feel restless.

She picked up her bedside phone and called Li C. Fu at his hotel. He seemed vastly relieved to hear from her and concerned to learn that she was in the hospital. She explained she was fine and would be home tomorrow; she had accidentally fallen down Saturday night and bumped her head.

He expressed polite joy at her imminent recovery, then told her he had visited her house yesterday, though he could not get in. He was very sorry to have to inform her that a dreadful fate had befallen the garage door — it was mortally wounded.

Minikin frowned trying to imagine what had happened, but assured him that Chalfonte would take care of it. She asked him to stay at the hotel until she could locate some keys to the new front door. He agreed, and she told him she would be in touch.

Li C. Fu drew a deep breath, "Mees Smawr, one thing more, please. At one o'clock today I meet Luk Tsi for lunch at Plaza. Where her violin?"

Incredibly, Minikin had forgotten the del Gesù.

"The CIA has it, Li C.," she hurried to explain in her gruff voice. "I don't think they plan to return it before Luk Tsi will leave for her tour. However, her insurance policy is ready and waiting at The Small Agency, and she is fully covered for any loss. Please tell her that I will see to it that she gets the violin back just as soon as the CIA releases it."

She hung up hoping Luk Tsi wasn't cursed with an artistic temperament and that Li C. Fu could make her understand.

Along about five o'clock, Detective Kake entered her room quietly. He hadn't brought flowers, Minikin noticed, but something much more thoughtful: her purse. She was glad to see him.

"I'm sorry I couldn't get here sooner," he drawled in his deep voice, "but we were kind of busy yesterday. And then I needed to catch up on some sleep."

He did look rested and freshly shaven and even carefully groomed. Minikin wished she had borrowed someone's hairbrush.

"What happened to St. Sinner?" she asked hoarsely. "Did they catch him?"

He shook his head. "Not yet. However, there is a police dragnet blocking all possible avenues of escape; I believe it's just a matter of time. Everyone's going crazy, especially the CIA."

Her feelings strangely mixed, Minikin said, "The film was destroyed; why are they so upset?"

He frowned at her, his look mildly reproving. "A double agent, working right under their noses for who knows how long? They've just realized all the secrets he was in on that he must have passed along, and it's turning their hair white."

She looked down and nodded quietly.

The big detective continued, "And to add to all their other troubles, an over-eager CIA man has created a big flap that you'll probably read about in the newspapers."

She glanced up. "What happened?"

"Well," Kake shifted uncomfortably from one foot to the other, "I just happened to be there at the time. We were at Kennedy Airport, and a guy named George Zengo was in charge. We all had photographs of Homer Rohm, but they had warned us to expect that he might be in disguise. We were looking for someone famous — a diplomat, or a movie star — someone outstanding, but ordinarily above suspicion."

Minikin suddenly visualized a Burt Reynolds look-alike in a stetson hat and cowboy boots, flirting with all the airline stewardesses.

"Anyway," he went on slowly, tugging at one ear, "here comes what's-her-name, the country western singer with the big platinum wig and the enormous, er, front. Zengo shouts, 'It's him, trust me!' and goes for her. Right at the gate he caught hold of the back of her fancy beaded vest with one hand, yanked off the blonde wig with the other, and yelled, 'You're under arrest, Rohm!'"

Paddy Kake's color began to deepen, and Minikin struggled to keep a straight face.

"The woman started screaming and was putting up a pretty good fight, so Zengo grabbed her by those phony-looking bazooms and tried to pull them off, and they were real. It *was* Dolly Parton."

"Good grief," Minikin said weakly.

He nodded quietly. "When all the yelling was over, our people tried to give a reasonable explanation for what had happened. Everyone apologized. We thought we had gotten all the photographs, but I guess we missed a few because they're in the newspapers today. Anyway, Miss Parton was very gracious about the whole thing—she's really very nice. But George Zengo is probably packing now for his new assignment in Zimbabwe."

Minikin didn't trust herself to speak, but the big Detective's eyes betrayed a twinkle, and there was a suspicious twitch at the corner of his mouth. Finally she could contain it no longer and began to rock with laughter.

Paddy Kake smiled while he looked her over appraisingly. She had some spirit, that one, and he rather liked that wild mane of hair. In fact, he decided, she was damned attractive. He planned to get to know her better. Perhaps, he thought, if she hangs around New York for any length of time, he might even teach her to ski. . . .

Meanwhile, on a flight high above the Atlantic, a fascinated matron in first class turned to her seating companion and whispered, "My dear, did you happen to notice how much the priest across the aisle looks like Bing Crosby? And a moment ago I swear he was humming 'The Bells of St. Mary.' "

# THE BEGINNING

Minikin didn't know when she actually decided to stay on in the house; it seemed to come about naturally. She arrived home one evening in The Slim, opened the new garage door with the remote control device, drove in and parked. Chalfonte had chosen a glossy black overhead affair that matched the front door, and the bill had been grudgingly paid by the CIA. She closed the garage door and entered the kitchen.

The newly finished room was redolent with the mouth-watering aromas of good cooking. Everett Orson had expressed a desire to try out her new kitchen and was making Italian dinner. Lacy had been invited and, looking *soignee* in a peach velour jump-suit, was helping Everett Orson with his seasonings and laughing musically at his mild protests.

Minikin glanced over at Li C. Fu. He was deeply engrossed in the instruction manual of the new personal computer, but looked up and smiled. She smiled back, glad to be home.

Unexpectedly, Walt Whitman's words whispered to her:

> "to be with those I like is enough,
> To stop in company with the rest at
> evening is enough,
> To be surrounded by beautiful,
> curious, breathing, laughing
> flesh is enough. . . ."

Slowly, Minikin crossed the room and stood gazing out of the vast greenhouse window, through the hanging plants, at the fairy lights in the garden outside. She realized she had completely rebuilt her life from the ground up; there were no dark or overlooked corners. She had work to do for The Small Agency, she had people here that she cared about, and she was heavily in debt to her decorator. She felt pretty good. Tomorrow she would ask Li C. Fu to get some goldfish for that pond, and then she would make reservations to fly over and close up her rented apartment in Cap d'Antibes.

The following day, she received a letter and a small wrapped box in the mail, from a New Jersey address. The handwriting was clear and carefully formed like that of a schoolteacher. She slit the envelope, unfolded the letter and read:

Dear Miss Small,

I would be pleased if you would accept this Chinese box from me. They tell me it is quite valuable and very old, yet for reasons too personal to explain it affords me no pleasure. I want you to have it because of what you did for Will — at a time when he was alone and needed someone to help him.

Our baby is due soon, and if it is a girl I plan to name her "Minikin." I find it an unusual and distinctive name.

My son, Gerald, joins me in extending to you our best wishes and

Kindest personal regards,
Gloria G. Grow

In September, Minikin received a birth announcement. It was a boy. He weighed 8 pounds 3 ounces, and was named William Telford Grow II.

# Acknowledgments

I would like to thank our insurance agent, Franklin Rosner, for his counsel regarding The Small Agency. I am indebted, also, to Dr. Richard B. Inglis for the information he provided. My sincere thanks to Myra Brooks Welch for the use of the excerpt from her poem, "The Touch of the Master's Hand."